All proceeds from this book benefit the upkeep and operation of the John Greenleaf Whittier Birthplace and the surrounding 69 acres of farmland in Haverhill, Massachusetts.

MURDER
AMONG FRIENDS

MURDER AMONG FRIENDS

MYSTERIES INSPIRED BY THE LIFE AND WORKS OF JOHN GREENLEAF WHITTIER

DAVID GOUDSWARD
editor

POST MORTEM PRESS
CINCINNATI

© 2017 Trustees of the John Greenleaf Whittier Homestead

Unless otherwise noted, all stories are copyright © 2017 by their respective authors and are original to this anthology.

"A Memorable Murder" by Celia Thaxter. First published in *Atlantic Monthly,* May 1875.

"The Murdered Lady" by John Greenleaf Whittier. First published in *Legends of New England*, 1831.

"A Mother's Revenge" by John Greenleaf Whittier. First published in *Legends of New England*, 1831.

"The Murdered Traveller" by William Cullen Bryant. First published in Specimens of American Poetry, ed. Samuel Kettell 1829.

"The Murderer's Request" by Lucy Larcom. First published in *Lowell Offering and Magazine,* July 1843.

A previous version of "The Flock" by Victoria Weisfeld was published in *Big Muddy: a Journal of the Mississippi River Valley*, Spring 2015.

Post Mortem Press, Cincinnati
www.postmortem-press.com

No part of this book may be reproduced in any form or by any electronic or mechanical means including information storage and retrieval systems, without permission in writing from the publisher. The only exception is by a reviewer, who may quote short excerpts in a review.

FIRST EDITION

ISBN: 978-1545208854

This book is dedicated to the memories of librarian Margaret Eager and journalist Tom Vartabedian. Each used different techniques but shared a common goal, the preservation of the history of Haverhill.

Table of Contents

Foreword xiii
    David Goudsward

Introduction xvii
    Tim Coco

Murder in the Summer Kitchen 1
    Edith Maxwell

The Murdered Lady 11
    John Greenleaf Whittier

On the Black Ice 15
    Pete Rawlik

The Flock 23
    Victoria Weisfeld

The Goodwife and the Bookseller 38
    Ken Faig, Jr.

The Murdered Traveller 59
    William Cullen Bryant

The Death Clock 61
    David Bernard

Miss Larcom Meets the Neighbors 83
    Susan Oleksiw

The Cricket in the Wall 95
    Kristi Petersen Schoonover

Antiques 109
    Gregory L. Norris

The Murderer's Request 121
    Lucy Larcom

Cane Fishing 123
    Rock Neelly

A Memorable Murder 138
    Celia Thaxter

The Mother's Revenge 163
    John Greenleaf Whittier

Exposed For Murder 168
    Judi Calhoun

The Skeleton on the Ski Lift 187
    D.G. Critchley

Contributors 200

Foreword

John Greenleaf Whittier, 1881
Detail from a photograph of the poet, distributed first as a cabinet card, then as an unmounted paper print. Much like postcards of his homes and the settings of his poems, images of Whittier were eagerly sought after by an adoring public. National Portrait Gallery, Smithsonian. Institution.

The following collection has few things in common, other than the fact all are mysteries – period pieces, noir, light-hearted, grim, cozies, and true-life crime. But the oddest mystery inspired by John Greenleaf Whittier involved his home in Amesbury, Massachusetts. And it's still unsolved.

After the poet's death in 1892, his niece Elizabeth(Whittier) Pickard leased the house to the Whittier Home Association as a memorial to the poet. To the dismay of Amesbury, Elizabeth's husband and her son decided to move into the house after Elizabeth's death in 1902. 72-year old Samuel T. Pickard, the editor of Whittier's biography and letters, was embarking one last book on Whittier – the landmarks from the poet's life and works. Repeated travel from their home in Portland, Maine into the area was just too grueling for him, so he set up shop in the Amesbury house. His son Greenleaf Pickard and his wife lived there as well. Greenleaf could tend to his father and was still close enough to

Boston to continue his work in the new science of radio. Samuel's position as Whittier's biographer and literary executor offered some cachet in the occupancy, but the welcome quickly wore thin when in 1903, he announced he was selling off Whittier's manuscripts and books to help restore the Amesbury house. He was also sending proceeds to the sale to Whittier's Birthplace in Haverhill, which had been devastated by a fire the year before.

In 1904, Samuel published Whittier-Land: A Handbook of North Essex, but had advised the Association he was not renewing their lease when it came due in 1906. The Association would no longer be allowed to maintain the front rooms as a literary shrine. The group could only watch in horror as the Pickards began adding on to the house, making it big enough Samuel, his nurse, his son, daughter-in-law, and a servant. The worst of the perceived desecration was Greenleaf's new 40-foot radio tower, built in the poet's old garden. The Whittier Home Association had had enough and requested Pickards sell the home to them. The Pickards refused. Some people took the refusal better than others.

The truth was that Samuel had no intention of leaving the Association in the lurch. He just was going to live in all of his house. The Association had been one of his late wife's projects, and she had left them a sizable bequest in her will, payable upon her husband's death. He made a counter offer to the Association's leadership. He would release half of their bequest to purchase the Colby house across from the Whittier House. The paperwork would not clear until 1907 and the transaction was kept secret until then. So, in the summer of 1906, it appeared to the general membership of the Association, and the town in general, that Pickard was dismantling Whittier's legacy.

Suddenly, the situation began to read like a mystery novel. On November 18, 1906, newspaper headlines across the nation reported that someone had tried to kill the Pickards by sprinkling arsenic on the beefsteak eaten for dinner. All became violently ill, and Pickard's nurse, Elizabeth Diegnan, hovered at death's door for 24 hours before beginning to recover. The attempt had taken place October 18, but the family had agreed to the police request to claim it was ptomaine poisoning, an accidental but potentially fatal case of food poisoning. This allowed the police to search the real culprit.

The mystery tropes abound. The intended victim was a beloved septuagenarian scholar. The unintended victim was his faithful nurse. His son Greenleaf, the stalwart amateur detective, verified the arsenic by testing the leftover meat in his lab in the addition to the house that was so hated by the Whittier purists. The red herring in the mystery was a cousin in Portland, who, although bereft of details, declared that the meat must have been treated with formaldehyde as a preservative (which was actually happening for a time), or spoiled on the train from Chicago. And then there were the suspects.

The first suspect was the former maid of Elizabeth Picard, who had left her position after Elizabeth's death because she disliked Greenleaf's young wife, who now ran the household. Rumor was that there was a bequest left to her by her beloved Elizabeth, placed in a trust until Samuel's death. The maid was supposed to have moved back to Maine, but police could not find her.

The second suspect was a former neighbor of the Whittiers/Pickards on Friends Street and a former member of the Whittier Home Association who had openly proclaimed her hatred of the Pickards and the changes inflicted on the Home. Even more clichéd, the woman had moved from Amesbury under a cloud of suspicion – she had been a suspect in a prior poisoning case in town. Her motive would have been to eliminate Samuel so the association received their bequest and could purchase the house from Greenleaf.

Sadly, the final chapter of the case of the poisoned Pickard remains unwritten. No arrests were ever made, and the case quietly faded away. Newspaper reports of Samuel's death in 1915 don't even mention the case. Some dedicated researcher needs to wrap up this case – the story practically wrote itself, but the lack of denouement is murder!

Dave Goudsward
Lake Worth, Florida

Introduction

John Greenleaf Whittier and I have parallels in our lives that make his works and life resonate with me as a kindred spirit. I am currently president of the trustees that protect his birthplace. I also operate non-profit WHAV-FM, a medium that was made possible by Whittier's grand-nephew Greenleaf Pickard's groundbreaking research in early radio. And there's the journalism connection.

ESSEX GAZETTE.
PUBLISHED BY A. W. THAYER.   HAVERHILL, MASS. JANUARY 2, 1930.   NUMBER 1....VOLUME IV.

Whittier edited a number of newspapers during his career – in Boston, Hartford, Philadelphia, and, most notably for me, Haverhill. Whittier edited *The Essex Gazette*, formerly the *Haverhill Gazette*, then the *Gazette and Patriot* after a merger, for six months, assuming editorship of *The Essex Gazette* with the January 2, 1930 issue. It was less prestigious than his former position in Boston, but he felt a need to be close to home as his father's health deteriorated. After his father's death six months later, Whittier departed again, this time to assume the mantle at the *New England Review* in Hartford, Connecticut.

He returned to the newspaper in 1836 for five months, two years before the paper changed its name yet again. Having also worked for the *Gazette*, I feel a journalistic comradery. It's difficult to know for sure what news stories attracted Whittier's attention, but no doubt the mystery and intrigue surrounding a murder caught his eye as it would any editor or reporter. It sells papers, can be covered for an extended period, and make or break a career. Like a good reporter, I'll cite sources, two of which are in this book. Celia Thaxter's firsthand account of the Smuttynose murders continues to generate books and even a 2000 film. Whittier's accounts of Hannah Duston's capture, along with Cotton Mather, are considered the original sources. Don't consider the Duston case a multiple homicide, fueled by revenge? You can thank Whittier.

When Dave approached the trustees with murder mysteries as the topic of this second volume of new stories inspired by Whittier and his world, there was hesitation. But then again, the first anthology *Snowbound with Zombies,* Whittier-inspired supernatural stories, had the same reaction and it worked quite nicely. And what a delightful mix – 16 stories of murder, mayhem, and malice. The mystery is which one will be your favorite.

Tim Coco
President
The Trustees of the John Greenleaf Whittier Homestead
Haverhill, Massachusetts

Murder in the Summer Kitchen

Edith Maxwell

Summer kitchen at the Whittier Home, Amesbury, Massachusetts
The small building nestled behind the Whittier Home is the summer kitchen, which originally sat next to the house. Summer kitchens were used to prevent cooking and baking from heating the main house during the warmer months. It could also be used year round for to keep foul smelling chores such as laundry out of the house. Courtesy of Edith Maxwell.

In the gloaming of the Eleventh Month afternoon, my attention had wandered from the literary conversation in John Greenleaf Whittier's parlor. The unmistakable crack of a gun brought me to my senses, and I jumped in my seat. Another report followed in quick succession.

All the eyes in the room went wide along with mine: John's, my niece Faith's, those of several other Friends, and Celia Thaxter's, John's famous friend whose work we Friends were here to discuss. Faith clutched my hand. A man name Zachariah leaped to his feet.

"What violence is this?" he cried.

The unflappable Celia raised an eyebrow. "Sounded like a gun to me." While not a Quaker, her dress was fully as plain as mine, although hers was adorned with a necklace made from seashells.

It had sounded like a gun to me, too. I'd witnessed the discharge of weapons on more than one occasion, and most of those times were not happy ones.

John tented his fingers. "Young ruffians sometimes prowl the streets of late. 'Tis a pity they cannot rightly be controlled by their parents." His high brow wrinkled in disapproval.

Mrs. Cate, John's housekeeper, clattered down the stairs from the quarters she kept with her husband, the Judge, and appeared in the doorway. "You're all right then, Mr. Whittier?"

"Yes, Mrs. Cate. Does thee know whence came this gunshot?" He stroked his snowy-white chinstrap beard.

"I do believe it was from the summer kitchen." She hugged herself, her mouth drawn down. "But why?"

"I'll go to investigate," Zachariah said. He was no taller than my five feet eight, nor much older than my twenty-four years.

"I'll come with thee," I said, standing.

"What has a midwife to do with guns?" Zachariah scoffed under sand-colored eyebrows.

"Rose Carroll is not only a midwife, young man," John came to my defense. "She's also something of a detective."

===

A few moments later Zachariah and I stood in the small outbuilding to the side of the house. Calling it a summer kitchen was a misnomer since Mrs. Cate cooked in it year round except in deep midwinter. No food preparation would take place here this evening, though. A man lay on his side on the wooden floor with his back toward us. Even in the twilight, I could see a dark ragged hole piercing his back. Blood stained his jacket and the floor beneath.

I pushed past Zachariah and knelt, feeling the man's neck. His skin was still warm, but his pulse was gone. I reached over his head and smoothed his eyelids shut before standing. I shivered, from the sight of another violent death as much as from the cold.

"Does thee know this man?" I asked.

Zachariah shook his head. "Never seen him before."

"Why, that's our handy boy," Mrs. Cate's voice came from behind me. "That's Mr. Price. John Price does odd jobs around the house and garden, don't you know. I daresay he was come to empty the ashes from the stove, just like I'd asked him to." She held a lit oil lantern high.

The light showed that, indeed, an ash bucket lay on its side near the man's feet.

I turned to Mrs. Cate. "Was he a surly man, likely to have enemies?"

"Oh, no, Miss Carroll. He was the sweetest fellow," she said. "Almost too sweet, if you get my meaning. A bit simple in the head, but an excellent worker. Quite trustworthy."

"Zachariah, thee must fetch Detective Kevin Donovan." I frowned. "He'll need to begin his investigation."

Zachariah pursed his lips and frowned back. "Very well," he finally said and made his way out.

Mrs. Cate set the lantern on top of the table and reached for the victim's shoulder as if to turn him. "We'll need to set this fellow to rights."

I grabbed her hand. "No, we shouldn't touch him."

She glanced at me in alarm. "And why ever not?"

"The police will want to see him exactly as he fell. They'll make a determination of where the shot was fired from and perhaps gain other evidence as to the identity of the murderer. I'll stay here. Thee can return to the house if thee likes."

"A young woman like you stay with a dead man alone? Why, I never. What if that killer comes back? No, I'll stay here with you."

In my profession as a midwife, I was not unfamiliar with death. In my recent investigations of murder in our town, I'd found a source of bravery in myself that had surprised me. Still, I didn't argue with her. It was a comfort to have the matronly woman at my side, even if she wasn't exactly an armed guard.

====

Twenty minutes later I was safely back in the parlor relating the details about both scene and victim to the gathering. "Kevin, the lead detective in the local police, arrived with several of his men and shooed us out. He'll handle the case from here on."

"He is an able investigator, our Kevin." John studied me. "But, Rose, I am seized with an unfortunate idea."

I waited for him to go on, imagining the workings of his creative brain, a mind which had produced so many lyrical poems. Celia cocked her head, stroking the head of a figure on one of the plaster scenarios of the Civil War that had been given to John in thanks for his abolitionist work.

"What idea would that be, Mr. Whittier?" the well-known author, poet, and artist asked. She was robust of figure, with an inquisitive face and curly white hair worn in a knot on top of her head.

Faith sat up straight, gazing at Celia. My seventeen-year-old niece, with her own dreams of becoming a widely read author, had been excited at John's invitation to meet his good friend.

"Thee might not know, dear Celia, that I am in the habit of making my own tea in the summer kitchen of an afternoon," John said. "Mrs. Cate works tirelessly all day long and I don't wish to bother her for my hot drink. What if –"

"The shooter mistook John Price for thee?" I asked. My heart chilled at the thought of losing this avuncular friend, this Friendly mentor, this national treasure. "In truth, the late-day light at this time of year is quite dim, with the sun leaving us well before five o'clock. And he was a tall, thin man, much like thyself."

"Exactly my thoughts, Rose," John said. "And he shot the wrong John."

"But surely thee doesn't have enemies," Faith said. "Who would want to kill thee?"

John gave her a kindly look. "The human species has the capacity for hurt feelings that far exceeds reason, my dear. Those who fought to keep the institution of slavery alive only two-some decades ago still harbor ill will against we who worked to destroy it. Also, some of the many fans of my little poems have expressed outrage that I cannot meet with them personally."

Celia rose and adjusted the array of late fall flowers and colorful leaves she'd arranged in a vase on the mantel. "An artist has only so much strength for such encounters, I agree." She nodded. "We must conserve our energies for our work."

=====

"But Rose, ain't it too early?" Prissy Gund said at seven the next morning as her latest pain ebbed. "My baby ain't supposed to come for another couple of weeks. Didn't you tell me that?" She flopped back on the bed pillows.

"A few weeks doesn't make much difference, Prissy," I said, smiling in what I hoped was a reassuring way. "The baby should be big enough to survive by now, and thee might have an easier time of the birth since your child will be a little smaller than at term."

My young apprentice, Annie Beaumont, and I had been at Prissy's small cottage in Patten Hollow for two hours now after Willard Gund had come to fetch me in the dark hours of the First Day morning. Annie, a good friend of Faith's, had quit her job at the Hamilton mill to apprentice with me, and I welcomed her assistance. The bedroom was small but clean. Willard had brought us basins and a kettle of recently boiled water.

"You'll take good care of my Prissy, won't you?" the first-time father asked me, looking both tender and terrified.

"Of course, we shall, Willard. Thee is not to worry. I'll bring thee news of thy baby as soon as the birth is safely accomplished."

He thanked me, wringing his hands. He planted a kiss on his wife's forehead, then left the bedchamber with a panicked look on his face.

"He just can't wait for our little one," Prissy said. "I've never seen him so excited about anything."

Now Annie wiped Prissy's brow as I picked up the Pinard horn to listen to the baby's heartbeat. "Let me listen to the heartbeat for a moment while thee is in between pains," I said.

The fetal heartbeat was strong and regular, an excellent sign.

"I want my mama," Prissy wailed as another contraction set in. But her mother was in far northern Maine. Prissy herself had recently been a mill girl until Willard offered her marriage and a modest living on his carriage factory wages.

I checked the watched pinned to my chest. Only two minutes had passed since the previous contraction. This baby would be along soon.

"I'll assess thy dilation after this pain."

Annie perched on the edge of the bed holding Prissy's hand. "You're going to be fine, Prissy," she murmured. "Try not to become tense."

I smiled. Annie had a naturally soothing manner about her even at eighteen. For a moment, my thoughts flashed back to the poor man on John Whittier's kitchen floor. No one would ever soothe him again.

After Prissy quieted again, I slid my hand inside her and measured the opening with my knuckles. I removed my hand and wiped it clean.

"Thy baby is almost here, Prissy. Take some deep breaths now while thee can. Thee will feel the urge to push soon, and we'll want thee to." I stood and checked the folded linens on the dresser next to a cross on a stand. I beckoned to Annie. "See if thee can find Willard. We'll need more than these two cloths."

Annie nodded. She glanced at Prissy, who was resting with eyes closed. "I heard about the body at Mr. Whittier's," Annie whispered to me. "That you found it."

"I did."

"What's this about Mr. Whittier?" Prissy called.

The mother-to-be suddenly had very acute hearing and I was sorry she'd overheard us.

"It's nothing, Prissy," I said, moving to her side. I motioned to Annie to go.

She set to groaning, a deep sound from her very core.

"Sit up a bit," I said, helping her farther up in bed. "Grab thy knees with thy hands and push."

Her face reddened with the effort and the groaning turned to an animal sound very much like a growl. When she was spent, she flopped back against the pillows and shut her eyes.

"Very good," I said. "A few more like that and you can meet your son or daughter."

"My husband hates Mr. Whittier," she murmured. "Despises him."

I narrowed my eyes. "Why, pray tell?"

"Willard's from North Carolina, and his family...ooh..." Prissy grabbed her knees again and produced another long guttural sound.

I couldn't pay attention to my roiling thoughts, but I wanted to. A southern husband who hated John? I hadn't noticed Willard's accent, but maybe he'd come to the north when he was a child. What if he– Not now, Rose.

I knelt on the end of the bed. Her opening was bulging and I caught sight of a smattering of dark hair, another good sign. But where was Annie? We were going to need those cloths, and soon.

When the contraction subsided, the top of the head slipped back out of view. "Prissy, with the next pain I want you to give a mighty push. Does thee hear me?"

"Yes," she said but her voice was faint.

I took a moment to close my eyes and hold her and her baby in the Light of God, that they would both survive this dangerous journey. True, women's bodies were designed to birth their young, but that didn't make it any easier for many, and babies often suffered in the process, as well.

Annie burst back in the room. "I can't find him anywhere," she muttered.

What if Willard had heard of his mistaken victim last night and had gone back to shoot John Whittier? My nostrils flared but I could do nothing about such a threat until Prissy's baby was safely born.

"Search the bureau for a clean chemise, a pillowcase, anything."

"Help me," Prissy wailed.

====

Help her, we did, and twenty minutes later a clean baby boy lay in the arms of his wide-eyed mother. Prissy gazed at her son and then up at me with full eyes.

"Ain't he beautiful?" she asked. "I want to show him to his papa." Her gaze fell back on the newborn and she stroked his cheek with her finger.

"I'll go and find him. Annie, thee stay with Prissy and help her with the first feeding."

Annie opened her mouth to speak, and then shut it, nodding. I wished I could explain my fear, but time did not permit.

=====

I was completely out of breath from pedaling my safety bicycle like a fury all the way uphill out of Patten's Hollow to John's home on Friend Street. I'd stopped at the police station and dashed in, but Kevin was not about. I told the young officer at the desk to find the detective and send him along to John Whittier's house with great dispatch. The bell at Saint Joseph's rang nine times as I passed the massive red-brick Catholic church.

Now I let my cycle drop at the back of John's house. I hurried to the summer kitchen, which was blessedly empty of bodies. The blood had been scrubbed from the floor and the stove was hot to the touch. Mrs. Cate would have prepared breakfast already and, as it was First Day, she and her husband had likely already left for their own worship services. I knew they were not members of the Society of Friends.

A horse snorted from Pickard Street at the side of the yard. I'd missed it when I arrived. My eyes widened to see it was the Gund's dappled mare harnessed to their simple open buggy. I was right. Willard was here. My heart set to thumping against my ribcage.

It was nine o'clock, too early for John to have departed for Meeting for Worship – the Meetinghouse was only a quarter mile down the road. Had Willard already killed him? How soon would Kevin arrive?

I crept up to the back door. Despite my gloves, fear had turned my hands icy, nearly numb. I managed to pull open the door without a sound. Voices drifted through the house from the direction of the parlor. I edged along the wall until I could peer in.

John and Celia sat side by side on the settee, with Willard pointing a gun straight at them. I barely kept from crying out.

"Now, young man," John said in a low and calming register. "Thee must lower thy weapon. We can discuss this matter in a peaceful fashion." He rested both hands on his silver-handled cane.

Willard shook his head, his dark eyes as wild as his thatch of unruly hair. He did not lower the gun. "No, we can't. You and your abolitionist friends ruined my family. We couldn't maintain our farm without no slaves. My daddy kilt hisself and my momma, she died of a broken heart. It's all your fault."

Celia sat back on the settee and folded her arms. "What good do you think it'll do to add two more murders to your list, Mr. Gund? You already killed the handyman, I hear. You shoot my friend Mr. Whittier and the law will see you hanged."

Willard glanced around quick, like a trapped weasel. "I didn't mean to kill that fellow. I thought it was Mr. Whittier here!"

I stepped into the room. "Thee killed the wrong John, Willard."

Willard whipped his head toward me. "Miss Carroll, what're you doing here?"

"I wonder the same, Rose," John added.

A little smile played on Celia's face, but she didn't speak.

"Thee has a newborn boy," I said.

Willard's face broke into a broad smile. "I do? A son?" His voice rose with joy but his weapon stayed trained on John.

"Yes, but he's very poorly." I added the lie because I had to. "Thee must abandon thoughts of murder and rush to his side." I caught John's gaze, looked fixedly at his walking stick, and tried to give him an unspoken message.

"Poorly? That can't be," Willard exclaimed. "What do you mean?"

I moved into the room to his side. "He's ailing. Please go to him and thy wife. She needs thee."

The distraught father stared at John. Willard's face glistened and the air smelled of desperation. If he decided to complete his terrible mission, he'd likely kill all three of us. My throat thickened as I tasted fear. The next few seconds lasted a year. Willard slowly lowered his gun. I let out the breath I hadn't realized I was holding.

"I'll hold that," John said, extending one hand. "Thee wouldn't want to have a gun near a baby."

Willard handed John the butt of the weapon. Willard took two steps toward the door before John stuck out his cane – aiming it in front of Willard's feet. He tripped and sprawled face first, crying out as he went.

In one move I hoisted the heavy plaster statuette of a southern woman and her babe and dropped it, shuddering as I did. I had to ensure Willard wouldn't rise in anger and attack John again. I'd aimed for Willard's head but the statuette fell onto his back and cracked into half a dozen pieces.

The front door crashed open. Kevin appeared in the hall with his weapon drawn. As the ruddy-faced officer took in the scene, he lowered the gun.

"Well, well, Miss Rose. Looks like you're not needing me after all."

"We'll certainly need you to throw this scalawag in the clink, Detective," Celia said with a wry smile.

Willard might have been a hopeful new father, but he was much more than a scalawag. My heart broke for poor Prissy, and for John Price's family, as well as for the unfortunate Willard himself. Justice, even when served, was rarely kind.

The Murdered Lady
John Greenleaf Whittier

Lovis Cove, Marblehead, Massachusetts
Lovis Cove, near Fort Sewall, offers a scenic view of Marblehead Neck. Also known as "Screeching Woman's Beach" or "Screaming Lady Beach," local folklore has repeated for centuries the gruesome folktale of murder and pirates that inspired Whittier. Courtesy of Peter Muise.

[In the 17th century, when the sea-robbers were ravaging the commerce of Spain, a vessel of that nation was brought into the port of Marblehead, by a pirate brig. For the better security of its rich cargo, the unfortunate crew were barbarously massacred. A lady was brought on shore by the pirates, and murdered, and afterwards buried in a deep glen or valley, at a little distance from the village. The few inhabitants of the place, at that early period of its history, were unable to offer any resistance to the fierce and well-armed buccaneers. They heard the shrieks of the unfortunate lady, mingled with the savage shouts of her murderers, but could afford her no succor. There is a tradition among some of the old inhabitants of Marblehead, *that these sounds have been heard ever since, at intervals of two or three years, in the valley where the lady was buried.]*

    A dark-hulled brig at anchor rides,
      Within the still and moonlight bay,
    And round its black, portentous sides
      The waves like living creatures play!—
    And close at hand a tall ship lies—
      A voyager from the Spanish Main,
    Laden with gold and merchandize—
      She'll ne'er return again!
    The fisher in his seaward skiff,
      Creeps stealthily along the shore,
    Within the shadow of the cliff,
      Where keel had never ploughed before;
    He turns him from that stranger bark,
      And hurries down the silver bay,
    Where, like a demon still and dark,
      She watches o'er her prey.

        * * * * *

The midnight came.—A dash of oars
    Broke on the ocean-stillness then,
And swept towards the rocky shores,
    The fierce wild forms of outlawed men;—
The tenants of that fearful ship,
    Grouped strangely in the pale moon-light—
Dark, iron brow and bearded lip,
    Ghastly with storm and fight.

They reach the shore,—but who is she—
    The white-robed one they bear along?
She shrieks—she struggles to be free—
    God shield that gentle one from wrong;
It may not be,—those pirate men,
    Along the hushed, deserted street,
Have borne her to a narrow glen,
    Scarce trod by human feet.

* * * * *

And there the ruffians murdered her,
    When not an eye, save Heaven's beheld,
Ask of the shuddering villager,
    What sounds upon the night air swelled
Woman's long shriek of mortal fear—
    Her wild appeal to hearts of stone,
The oath—the taunt—the brutal jeer—
    The pistol-shot—the groan!

With shout and jest and losel song,
    From savage tongues which knew no rein,
The stained with murder passed along,
    And sought their ocean-home again;—
And all the night their revel came
    In hoarse and sullen murmurs on,—
A yell rang up—a burst of flame—
    The Spanish Ship was gone!

The morning light came red and fast
    Along the still and blushing sea;
The phantoms of the night had passed—
    That ocean-robber—where was she!—
Her sails were reaching from the wind,
    Her crimson banner-folds were stirred;
And ever and anon behind,
    Her shouting crew were heard.

Then came the village-dwellers forth,
    And sought with fear the fatal glen;—
The stain of blood—the trampled earth
    Told where the deed of death had been.
They found a grave—a new-made one—
    With bloody sabres hollowed out,
And shadowed from the searching sun,
    By tall trees round about.

They left the hapless stranger there;
    They knew her sleep would be as well,
As if the priest had poured his prayer
    Above her—with the funeral-bell.
The few poor rites which man can pay,
    Are felt not by the lonely sleeper;
The deaf, unconscious ear of clay
    Heeds not the living weeper.
They tell a tale—those sea-worn men,
    Who dwell along that rocky coast,
Of sights and sounds within the glen,
    Of midnight shriek and gliding ghost.
And oh! if ever from their chill
    And dreamless sleep, the dead arise,
That victim of unhallowed ill
    Might wake to human eyes!

They say that often when the morn,
    Is struggling with the gloomy even;
And over moon and star is drawn
    The curtain of a clouded heaven—
Strange sounds swell up the narrow glen,
    As if that robber-crew were there—
The hellish laugh—the shouts of men—
    And woman's dying prayer!

On the Black Ice

Peter Rawlik

Whittier, Alaska
The nearby Whittier glacier was named for the poet in 1915. During World War II, the United States Army constructed Camp Sullivan near the glacier. Camp Sullivan remained until it was decommissioned in 1960. The town of Whittier, named after the glacier, was incorporated in 1969. Most of the citizens live in a single building, a 15-story former barracks. Today, Whittier has become a port of call for cruise ships. Library of Congress Prints and Photographs Division

Camp Sullivan, January 8, 1944 –

Captain James Chan stared at the horizon, thinking about the events of the last three days. The wind was whipping down off of the Whittier Glacier and he could hear the ice creeping, cracking as it shifted and moved. It had existed for ages, a frozen memory of the world how it used to be. In places, when the light hit it just right, it was a cavalcade of colors, blues mostly, swirled with whites and dusted with brown from ancient sediments that still churned up now and again. But that was in summer. In the dim light of winter, the ice looked black, serving as a reflection of

Chan's own mood. He had been walking at the edge of the glacier for hours, not a safe place to be, not an authorized place to be, but after what he had done, after what he had been asked to do, he just didn't care about rules anymore.

His father would have reprimanded him, gently of course, but it would still have been a reprimand. He grinned at the thought of the old man wagging a finger at him. He had served as his father's assistant for so many years, but he hadn't learned the hard truth. Playing detective was easy, even exciting. There was something terribly enjoyable in investigating a crime, using not only your knowledge, but your wits, and on occasion physical confrontation to bring a man to justice. It turned out he didn't have a taste for the aftermath.

That was something he had never thought about before, the dark side of what his father did for a living, and what he and his brothers all had hoped to do as well. It was a black task, and James had always felt that justice was a bright light of truth, chasing away evil. But he had never testified in a courtroom. He had never seen families destroyed by that truth. He had never seen men hauled off to prison and slowly rot, their minds and souls destroyed by the slow passage of time until they were finally taken to the electric chair. His father made sure of that. Maybe the old man had done him a favor, maybe not. Maybe he and his brothers should have known what it was really like to watch a man die.

It had the worst three days of his life, but it hadn't started that way. It had started with an order to report to his COs office.

"Chan!" When Colonel Nichols barked his name it wasn't usually for anything good. Nichols wasn't exactly happy with his command, he had wanted to be at Dutch Harbor, in charge of the reconstruction there. Alternatively, he could be at Kiska, at the end of the Aleutians, where the enemy had been weeded out and the army was fortifying the harbor for a likely invasion of Hokkaido. He had no desire to be at Camp Sullivan making sure that soldiers and supplies were properly distributed. Sullivan was little more than a waystation and that didn't sit well with Nichols, and he tended to take it out on Chan.

"Yessir?" Chan dashed into the office from the anteroom where he had been waiting. He stood at attention, feeling awkward in his winter uniform. He was a long way from his native Hawaii and the light cotton suits he was accustomed to.

The Colonel motioned for him to sit, and Chan did so. "You saw the troop transport paperwork come in this morning?"

Chan nodded. "Yessir, regular rotation out from Kiska. A few minor casualties, guys with frostbite in their fingers and toes."

Nichols frowned. "There's also three prisoners. Wong, Miao and Gu - all ABCs."

Chan took a deep breath and slumped in the chair. He hated the abbreviation, he hated the designation, American-Born Chinese. As if they were somehow different than all the other second-generation immigrants in the United States. "What's the crime?"

"Apparently they were out on patrol and killed their commanding officer." Nichols slid a rather large folder over the desk. "I need you to act as their advocate."

Chan glanced at the file. "Me sir, wouldn't Hanes or McBride be more qualified?" He had never actually defended anyone before, and this would be a capital case.

Nichols' eyes slid away and stared out the window. "Hanes will be acting as the prosecutor, and McBride – let us just say that McBride isn't impartial in the matter."

Chan's jaw clenched. "You mean McBride is a bigot and he's already made his mind up that these men are guilty."

The Colonel's fist came down on the desk. "Damn it, Chan! Yes, McBride's a son of a bitch, and so are half the men in the army. Chances are these men are guilty – Hell they've all confessed. But we need to have a fair trial. I'm not sending these men in front of a court-martial without a decent defense. You may not be the best we have, but you won't sell them down the river before things even get started."

"Because I'm Chinese."

"Yes, because you're Chinese, but also because you're smart and a decent human being."

Chan grabbed the file and headed for the door. He paused and stared at his CO. "Says a lot about the service that you can't find any decent white officers to represent these men."

As Chan left, the cutting words brought the Colonel to his feet. He opened his mouth to say something but then shut it and in his mind cursed at the smart-mouthed kid, not because he was insubordinate, but because he was right.

The next day Chan found his clients in rather poor condition. Wong had a black eye, Miao a broken wrist, and Gu was missing several teeth. They had been fed the night before, but this morning the guards had not yet brought their breakfast. Chan found it unconscionable and sent a private on the errand immediately, he then sent for a medic. He waited till both medic and breakfast were finished before he began questioning the men in his charge.

They were reticent to speak to him. His father would have had some colorful phrase to describe them, the old man had been a master of fortune-cookie wisdom, but James had never found such things useful, particularly as he had often been the target of their so-called wit. It was the appeal he made to them concerning the time that finally got them to speak.

It was Wong who took the lead, his voice gruff and stilted, not at all what Chan had expected. "Gatiss was an asshole." He said it as if that explained everything; as if Chan should have known that their commanding officer, Captain Spaulding Gatiss deserved what had happened to him. Wong sighed and half-turned his head in frustration and then snapped back to look at Chan in the eyes. "The Captain had us up at dawn on Christmas, dressed and ready for an impromptu patrol. The Captain wanted to go and see the old Chichagof Harbor, a cove about five miles north of the airfield. There was no road, and Gatiss didn't like boats. Imagine that, being stuck on an island and not liking boats. Anyway, to get to the harbor we were going to have to march over the low mountains that made up the spine of Attu, so it was going to be hard going. When we pointed this out Gatiss just sneered and told us that we had to quit being so mouthy and that everyone knew that Orientals could handle more stress than Whites, but they were just lazy and complained more." Wong paused and let that sink in. "When Gu complained that he would be missing Morning Mass, Gatiss told him he wasn't a real Catholic, but a heathen pretending to be Christian so that he could benefit from Western Society. After that, we all shut up and just followed him as he marched off the base."

"Attu is a bitterly frigid place," groaned Miao. "When we took it back from the Japanese, we lost 550 men, and had another 1150 wounded, but over 2000 men came down with frostbite severe enough to force their evacuation. The wind blows down from the arctic and comes off the sea not only cold but dry as well. It tears into a man, cutting into him, searching out holes in his coat and weaseling its way inside to cut at bare skin like a frozen knife. There are no trees to block that piercing gale. Sometimes, you can find shelter in the shadow of a hill or mountain ridge, but never for long. The squall-like winds shift and dance, coming at you from all directions, redirected by the very mountains and valleys that you hope to find shelter in. It is a horrible place, not fit for men, whether they're white or yellow."

Wong put a hand on his friend's shoulder. It was an act of comfort, a small gesture of humanity, something Chan had not expected to see amongst men who had been accused of murder. "About an hour in, we were crossing a rather treacherous ridge. Miao moved across first and then threw back a rope to help the others. Gatiss crossed over and then Gu. When it was my turn Gatiss watched as I proceeded, lost my footing and nearly slid down a ravine. Miao and Gu had to haul me back up as I scrambled to find a handhold in the loose rocky soil. When I finally got back up, I was doubled over, trying to catch my breath. Gatiss came over and ordered me to stand up straight so he could get a look at me. When I complied he hauled off and punched me in the eye." The man's hand gestured to the bruise around his one socket. "He said that I was lucky that they hadn't just let a worthless chink like me fall, and that if he had been on that rope I would probably be dead. I can remember my fist clenching and the rage boiling up inside me, but Gu was looking at me shaking his head back and forth silently begging me not to do anything. So I didn't. I sucked all that hate back in and buried it."

Gu took over the narrative. With his missing teeth, his speech was tinged with a weird hissing lisp. "Hourth later we were coming down off the ridge, thuffling through the loothe rock, trying to keep our balanthe. I wath in front, walking thidewayth. Gatith wath in back, when thuddenly he yelled. He had lotht hith footing and wath now running down the thlope trying to keep from tumbling over or thlamming into the rocksth and boulderth at the bathe. Ath he pathed me he grabbed my arm and pulled me in front of him. I had become a human cuthion and he uthed me to break hith fall. He thood up uninjured, but my mouth wath a math of blood and I had thwallowed three of my teeth."

Miao picked up where Gu left off. "Gatiss demanded that we keep going, but Gu clearly needed medical attention. I made the mistake of standing up to him, and while I was demanding that we return to base Captain Gatiss took off his helmet and smashed me in the arm with it, breaking my wrist. Like Wong I wanted to strike back, but I was able to beat that feeling down. Together the three of us turned and walked away from the man. Leaving him there alone, screaming at us to come back. We didn't make it to base until long after nightfall."

Wong stepped in. "The next day a search party found Gatiss about a mile away from where we left him. He was half buried in grass and dirt with the remnants of a fire nearby. He had apparently tried to weather the night and died from exposure. We told our story to the base commander, just as we told it to you, but they still suspect us of doing a little more than just leaving him behind."

"They think you killed him," Chan offered. "His gun was empty and there were powder burns on Gu's coat. How do you explain that?"

Wong shook his head. "We're soldiers, it would surprise me if there weren't powder burns on our coats. As for Gatiss's gun being empty, who knows? Perhaps he used it to try and signal for help."

Chan sighed. "The case is purely circumstantial. I should have no problem proving your innocence. You'll be free men soon enough."

"No – No we won't," It was Gu who interrupted. The other two tried to stop him but he would have none of their interference. "Captain Chan, we killed Gatith. After he knocked my teeth out I drew my gun and Wong and Miao took hith weapon away. We thtayed out there and uthed Gatiss'th own gun to keep him away from our fire until he thuccumbed to the cold. Then we buried him and ran back to camp."

Gu's companions slumped back in their chairs, but whether that was in exasperation or relief Chan couldn't say.

In fact, Chan couldn't say much of anything. Instead, he closed up his files and walked out. He walked out and then went straight to Nichols office.

"You knew didn't you?" yelled Chan as he burst through the door. "You knew and you let me go anyway!"

Nichols folded his fingers together. "Yes I knew, and you didn't have any choice in the matter. I needed you to go. I needed you to hear their confession. They were just waiting for the right person to tell it to."

"Why me?"

"I told you, Jimmy, I needed someone to be fair to them. You've heard what Gatiss was like, and you've heard what they did. You'll argue on their behalf now, and it'll be a fair hearing. I need that. The world needs to be like that. Even when it must do terrible things."

Chan threw the file across the room but Nichols didn't even flinch. As the young man stormed out fuming, he slammed the door behind him. Nichols thought of putting the young man on report but then decided against it. It would have added insult to injury.

The trial was held the next day and was little more than a formality. Chan argued for leniency but to no avail. Three soldiers had killed their commanding officer, and regardless of the circumstances, a man was dead. The tribunal ordered swift justice. Chan appealed but his pleas fell on deaf ears. As his clients were marched back to the stockade Chan sat at his table and stared at the wall wondering if placed in the same position, would he have done anything different.

He was still thinking about that issue a day later as he walked out of camp and stood in the shadow of the Whittier Glacier. The great mass of ice had been named after some ancient New England poet, one that Chan had studied at university. Some of the man's words still lingered in his memory,

The sun that brief December day
Rose cheerless over hills of gray,
And, darkly circled, gave at noon
A sadder light than waning moon.
Slow tracing down the thickening sky
Its mute and ominous prophecy,
A portent seeming less than threat,
It sank from sight before it set.

In the distance, Nichols marched a line of six men out from the camp and had them take up positions opposite each other. Chan forced himself to watch as one line of men marched about ten paces from the other and then turned. This was the hard part, the part his father had never really prepared him for. He heard Nichols bark an order and the one group aimed their rifles. It was necessary he supposed, the order of things. Justice was more than just finding out who had committed a crime and then having a trial. Nichols bark again. Punishment had to be meted out. Gunfire erupted. Even from this distance, he could see the smoke of the barrels. The other men fell. If they made a sound he couldn't hear it over the echoes of the shots as they reverberated off the ice.

Chan thought there should be more than that. Three men had been put to death for the murder of a fourth. There should have been something biblical, a great ominous crack, an avalanche, something.

But the ice, that black ice that loomed above them, just stood there watching, waiting, as it had for thousands upon thousands of years. As if the men beneath it and the war they waged meant nothing. As if it knew deep within its crystalline heart that this horrid human conflict that made men do terrible things would someday pass.

Somehow Captain James Chan took comfort in that. It was a cold comfort, but it was still a comfort, and that was enough.

The Flock
Vicki Weisfeld

Goodwoman Eunice Cole, Hampton, New Hampshire
On the grounds of the Hampton Historical Society's Tuck Museum is a cenotaph to "Goody" Cole. Formally accused of witchcraft three times, she is the only woman convicted of witchcraft in New Hampshire. Her gravesite is, of course, unknown but is believed to be near the former site of her hut, now the land of the museum. Whittier makes Goody the antagonist in two tales of old Hampton, "The Wreck at Rivermouth" and "The Changeling." Courtesy of Scott T. Goudsward.

The speck of Indiana called Waverly rests in a placid region near the banks of the Wabash, where the river loops and wriggles, coyly postponing its inevitable rendezvous with the Ohio. The surrounding hills rise unassumingly above the horizon and, in the late 1800's, this modest topography pretty well reflected the local opinion of how people should behave.

At that time, a newcomer could easily disrupt the regular thrumming of Waverly's carefully controlled existence. And one particular December, it happened. The townspeople knew two things about the new arrival for sure. Her name was Mary Bight (the postmistress had told them that much), and she'd moved into old man Thompson's tiny cottage soon after it was empty, Thompson now occupying an even smaller and more permanent space in the cemetery behind the Methodist church.

Word was he'd caught a chill from sleeping with the bedroom window open past Thanksgiving. "Never had a lick of sense," the neighbors said, and the deteriorating condition of the cottage, with its reclusive tenant, confirmed it. They predicted the house wouldn't last the winter, and the women of the town shook their heads and tsk-tsked as they hurried by on their way to Mr. Grassley's store, as fast as the frozen puddles allowed.

No one knew where Mary came from, why she was there, or who her people were, providing a vacuum they filled with endless speculation. Mary thanked Rev. Applewood for his brief visit, but she didn't appear at church. She nodded to postmistress Quaid when picking up her parcels, but turned away, studying the return addresses, unmindful of Miss Quaid's affronted eagerness. Mary politely greeted the women who paid calls shortly after her arrival but did not invite them inside. The tiny house was "too much of a mess," she said, and their invitations to Christmas teas and open houses were neither accepted nor reciprocated.

In the winter, when Mary should have shoveled the front walk and knocked the heavy snow off the evergreens—and since she didn't do this, several of the yews had become grotesque topiaries—she put on her crimson coat, and the townspeople saw her ramble across the fields that edged the town, a drop of red on snow clean as bandages.

In spring, when Mary should have planted her peas and lettuces and later her annuals and still later her tomatoes and peppers, she instead sat at a deal table by the open front window and clattered away on her new typewriting machine. Grassley's young clerk, Tom Cooper, had delivered the big wooden crate on a handcart and would have helped her with it, but Mary told him to leave the box on the porch and prized it open herself. Stenciling on the box showed it arrived by train. If the new railway service, not yet a year old, brought goods that filled the crowded shelves of Grassley's store, it also brought unfamiliar people—including Mary Bight—and noisy typewriters and city newspapers, and it made the places along its lengthy route seem closer than they ought to be.

Mrs. Parker next door complained far and wide that she had to listen to the unsettling sound of Mary's clackety-clack-ping! clackety-clack-ping! morning to night. Mrs. Parker, whose few ideas were doled out by a parsimonious husband, couldn't for the life of her figure out what Mary could be writing, day after day. Who could she be writing to? How could she have so much to say? Why couldn't she use a pen, like regular folks? Curiosity flamed and crackled.

Postmistress Quaid, who regularly sharpened her eyes, nose, and tongue on the whetstone of local gossip, swore Mary Bight wasn't writing letters. She hardly ever mailed or received a one. "Books, books, books. That's it."

As spring arrived and Indiana turned its face to the sun, Waverly's menfolk passed the Thompson house at a stroll, hands in pockets, as if they had nothing really to do and might be available for any odd job, should Mary appear at the front door with its sagging screen and call out to them. Their palms fairly itched as they considered how a hammer and some strong nails could repair the sprung boards on the porch and right the tilting shutters. And, what they could do with a brush and a couple gallons of Grassley's white paint!

Mary was a good-looking young woman, and the men hoped to (but never did) catch a glimpse of her bending over a laundry basket or trimming the distorted shrubbery, chestnut hair pinned away from her face, lissome arms stretching overhead.

So, she lived among them, almost unseen but very present, when the events began that were fixed in the memories of Waverlians as distinctly as photographs glued to the crackling pages of a family album. Even townsfolk who only heard the story many years later, as it was passed parent to child, could recount some version of the debacle, which had about it the mingled clarity and confusion of a dream.

The townspeople awoke that June Sunday to weather so fine it must have been sent directly from God to encourage churchgoing. Along Mary Bight's street came the weekly procession of straight-backed ladies done up in corsets and restless men choking in their neckties, all of them in their too-tight Sunday shoes, truly church-bound. But their progress halted at the Thompson cottage, where a growing cluster of citizens gathered, heedless of the church's nagging bell.

A length of clothesline stretched across Mary's yard, and pinned to it like miniature bedsheets and waving from the lower branches of the new-leafed trees like starched handkerchiefs were pages and pages and pages covered with Mary's typing. From outside the yard's tired fence, the torrent of words blurred gray. Several larking older boys tried to reach over the splintered pickets and grab one of those tantalizing papers, but they were just out of reach.

"Who does she think she is?" stout Mrs. Grassley asked, a sufficiently vague and all-purpose indictment.

"That's a lot of writing, surely," said young Tom Cooper, awestruck. The church bell rang insistently, and, out of lifelong habit, they at last responded. For generations the bell had been the town crier as well as its timepiece, even though the bell's latter role was somewhat supplanted by the ear-piercing whistle of the 12:15 pm train arriving from points west, the 5:30 pm en route to Chicago, and finally the 8:27 pm speeding south, all the way to New Orleans.

On that Sunday, after the opening hymn and before the benediction, a bank of dense clouds rolled across the darkening sky, accompanied by a west wind that scoured the churchyard, sought out the desiccated leaves lodged against untended gravestones, swept them neatly into corners, then scattered them again. The wind slipped through an open church window and danced with the feathers on Mrs. Grassley's fashionable hat and startled Mr. Grassley awake. And it played with the papers hung in Mary Bight's yard, teasing them down from the trees and off the clothesline.

When the good folk of Waverly arrived home, a few found one of Mary's pages skipping across their lawns or wind-plastered to their porch rails, and what would have been a drowsy chicken-and-dumplings afternoon became a scavenger hunt, as older children were sent to find more of the intriguing pages if they could.

In all, twelve sheets were found. Their contents mystified the families possessing them. Neighbors compared pages, and the puzzlement deepened. The suggestion quickly spread that those who had pages should bring them to the church that evening, in the hope that, all together, they might make sense. No one entertained the most obvious thought, to return them to Mary herself, the stranger in their midst.

After evening services, they congregated in Fellowship Hall but soon discovered the random pages were still too random. In fact, reading all of them—in whatever order they attempted, since the pages were not numbered—made no more sense than reading them separately.

In a clear voice, young Evan George read out the paper his family had found. Evan had attended one semester at Indiana University, and the congregation deemed him well prepared for oratory.

Evan's page started near the end of a sentence. " . . . the means. But if he had not, would events have unfolded differently? Definitely not, thought those who claimed to know the doctor and his depraved intentions, who recorded his dabbling in the Black Arts. Most people avoided passing his noisome laboratory after dark. They heard frightening nighttime shrieks; the village's many stray cats had disappeared. A vagrant who helped him move some firmly padlocked chests claimed the laboratory's shelves held skeletons of small animals, baskets of dark, bitter-smelling herbs and roots, and loathsome things floating in jars. All this so unnerved the poor man that he refused to return for his meager pay." A murmur from the crowd. "The doctor claimed he engaged in strictly scientific pursuits, but the eerie glow from his laboratory fed doubts. A pale and breathless stranger stopped by the tavern late one November evening and told the publican he'd peeked through the laboratory's grime-streaked window and seen a green luminescence coil and swirl like mist, until it formed a grinning mask. The doctor spoke to it in an unfamiliar language. Its guttural reply made the . . ."

Mrs. Belden, one of the church's eldest parishioners, gasped and came close to fainting—whether because of the frightening text, the heat of Fellowship Hall, or the constriction of her implacable corsetry. While several church ladies chafed her wrists and brought cold water, the others decided it best to move on, and Evan George sat down, disappointed.

Postmistress Quaid had left for the church in such a rush that she brought the wrong piece of paper, but she peered over her steel-rimmed glasses and in a pinched voice explained it contained a vile chemical concoction. Her elaborate description evoked sulfurous high school science experiments. She distinctly remembered a "bubbling cauldron" and a list of unsavory ingredients that made her hearers shudder.

Her dark expression prompted uneasy glances at Mrs. Belden, still vigorously fanned by Mrs. Parker. Doc Murray, the pharmacist, said the ingredients Miss Quaid cited were fantastical and that she must have gotten them wrong. Her vehement denials reinforced the muttered notion, repeating through the assembled group like the refrain of some popular song, that someone, somewhere was "up to no good."

"Pure gibberish," Doc Murray pronounced and shook his head.

The next page contained only four lines:

"midnight sun and again
the wash of strongest light
months pass fleetly by
til Aurora paints the star–specked night."

The reader—the shy clerk Cooper, who harbored a romantic streak—thought it might be the end of a poem, but Grassley declared there was nothing poetic about it. His clerk sank into chastened and accustomed silence.

"Well, it rhymes," said Mrs. Grassley, puckering her mouth in opposition to her husband.

Grassley snorted. "It ain't grammatical. Wouldn't a poet know their grammar?"

The other pages likewise raised unanswerable questions. The group finally laid the matter at their minister's feet. Rev. Applewood had sat quietly through the recitations, gazing heavenward—or at the stain on the ceiling he'd just noticed, which would require costly repairs to the church roof—pinching his chin thoughtfully.

"What does it mean?" the parishioners asked.

"Is it dangerous?" Mr. Parker refined the question.

"It's subversive," said Grassley.

"She frightens me," said Mrs. Parker, a statement all the weightier because of her family's unlucky proximity to the author.

Postmistress Quaid snatched a paper from the hands of the woman next to her, and in an excited voice read:

"Rake out the red coals, goodman –
For there the child shall lie,
Till the black witch comes to fetch her
And both up chimney fly.
"It's never my own little daughter,
It's never my own," she said;
"The witches have stolen my Anna,
And left me an imp instead."

"Ha!" she concluded, the whole matter settled to her satisfaction (and, it's fair to say, barely concealed delight) on the side of evil-doing.

Rev. Applewood was a quiet, self-contained man, a plausible vessel for keeping Eternal secrets. Because he had trained at a leading Methodist theological school—Boston or Drew, no one could remember which—he was expected to voice a considered and definite opinion. He sighed.

"It's a puzzle, all right. We need to know more." He heard the restless shuffling. His congregation wanted answers, not intellectual shilly-shallying. He quickly went on, "and I think it would be unwise—un-Christian," he retreated to high ground, "to come to rash conclusions." This didn't sit well, either, so he ended with an ambiguous "one way or the other." Much better. A few people understood this final emendation as laudably even-handed, but most fixated on its delicious hint that something dire remained possible. They went home uneasy, but oddly satisfied.

By the next morning, Mary Bight had taken down all the papers. Meanwhile, a dozen Waverly families laid out the mysterious sheets on their kitchen tables for intensive study. The post office became the central reservoir for growing speculations and overheated reactions, and few patrons went away without dipping from Miss Quaid's overflowing pool.

One of the twelve papers was especially troublesome. It described an enormous monster, white as ice, with a devil's cold and malevolent gaze. The monster struck the unfortunate men who encountered it with overwhelming terror, and the certainty it would be nearly impossible to destroy. Two members of Dr. Waylon's family, which possessed the page, were acutely affected. Johnny Waylon, age eight, had screaming nightmares. Mrs. Waylon "heard things" in the night and, between comforting Johnny and repeatedly bolting out of bed to check the house's previously unused door locks and window latches, barely slept four nights running.

"Take that thing down to Rev. Applewood," she said to her husband Thursday at dinnertime, pointing a shaking finger at the paper. "I don't want it in the house." He promised to do so first thing in the morning, but just as the Waylons prepared for bed, a man pounded on the back door and pleaded with the doctor to hitch up his horse and hurry out to the farm to help his wife, struggling with a difficult labor. Dr. Waylon did not arrive home until nearly noon the next day. Exhausted, he lay down to rest while his wife cooked his lunch.

A shriek from the kitchen woke him, and he rushed in to find Mrs. Waylon bent over a bowl of potatoes, blood dripping from a cut on her hand, staining the white slices. He whipped out his handkerchief and fashioned a tourniquet. They sensed movement in the doorway and turned. The menacing page had blown off the hall table and lay on the floor, fluttering lightly.

Mrs. Waylon shrieked again, and her husband had no choice but to carry that page to Rev. Applewood as soon as he had properly bandaged her wound.

The story of the papery attack on Mrs. Waylon flew around town as fast as Johnny Waylon could run. Shortly thereafter, Rev. Applewood possessed all dozen riddle-pages. Mr. Parker rushed to buy tickets for his wife and children on the 5:30 Chicago-bound train, penning a short letter for her to take to his sister, explaining the precipitate visit.

The following Sunday, when the Methodist Church's bell summoned the town, many congregants looked uneasy as they slipped into their familiar pews, their usual good humor and benevolent nods set aside. Rev. Applewood chose as his text, Joshua 1:9, "Be not afraid."

During the week he had felt the blood quickening in the townspeople's veins. "Do not let your imaginations take control of you, just because of a few puzzling sheets of paper," he said. But his warning went unheeded, and that night, in the shadows of the trees across from the Thompson cottage, two or three men gathered, watching for they knew not what.

On Monday, the event the town had vaguely expected became all too real. Helen Jackson found her three young children behind the barn, vomiting clotted blood and moaning "as if possessed," a neighbor said. Desperate, Mrs. Jackson sent for Dr. Waylon, but he was several miles outside of town, tending a farmhand whose horse had kicked him in the chest. The story of the poisoned children reached every corner of the nerve-wracked town before Dr. Waylon could return, apparently just in time.

As ever, good news travels at leisure, while bad news takes the express, and only several hours later did everyone who had heard about the poisoning learn about the children's recovery, time enough for the idea that confirmed their prejudices to become rooted in many minds, free of discordant facts.

That night, eight or ten men loitered outside old Mr. Thompson's house, and they carried guns. They'd brought out two or three hunting rifles, Grassley's father's Spencer carbine, and several revolvers not loaded for decades and more likely to explode in their owners' hands than to hit any target. The small guns stuck ostentatiously from the belts of men lucky to be sober. They stared at Mary's night-blackened house, alert to every noise, but saw and heard nothing.

Rev. Applewood might not be a man to act precipitously, but he could detect the brimstone odor of moral danger. He sniffed it now. He called on Waverly's leaders: Dr. Waylon, attorney Horace

Silpatt, who was also the town's mayor, and Doc Murray, the pharmacist—the town's most respected and level-headed men, men with "a sense of consequences," he said to Mrs. Applewood. "And we need Miss Byron's good sense. She can calm the children."

Janel Byron, Waverly's schoolteacher, had spent the last month of the school year in St. Louis, attending her mother's final illness. They expected her back in Waverly on the 12:15, and when the train clamored into the station screeching its brakes and whuffing steam, the four men stood silently waiting.

"I didn't expect such a prestigious welcoming committee," she greeted them.

"We surely would not descend on you in this way, out of consideration for your loss," the Reverend said, "if it weren't absolutely necessary."

Questions flew to the woman's lips, but before she could ask them, Dr. Waylon said, "This is unpardonably rude, but can you come with us now, to the church?"

"Now?" Miss Byron looked around the platform for her luggage. She gave a young man leaning against the station wall a dime to carry her bags the several blocks to her rooming house. On the walk to Rev. Applewood's office, the men condoled with her by describing in detail the agonizing deaths of their own parents.

They'd soon told the whole tale—the mysterious pages, the growing anxiety, the odd events that fed the fear mongers. And, in the midst of everything, Mary Bight, secluded, unaware, and going about her work, whatever it was.

"Let me see the pages." The men sat silently as she studied them. The church bell chimed one o'clock. Miss Byron looked up.

"Well?" A chord of voices.

"First we must talk to Mary Bight." Miss Byron's obvious suggestion was a chink of light that immediately brought them to their feet.

"We've meant to do that, but," Rev. Applewood reddened, "we don't really know her, and we thought it would go better with you there."

"And the situation has gotten worse so quickly," said Mayor Silpatt.

"We'll go now." Miss Byron said.

If Mary was surprised to see Waverly's five leading citizens on her sagging front porch, she did not reveal it and promptly invited them inside. Unlike the house's shabby exterior, the inside, though tight on space, was clean and orderly. True, boxes and piles of books outnumbered pieces of furniture, but even without knowing the volumes' contents the visitors could see there was a method to their arrangement. By the window sat the typewriter that punctuated Mrs. Parker's days, flanked by a stack of clean paper on the left and typed sheets on the right. Less than an hour later, Mary's visitors departed.

At six-thirty that evening, the church bell's urgent summons boosted husbands out of their chairs to put on their coats and prompted wives to set aside the dish-washing, dry their hands, and gather the children. Only an urgent matter would call them out at this unusual hour, and they guessed what it was.

The townspeople approached the church afraid to learn what new depredations might have been revealed that day and keen to hear about them. They filled the sanctuary quickly and quietly, eyes fixed on the five town leaders who sat in front of the altar, facing them.

Rev. Applewood stepped to the lectern. "Dear friends, a pall of fear and confusion has lain over our town these last days. I know certain strange events and coincidences have alarmed many of you." His audience stirred on the uncushioned pews, alert, backs straight, eyes on him. "Some rather wild speculations have circulated. And some of you believe these rumors justify strong actions." Nods and mutterings of assent rumbled through the congregation.

"I've called you here tonight with great relief because we can finally put these matters to rest." He told them how he and the others had visited Mary Bight that day. "She made a good impression on all of us. She's bright, studious, and completely absorbed in her work, as we've all recognized."

"The Devil hath power to assume a pleasing shape," a rumbling voice called out from the back of the sanctuary.

Rev. Applewood held out his arms in a mollifying gesture. "We are very, very far from needing to think along those lines," he said. "I'd like Miss Byron to explain."

"When these gentlemen showed me the twelve sheets today," the schoolteacher said, "I observed a theme—a thread—among them. A thread related to their purpose, not their content." The audience looked wary. "When we spoke with Miss Bight, we found my supposition was correct.

"Far from being alarming or dangerous, these are pages of a scholarly work. Miss Bight recently received her doctoral degree in English literature and is writing a textbook exploring many of its masterworks."

"What about my page—the chemistry problem? That's no literature," Miss Quaid interrupted.

"I'm surprised no one recognized it," Miss Byron said and turned to Doc Murray, who stood.

"I said the ingredients sounded odd, and I couldn't understand the 'Hell broth boil and bubble,' that Miss Quaid recalled for us. But today when I saw the actual paper," he paused, "it's Shakespeare! We read it in high school!"

The crowd shifted in their seats. "Many of you surely remember the three witches who foretold Macbeth's fate," Miss Byron said. "'Double double toil and trouble, fire burn and caldron bubble?'" She looked at them expectantly. "Miss Quaid's paper had a fragment of that speech. And, yes, the witches' cauldron did contain odd ingredients, like 'eye of newt and toe of frog.'"

Miss Quaid fumed. Mrs. Grassley jabbed her husband with her sharp elbow. "You should've got that," she muttered.

"What about the witches, and the devil child, the imp?" Miss Quaid said.

"I should have remembered those lines," said Rev. Applewood. "They're from a poem by my favorite Quaker poet, John Greenleaf Whittier."

"'The Changeling.'" Miss Byron patted his arm. "Whittier was very prolific - You can't remember them all."

Unconsciously clutching her bandaged hand, Mrs. Waylon asked, "What about the white devil?"

"Part of a summary of Melville's Moby Dick," Miss Byron said. "The Great White Whale."

"But, my hand?" she asked in a weak voice and held it up.

"I'm sorry, my dear." Her husband smiled gently. "I'm afraid you are somewhat prone to household accidents." Before she could take offense, he added, "It's one of the chief reasons I'm glad I'm a physician." The audience chuckled, and she blushed but returned the smile.

"The man in the laboratory?" someone inquired, cobwebs of uncertainty still clinging to him.

"That page describes a type of story that uses science to give its plot a base of plausibility, then erects on it a most unscientific edifice. You may have read or heard about Robert Louis Stevenson's new story, 'Dr. Jekyll and Mr. Hyde,' or remember Mary Shelley's Frankenstein."

Like balloons losing their air, the townspeople gradually slumped. Their heads sank further with each benign explanation.

Miss Quaid launched a flanking attack. "But why did she hang those papers outdoors like that?"

Rev. Applewood returned to the lectern. "In a way, she had the same problem we did. She'd neglected to number the pages. She went shopping on Saturday, and a sudden thunderstorm came up. The wind through the open window blew a good many of her papers onto the floor and hopelessly scrambled them. She didn't have room to lay them out inside the house and had the idea of hanging them up so she could see them all and put them back in order. Which, in fact, she did."

"What about the Jackson children?"

"Ah," said Rev. Applewood. "That was unfortunate. But it had nothing to do with Mary."

Dr. Waylon spoke up. "The children spent the afternoon climbing in their neighbor's cherry trees. They ate too much fruit, plain and simple. Nothing supernatural about it." A few people nodded, having had children of their own.

After a prolonged silence, a woman's peevish voice asked, "Why don't she take better care of that place?" Everyone burst out laughing, including Rev. Applewood.

The mayor spoke up. "Mary is renting the Thompson house for a few months, just until she finishes her book. Meanwhile, Sarah and Hiram Thompson took some of the old man's money—yes, he had quite a hoard, believe it or not—and went to Europe." The townspeople shook their heads. "When they return to Indianapolis, they'll see about the house."

"By the way," Rev. Applewood said, "Mary did number the pages, once they were all in order. She realized some were missing and was pleased to get them back."

There were no more questions, and soon the church emptied, the people seemingly embarrassed to have needed such an explanation.

"Mrs. Parker's idea, the trip to Chicago," Parker said to the Grassleys, as they walked toward home. "I knew that young woman wasn't a witch."

"Of course not," sighed Mrs. Grassley and glared at her husband.

"Hmph," said Grassley, muttering, "'eye of newt.' Hmph." He hoped no one remembered he'd suggested the guns.

Miss Quaid, head held high, turned off at the next corner. "I just can't believe how gullible people are, letting themselves get carried away like that," she said.

Behind closed doors that night, the townspeople gradually came to accept this alternate and benign set of realities. A lot of conversations that started out talking about "protecting my family" and "can't be too careful" ended up with "benefit of the doubt" and "jumping to conclusions," as well as "sorry." The men who'd held the guns said little, but their hands trembled. Just one more step, which the night before had seemed almost inevitable, and they would have fallen into an abyss of error and regret.

Over time, the people of Waverly drew upon this lesson again and again, as they confronted new challenges to their established ways—the prejudices sparked by immigration, the hatreds born of wars, the meanness of the Depression, and all the other upheavals in small town life whose beginning they dated to the arrival of the railroad, so many years before.

On the morning after the community meeting, Mary Bight opened her front door to find a bouquet of garden flowers, two pies, and a loaf of fresh-baked bread. Mid-morning, half-dozen men carrying tools strode up her walk. By Sunday, the porch floor was secure, the shutters straight, and, most surprising of all, Grassley had donated several gallons of white paint that the men put to good use. She'd learned a lesson, too, and regularly appeared at church and took the time to know her neighbors.

As I grew up, I often heard this story from Waverly's old-timers. And I know that Johnny Waylon, my grandfather, lived its lessons throughout his own generous life. Still, whenever he told it, I could hear, just dusting his dry voice, a small boy's disappointment that the most exciting event of his childhood had evaporated like a mysterious green mist.

The Goodwife and the Bookseller
From the Casebooks of Wilmott Watkyns
Ken Faig, Jr.

Whittier at age 26
This 1833 portrait of John Greenleaf Whittier by Deacon Robert Peckham hangs in the National Portrait Gallery in Washington DC, on loan from the John Greenleaf Whittier Homestead. Whittier was still editing newspapers, but his abolitionist stance and poetry were beginning to garner notice.
National Portrait Gallery, Smithsonian

Back about two years before my friend Kathe Koellner died, she made what she thought might be a major literary discovery. Kathe was the proprietor of Koellner's Kabinet, an antiques emporium which she maintained for four decades in a small twelfth-floor office in an older building on Sixth Street in downtown Cincinnati.

Kathe was always looking for inventory for her store, and while browsing the $5 shelf at Bertrand Smith's Acres of Books she found a nineteenth-century, leather bound duodecimo volume bearing the stamp Baptist Miscellany on its spine. In days of yore, ministers were known to bind up various printed sermons in such volumes, and Kathe's discovery appeared to belong to this genus. There was no title page exhibiting a publisher, a place or a date of publication, or even a table of contents or index. Many of the individual sermons had been printed by the firm of W. & W. R. Collier of 13 Merchants Hall in Boston between 1828 and 1833. A few had been printed earlier—between 1813 and 1827—by the firm of William Collier. One sermon had the ownership signature of Mary Anne Collier, but otherwise, there did not appear to be any identification in the book. However, Kathe noted one small chapbook of poetry tucked in with the sermons—printed by W. & W. R. Collier in 1829. It bore the title Goodwife Wilson of Salem Town and contained one poem of 324 lines. The chapbook had tan paper covers and identified the author only as "J. G. W."

Kathe was old-school and still fond of Whittier even though his star has diminished. A copy of the 1945 Heritage Press edition of his selected poems was on the narrow shelf of favorite works (not for sale) in her shop alcove. So, when she saw the author's initials J. G. W. on this chapbook, she immediately thought of her favorite poet John Greenleaf Whittier. Book scouting was just a sideline for Kathe, and she rarely paid as much as much as five dollars for an acquisition, but she willingly paid Acres of Books its asked-for price for the volume. It didn't take her long to consult Pickard's 1894 Life and Letters of John Greenleaf Whittier at the local library. She found that Whittier had gone to Boston in December 1828 to live in the home of Baptist clergyman William Collier at 30 Federal Street. Collier was associated with his son William Robbins Collier in the firm of W. & W. R. Collier, publishers and printers, at 13 Merchants Hall. Beginning with the issue of January 1, 1829, Whittier became the editor of the

Colliers' weekly Whig-leaning American Manufacturer and their weekly pro-Temperance newspaper, National Philanthropist. The Colliers also published the monthly Baptist Preacher, but the Colliers did not entrust the Quaker Whittier with those editorial duties. He resigned his position to return to Haverhill to care for his ailing father. That much Kathe discovered from her consultation of Pickard's biography of Whittier.

As for the J.G. W. poem Goodwife Wilson of Salem Town, Kathe found that the subject was seventeenth-century Quaker named Deborah Wilson who was so upset by the harsh persecution of her fellow Friends by the Salem authorities that she determined to walk through the town naked in the summer of 1662 in protest. Quakers of both sexes were often stripped to the waist and tied to the cart's tail to receive their sentences of whipping. Their crime was heresy – they were not Puritans. Mrs. Wilson considered such punishment of women—which bared their breasts to public view—immodest. Mrs. Wilson took her infamous naked walk on June 9, 1662. She was accompanied by her mother Tamoson Buffum and her step-sister Margaret Smith, both fully clothed, on her walk. Mrs. Buffum carried her daughter's cloak and Margaret Smith carried a wooden sign proclaiming her half-sister "A Naked Sign." Some months later, on a bitter November day, the three were tied to the cart's tail to receive their punishment. Mrs. Wilson was stripped to her waist to receive her sentence of twenty lashes, reluctantly imposed by the constable Daniel Rumball. Her mother and her half-sister were stripped only to their shifts and received no lashes, although Mrs. Buffum protested loudly when a lash intended for her daughter struck her own exposed shoulder. Mrs. Wilson only lived a few years after being punished for her infamous walk. Her husband Robert Wilson pleaded illness when she was subsequently cited for absences from the public services of the established church. Deborah Wilson died about 1669, leaving a widower and three young children. Robert Wilson soon remarried and had more children by his second wife Ann Trask.

As for J. G. W.'s poem, it was quite evidently a beginner's work. It began:

> Tamsin Buffum one fine June day
> Watch'd fair daughter cast her clothes away.
> "Mother, I will no longer hide
> My strong hate for Salem's churchly pride."

    The poem continued for 324 lines, basically telling in verse the story which Kathe had discovered. Mrs. Wilson's judge was the overzealous persecutor Major William Hathorne, whose son John Hathorne would be involved in the Salem witchcraft trials later in the century. Major Hathorne was also author Nathaniel Hawthorne's paternal great-great-great- grandfather.

    Somewhat lascivious by standards of those times, the subject of the poem nevertheless seemed to be one which might have appealed to the Quaker Whittier. In one portion of the poem, Robert Wilson reproved his wife for showing herself on the streets of Salem. He told her that he would rather have had her commit adultery in private than show herself on the public streets. Mrs. Wilson defended her virtue and told her husband that her naked walk was more painful for her than for him. So, the husband forgave his erring wife.

    Kathe was at a dead end on how to pursue her discovery. There was no mention of Goodwife Wilson of Salem Town in Pickard's biography of Whittier. A hoped-for subscription edition of Whittier's verse proposed in 1828 was never published. Kathe did discover that Whittier had commented unfavorably on the excesses of Mrs. Wilson and several other seventeenth-century Quaker women in later prose writings. But beyond the presence of several works printed by W. & W. R. Collier in the Baptist Miscellany and the signature of Mary Anne Collier on one sermon, there was nothing to connect Goodwife Wilson of Salem Town with Whittier apart from the initials and the Quaker-related subject of the poem.

    At a loss, Kathe called me in to view her treasured discovery. She asked if I could assist her in the validation of her theory that Whittier was the author of the poem and promised ten percent of the sale proceeds if we succeeded in selling the book as a rare piece of Whitteriana. I knew Kathe was of modest means and was lucky to clear the rent for her shop each month. An only child, she had remained single all her life and had inherited her little bungalow out in Oakley from her parents. She owned the bungalow free and clear and lived mostly on her modest SSI checks. So, I agreed to her proposed terms. I took the book with me for safe keeping and promised to keep her involved as my investigation proceeded.

I've done research far longer than Kathe, I quickly found that Baptist clergyman, printer, and publisher William Collier was born in Scituate, Massachusetts in 1771, and died in Boston in 1843. He had six children, including a son, William Robbins Collier, who was born in Charlestown, Massachusetts in 1809. The younger Collier was not yet twenty years old when Whittier, slightly more than a year older than he, took over the editorship of the Colliers' weekly newspapers. I found that the household of W. R. Collier, male, age 41, clerk, in Boston in the 1850 census. Also in Collier's household in that year were Ann Collier, female, age 65, and Mary Anne Collier, age 39. I theorized that Ann Collier was a sister, or perhaps a widowed second wife, of the head of household's deceased father, and that Mary Anne Collier was a sister of the head of household. Presumably, Mary Anne Collier was the same person signed her name on one of the sermons included in Kathe's Baptist Miscellany volume. The 1865 Massachusetts state census recorded W. R. Collier a 56-year-old single man living in Boston. W. R. Collier died at the Home for Aged Men in Boston in 1886. His remains were interred in Mt. Hope Cemetery. The informant for his death record was one G. Tinkham.

I verified that no poem resembling "Goodwife Wilson of Salem Town" appeared in the collected edition of Whittier's poems, even among the juvenile poems printed as an appendix to the work. In fact, Whittier was known to have zealously destroyed examples of his early newspaper verse which came into his hands. An unknown early chapbook of one of Whittier's poems would be something of a bombshell in the literary world—albeit a mere firecracker pop compared with a newfound copy of Edgar Allan Poe's Tamerlane. I have a friend, Joel Baker, who is an antiquarian bookman in the field of American literature, so I decided to give him a call and lay out the facts, on the promise of confidentiality.

"The problem is that you have only an attribution to Whittier," Joel told me. "The Quaker subject of the poem and the signature of a Collier family member elsewhere in the volume are in favor of your case, but otherwise, you have nothing to prove that the poet J. G. W. was indeed Whittier. Nothing short of a verifiable dedication signature in Whittier's own hand or independent evidence that Whittier actually wrote Goodwife Wilson of Salem Town would turn your friend's discovery into a sure thing. Even so, I'd caution you on the valuation. With a verifiable Whittier signature (preferably a dedication to a Collier family member), your chapbook (left in the bound volume) might, and I emphasize might, command $25,000 at auction. Lacking such a dedicatory signature, we are dealing with the domain of attribution. With no attribution from recognized scholars, your chapbook might command $5,000 based on the arguments for your case. Written attributions from two or three recognized scholars might stretch this to $10,000. I hate to tell you, but this volume is not going to make your friend rich. Since it is bound with contemporary sermons, I don't think there is much doubt that the chapbook is properly dated 1829. Of course, it could have been interjected after the original binding of the volume. You never can tell. If the poetry chapbook is a forgery, it's a devilishly clever one."

Joel promised me a call back on the subject of Whittier experts. He fulfilled his promise a couple days later. "Whittier scholarship is not a large field these days," he explained. "A century ago your friend's discovery would have stirred a very lively debate, and likely realized a higher price, even allowing for inflation. Retired Professor William Emery of Colgate University is the recognized Whittier authority today. Lucky for you, his retirement home is in Dayton, Ohio. Richard Branigan is today's "young Turk" of Whittier studies and is likely to disagree with any opinion of Emery. He's at Florida State University. A third name is Emerson Brewer of Carnegie Mellon University. I hope the names help. If you can get two or three written opinions from recognized scholars favoring the authenticity of your attribution to Whittier, you're likely to be able to stretch the auction price from the $5,000 range to the $10,000 range. If the professors are lukewarm or divided, perhaps $7,500 is the likeliest ballpark. I'd offer you $3,000 sight unseen. No auctioneer's fees, no publicity. My objective would be to make a private sale in the $8,000 range."

I thanked Joel and told him that Kathe would consider his offer. But first I wanted to touch base with Professor Emery in Dayton. Before I called Emery, I grabbed the Baptist Miscellany and went to downtown to Kathe's shop to update her on the status of my investigation and ask her if she wanted to come with me to show the volume to the retired professor. As I opened the door, I caught a familiar scent. Kathe's one indulgence with her limited budget was that each afternoon, regardless of how busy the shop was, she brewed a cup of elderberry tea from a stash of frozen berries she kept in a small freezer in the back room. Her mother had planted an elderberry bush behind the house, and Kathe had continued the tradition. Personally, I found the tea to be cloyingly sweet, but it was Kathe's mother who had devised the recipe, so it was sacrosanct as far as Kathe was concerned. She was sitting at the counter sipping the reddish purple brew from her favorite bone china tea cup that had permanently been stained lavender by the tea.

I placed the book on the counter. "Kathe," I said, "I talked to Joel Baker about the Whittier chapbook."

Kathe glanced down at the book. "Let me guess. It's worthless." She sipped her tea.

"Not quite that bad," I started. "Joel says that without definite proof, you'll be lucky to clear $5000 from the sale."

Kathe looked astounded. She put her tea cup down so hard is splashed on the counter. We quickly cleaned up the spill. To our dismay, some drops had splattered across the Baptist Miscellany. We dabbed them dry with a dry cloth and fortunately, there were no stains on the leather. Kathe carefully moved the cup off the counter and sat again.

"$5000 would be wonderful," she said. "But how do we get proof?"

I explained what Joel had said about attribution by a Whittier scholar possibly raising the value. She consented immediately to a consultation with Professor Emery.

I called the professor the next day and he readily agreed to meet us. We set up a meeting for a few days later. I picked up Kathe and we made the trip to Professor Emery's Dayton home in less than an hour. He greeted us at the door of a modest home—not quite as modest as Kathe's, but still modest—and led us into his book-lined study. Professor Emery appeared to be about sixty-five years old, middle build, balding with sandy hair. He wore the professor's proverbial tweed coat. He greeted both Kathe and me with a broad smile, and eagerly examined our hoped-for treasure once we were seated in his study. We suppressed chatter and let the professor proceed with his examination.

"Quite a find," he finally proclaimed.

"So you think it is Whittier?" we asked, simultaneously.

"I have no doubt," he replied.

"And you'd be willing to give your written opinion on the attribution?" Kathe asked.

Emery paused. "Well, on that matter, I need to say a few more words," he told us. "I know a tiny bit about this work, or rather the rumor of it, even before your visit. My old professor at Baylor, Bartholomew Southwick, knew a fellow named George Tewksbury, who had known Whittier personally.

Dr. Southwick recalled when he was talking to George Tewksbury and the subject came up of lost Whittier items. Tewksbury told Southwick that Whittier actually had two poetry chapbooks printed by the Colliers in editions of fifty copies each. Whittier had been disappointed by the failure of a proposed subscription edition of his poems in 1828. So as a favor, or perhaps a partial compensation to Whittier for his editorial work, the Colliers printed these two chapbooks and gave the entire editions to Whittier.

Apparently, he gave out very few copies, and later recalled most of those that he had given. Whittier himself would not discuss the chapbooks with Tewksbury. But through George Tinkham, a mutual friend, Tewksbury found that William R.

Collier, the junior partner in the printing and publishing firm which had employed Whittier in 1829, was still living. So, around Christmas of 1885, Tewksbury went to visit Collier at the Home for Aged Men, where he lay partially paralyzed by a stroke. He asked the professor to convey his greetings to his old friend Whittier. He recalled the two chapbooks and said that Whittier, by 1833, had recalled all the copies he had given away, except for the copies given to his sister Mary Anne, who would not relinquish them. 'Johnny will just pitch his beautiful poems into the fire, so I intend to save them,' Collier recalled his younger sister proclaiming. He recalled little of the chapbooks, except to say that he thought the title of one was Household Verses and that the other concerned a Quaker woman who had walked naked in the streets to protest something or other. I don't know that Whittier ever visited Collier after the poet returned to Haverhill in August 1829. Collier died just four months after his interview with Tewksbury."

"I can provide you just one more bit of information," Professor Emery continued. "I've copied something out to read to you," he said, withdrawing a folded piece of paper from his jacket pocket. "This is a transcription of a letter from notorious forger Thomas J. Wise to an accomplice H. Buxton Forman which dates to November 14, 1892, a couple of months after Whittier's death. 'I hear tell,' Wise writes Forman, 'that there are no legitimate juvenile publications of Whittier's writing except what has survived in newspapers, which I do not care to collect. Some years ago, I heard rumor of a chapbook of poems, dated 1829, ascribed to a poet with the initials 'J. G. W.,' but my client, the collector John Henry Wrenn, informs me that the author of Household Poems was one Joseph Grimes Wilmer, not John Greenleaf Whittier. Given that Whittier so ruthlessly suppressed his early work, I don't believe the potential profits from an alleged hitherto-unknown early chapbook of Whittier's verse would cover our costs. We'd either have to take poems from the appendix of the standard edition, search for obscure newspaper verse, or hire someone to write poems like Whittier's. Not a proposition I care to undertake, despite the posthumous vogue for the poet and his works.' So ends the relevant passage from Wise's letter to Forman," said Professor Emery, refolding the paper and returning it to his jacket pocket.

"I've never been able to find any trace of Joseph Grimes Wilmer," Professor Emery continued. It remains a possibility that Wise did publish a forged chapbook of Whittier's alleged early work. Of the content of Household Verses—note the difference in title from Wise's account—I can tell you just one other bit of information, also secondhand from Professor Tewksbury. Professor Southwick told me that Whittier was embarrassed by some of the erotic content—quite mild of course—of his early verse.

If Household Verses had mildly erotic content, that chapbook would be a find indeed. There was lots of colonial folklore concerning sex, courtship, and marriage, with which would have been familiar to Whittier. In any case, the subject of Goodwife Wilson of Salem Town is good evidence that Household Verses, published at about the same time, might also exist."

"With all this in its favor, why do you hesitate to provide a written attribution to Whittier?" asked Kathe. "We'd give you a cut of the sale price."

"So you are partners in this endeavor?" Professor Emery asked in response.

"Yes, partners," said Kathe. "I made the discovery. My friend Wilmott has been doing the research. I have promised her ten percent of the proceeds."

"How much do you envision this volume might be worth?" asked Professor Emery.

"An antiquarian bookseller friend to whom I described the content expected a baseline auction price of $5,000," I responded. "With a couple attributions from recognized Whittier scholars, he thought we might stretch that to $7,500 or $10,000," I added.

"I think he's in the right ballpark," said Professor Emery. "I have modest means in retirement—as you can see from my house—but I would myself pay you $5,000 for your discovery. In fact, I'd prefer to make a private purchase, with no publicity. The fact is that my young rival Professor Branigan is going to disagree with any attribution I might make. I don't want to kick up a controversy. If I say yes and Branigan says no, you might not even achieve the baseline asking price. If Branigan says no and Brewer and I say yes, I think you're likely to get the $5,000, but not much more. So I hope you will sell the book to me privately, and save yourself the bookseller's markup or the auctioneer's fees. Not to mention the resulting publicity. I can assure you that your discovery and the differing opinions on its attribution to Whittier would be a one-day event in the news arena—perhaps a little more prolonged in the scholarly world. However, the unwanted attention and resulting inquiries might prove to be a major irritation."

"If we sell the volume to you, what will you do with it?" Kathe asked.

"That's between me and Whittier," said Professor Emery. "I intend to go over Goodwife Wilson of Salem Town with a fine-tooth comb and then make my decision. You and I know what Whittier himself would say."

"You'd consign the entire volume to the flames to honor the poet's wishes?" Kathe asked.

"No," said Professor Emery. "I would not destroy the volume. I would cut Goodwife Wilson of Salem Town out with a razor. I can do it carefully, so that the deletion will be difficult, if not impossible, to detect. Then I will sell the bound Baptist Miscellany volume to an antiquarian theological bookseller who will be interested in it. I might realize $100."

"And what will you do with the chapbook once you excise it?" Kathe asked.

"Again, that decision must remain between me and Whittier," said Professor Emery. "Neither of you will be privy to that decision. Years ago, not long after Professor Southwick told me the secondhand story from Professor Tewksbury, I had a dream. I was still a young man, doing my first teaching and working to finish my Ph.D. thesis. To this day, I seldom dream. But I have always remembered my dream of Whittier distinctly. The poet appeared to me in his study. He was nearing the end of his days. A fire was burning in the grate. He went to a roll-top desk and opened it, extracting a thin stack of what appeared to be chapbooks, with tan covers. He did not open or examine the chapbooks, but walked over to the fire, and cast them in. I saw him smile as the flames consumed the material. At the time, I had no idea of the meaning of my dream. Now, I think Whittier was showing me what he wanted me to do with any surviving copy of Goodwife Wilson of Salem Town."

"So, you and Whittier have already reached a decision in the matter?" Kathe asked.

"By no means," Professor Emery answered. "I'm just telling you how Whittier will vote, and why. If the chapbook is to survive, I must leave it in the bound volume Baptist Miscellany to prove that it is contemporary and not a Thomas J. Wise forgery. I have by no means decided what I should do. If I keep the volume, I might donate it to the Whittier Collection at the Haverhill Public Library and ask that it be held confidential until we celebrate Whittier's two-hundred-fiftieth birthday on December 17, 2057. I don't think even Branigan will still be living then. Frankly, I don't ever want to read what Branigan might write about Goodwife Wilson of Salem Town."

"So, scholarly rivalries dictate that Goodwife Wilson of Salem Town be consigned to oblivion?" I asked.

"By no means," Professor Emery answered, but his tone was beginning to change. "You and your partner can do as you wish with Baptist Miscellany. I'm just telling you why I'm not going to give you a written opinion on the chapbook."

"Even for a share of the proceeds?" I asked.

"Most especially not for a share of the proceeds," Professor Emery answered. "Receiving payment could be interpreted as an undisclosed interest casting doubt upon my attribution. I have explained to you why I don't want to give you a written opinion, and I have given you my private opinion verbally. Your chapbook is genuine Whittier. As I said before, you and your partner can do what you wish with Baptist Miscellany. I offer you $5,000—in cash if you prefer—for the volume."

"We'll consider your kind offer," said Kathe. "I don't suppose you want to keep Baptist Miscellany for further study?"

"I will study it further when and if you decide to sell it to me," said Professor Emery. "I am grateful to both of you for giving me the privilege of seeing it. I have told you what I think."

"Do you think the other chapbook Household Verses might ever turn up?" asked Kathe.

"You can never tell what will surface in the antiquarian book market," said Professor Emery. "I don't expect to see it, but you never know. I never expected to see the chapbook you brought today."

So we said our farewells. "Please consider my offer and let me know your decision," were Professor Emery's final words. Kathe and I were mostly silent as we drove back to Oakley. We had a lot to think about.

"I think I should leave the book with you," I told her once we had pulled up to Kathe's house. "I've gone about as far as I can with my research unless you want me to pursue opinions from Branigan and Brewer. It's going to be expensive to ship the book to them to get their opinions. Without a written appraisal, you might have difficulty collecting $5,000 of postal insurance in the event of loss or damage. If you're as concerned as I am about Professor Emery destroying the chapbook, my advice would be to sell to Joel. Joel only offered $3000, but we may be able to haggle."

"I'll take the book," Kathe said. "I'll let you know what I decide to do. I have a lot to think about"

So we bade each other goodnight, and I drove home. It had been a long day. Frankly, I hadn't been too impressed with Professor Emery. He exhibited some signs of deviousness. It shocked me that he even mentioned the possibility of removing Goodwife Wilson from the bound volume Baptist Miscellany. I also thought it odd he wouldn't allow us to have a look at the letter from Wise to Forman that he read to us. Overall, he seemed totally fixated on the subject of Whittier. My gut feeling was that Kathe would be better off to sell to Joel Baker. The offered price was lower, but I trusted Joel not to destroy the chapbook because of a dream.

I didn't hear from Kathe for several weeks. So, after grabbing lunch at Mills' Cafeteria one day when I was downtown on other business, I walked over to the building containing Kathe's shop.

Kathe had a few noontime browsers, so I browsed until they left.

"Any decision on Whittier?" I asked her.

A cloud briefly passed over her face and she forced a smile. "I should have called you," she replied. "Professor Emery came down from Dayton about a week ago. He paid me $5,000 cash for Baptist Miscellany. I have your money in the drawer for you."

"Kathe, you don't really have $5,000 in cash in your drawer?" I protested.

"No, of course not," she answered. "I put the money in the bank the same day Professor Emery paid me. I specifically asked the Professor for one hundred fifties, and I deposited ninety of them in the bank. I have 10 of them in an envelope for you," she answered.

Kathe's story sounded a little fishy to me. However, I merely protested, "I really didn't earn it. A couple hours of research, one field trip to Dayton to show your discovery to Professor Emery. It doesn't amount to much."

"It amounts to $500 cash. Or you can have $1000 shop credit," she said.

"I'll take the shop credit," I told her.

"Your decision," she said. "I'll put your ten fifties in the bank. I usually don't keep that much currency in my drawer. One hundred dollars in smaller bills is usually the most you'll find in my drawer. Even so, I've been robbed once at gunpoint and burglarized twice."

"You know how my mother loves antiques," I told her. "I can buy her something really nice with my shop credit. Perhaps for several years in a row."

"I'll appreciate the patronage, just as I appreciated your help with Baptist Miscellany," she said.

"Did Professor Emery have anything more to say?" I asked.

"Just thank you," said Kathe.

I don't think I ever used my shop credit, although I probably saw Kathe half-dozen times more before she died. I looked over the contents of the shop each time for a potential purchase, but I never saw anything that I thought would suit my mother's "high-end" tastes in antiques. On one of my last visits, Kathe had a rather battered cigar store Indian that I thought my father might like, which she urged me to take in return for my $1000 shop credit, but I demurred, thinking that my mother would not react favorably to the new addition to her household.

My immediate reaction to the news of the sale of Kathe's discovery was surprise. I thought Kathe would consult me before selling Baptist Miscellany to Professor Emery. I wondered if she had intended to forget about the matter of my commission if I failed to make further inquiry concerning the volume. Nor did I think my friend was stupid enough to keep $500 in cash in her drawer after being robbed once and burglarized twice—which is to say, I doubted that she really had my money waiting for me when I stopped by her shop. However, I decided to think better of my longtime friend. It was clear she didn't want to discuss Baptist Miscellany any further with me—perhaps Emery had even sweetened the deal. Fine by me.

I never expected to hear another word of it. But then a week later I saw a shocking headline on the third page of the Enquirer:

RETIRED PROFESSOR MURDERED IN HIS STUDY
POLICE SEEK INFORMATION

The victim was Professor William Emery, age 73. He had been killed by a gunshot wound to the heart and had bled out on the floor of his study. There was some scattering of papers on the top of his desk, and an empty metal container, about a foot square and four inches deep on a side table, but otherwise no major disruption of his study. Of course, in a study lined with several thousand books, it was impossible to assert that nothing was missing. The police were asking for assistance from anyone who might have seen a stranger around the Emery home or who knew of anyone involved in a dispute with the professor. The professor had lived alone, and had not even employed a housekeeper. Like

Kathe, he did his own cleaning and cooking and kept his little home immaculate. Orderly personalities, both of them.

After I read the article, I couldn't help calling Joel Baker. He answered on the second ring.

"Wilmott, I knew you'd be calling," he said. "But let me guess the subject of your call. Professor William Emery. Murdered in his home up in Dayton. Did the empty box contain his copy of Baptist Miscellany and the precious Goodwife Wilson of Salem Town? Did a scholarly rival beat the professor to the punch?"

"You're way ahead of me," I told my friend. "I'm still digesting the news."

"I heard from Emery about three days before he was killed," replied Joel, "and I've already reported the gist of the conversation to Sergeant O'Halloran of the Homicide Squad of the Dayton Police Department. Emery seemed paranoid that someone was out to deprive him of his treasure. He said he'd spent nearly a decade on the definitive article on his acquisition, and he didn't mean to be deprived of his work now. He asked me if I'd seen the alleged image of Household Verses, on the internet, and I told him no."

I interrupted Joel – "what image of Household Verses?"

Joel had me fire up my computer and then dictated a string of what must have been forty symbols. After a few miscues, I finally got it right. There appeared on my laptop the image of the salmon-colored cover of what appeared to be a pamphlet or tract:

> HOUSEHOLD VERSES
> By J. G. W.
> W. & W. R. Collier: Printers
> 13, Merchants Hall
> Boston, Massachusetts

"Do you know who posted this?" I asked.

"That's what Emery was asking me," he said. "He was rather upset. He accused me of entering the Thomas J. Wise con game in my own right and claimed I was destroying all the value of the book for which he paid $5,000 to your friend Kathe. I told him I didn't even know that he had purchased the copy of Baptist Miscellany until he called me. Then he wanted to know if I'd ever discussed Kathe's find with Branigan, Brewer, or for that matter anyone else. I told him that I'd never used his name in connection with Kathe's discovery since I didn't know he had purchased it. I did tell him that I had called some academic colleagues to try to develop a list of possible academic opinion-givers for you and Kathe.

Several sources told me that stories regarding early Whittier chapbooks had been circulating in the academic world for decades. The knowledge was not unique to Professor Emery. I hope I haven't created any problems for you. I was sorry to learn of Professor Emery's death, despite his abrupt manner with me. It amazes me to think that anyone would kill for the sake of a Whittier chapbook. The thing is not that valuable, certainly not worth a life."

"Life can be cheap, Joel, particularly if someone considers that his life's work or his integrity is being challenged."

"The Dayton police will likely contact you and Kathe," Joel said. "I hope you don't mind."

"I will help them however I can," I said.

"You know," said Joel, "Kathe's Baptist Miscellany is not unique. Thomas J. Wise gave a copy of the same compilation to the British Library in 1899. I don't know whether the British Library copy contains any alleged Whittier chapbooks. I assume you know about Wise and his forgeries."

"In outline," I said. "When we visited him, Professor Emery read an extract from a Wise letter to H. Buxton Forman which suggested a possible interest in forging an early Whittier chapbook. Wise's client apparently told Wise that the chapbooks existed, but that a man named Joseph Grimes Wilmer was the actual poet."

"Things get murkier as we progress," Joel commented. "I expect that the Dayton cops are going to be getting the FBI's intellectual property unit involved in the case. Given the Wise connection and the presence of a bound copy of Baptist Miscellany in the British Library, it wouldn't surprise me if Interpol gets involved, too."

"Once the FBI is involved, it's going to get more complicated," I said from personal experience.

I was duly contacted by Sergeant O'Halloran of the Dayton Police Department, and I told him the whole story, as much as I knew.

He said they were working hard to find the source of the internet post of the alleged cover of Household Verses, but that the poster had already taken it down. They recovered an archived copy of the image on Emery's computer, but the original hosting site was proving difficult to identify.

"We've got some prints from Emery's study," O'Halloran told me. "We're checking to see if the Florida State and Carnegie Mellon employment files on Professors Branigan and Brewer contain fingerprints. Not very likely. We're consulting with the FBI as to whether there is enough information to get search warrants for Branigan's and Brewer's homes and offices. We have to be very careful, though, because of academic sensitivities. Accusing professors of wrongdoing is always risky business. The FBI may wish to consult with you. So far, we've been working with Inspector McNichol, in charge of the Dayton FBI office. But the matter has already been referred to the FBI's Washington DC headquarters."

I thanked O'Halloran for being so candid with me and offered whatever help I could provide to law enforcement authorities. He told me they were also working with my friend Joel Baker. Before I hung up, O'Halloran told me, "The FBI has already asked their counterparts in London to take a look at the British Library's copy of Baptist Miscellany. A full collation has been promised by the British Library staff."

The next call was from Kathe, who was frantic with concern. She had also heard from Sergeant O'Halloran. I was able to calm her down. I explained that the transaction was legal and that since she didn't tell anyone but Joel and myself about the book, the murderer had to have learned about the Whittier chapbook from

Emery himself. She seemed better, but I knew she'd dwell upon the matter until the killer was apprehended.

The next word I had was about two weeks later from Joel Baker. "They managed to trace the Household Verses image back to Professor Brewer's computer in Pittsburgh," Baker told me. "So they executed search warrants on Brewer's office and home. They found two copies of Baptist Miscellany in Brewer's office. One with Household Verses and one with Goodwife Wilson. The problem is that there's no way to prove that the copy with Goodwife Wilson is the copy which Kathe discovered. Brewer claims he's spent years looking for copies of the two chapbooks as part of his research, and the FBI thinks a jury might believe him, considering his credentials and the fact we really don't now how many copies of Baptist Miscellany might be out there with or without the Whittier chapbooks. FBI's intellectual property unit is convinced the chapbooks are forgeries deliberately placed within the Baptist Miscellany by Wise and the police are convinced Brewer is lying, but without proof that Brewer's copy is the Emery copy, his lawyer wants him released as soon as possible."

A thought suddenly struck me. "Joel, I need to make a quick call. I'll call you back tomorrow."

I quickly located the phone number for the Dayton Police Department and asked to speak to Sergeant O'Halloran. I quickly explained my little brainstorm. O'Halloran seemed dubious but promised to pursue my lead. I sat back and relaxed. Perhaps there would be justice after all.

The next morning, I decided to look at Kathe's wares to spend my store credit. "Kathe rushed over as soon as I strolled in the door. "Wilmott, I had the oddest phone call from the Daytona Police last night. They were asking me about the Baptist Miscellany."

I nodded. "I thought they might."

Just then the phone rang. Kathe answered it and looked puzzled. "It's for you"

I took the phone. It was Joel Baker. Kathe's phone was an antique itself but it did have a speaker phone so she could talk to customers while checking the shelf for them. I punched it on speaker so Kathe could hear. "Wilmott Watkyns, what did you say to Sargent O'Halloran?"

I couldn't help but smile. "Why Joel, whatever to you mean?"

"Professor Brewer has been arrested and charged with the murder of Professor Emery. Apparently, he confessed when O'Halloran confronted him with some new evidence. Extradition papers are being filed in Pennsylvania."

"Joel. I simply remembered something."

"Simple my eye. You just caught a murderer."

"Joel, when I was here with Kathe, she sloshed her elderberry tea, and some got on the book. It was just a minor little accident."

Kathe nodded. "The police asked me about that last night."

I continued. "The tea didn't stain the leather, but the leather is so old, it had to absorb a little of the liquid. I suggested that the police have their officer with the best nose take a good sniff and see if there was that sickly sweet scent of elderberry lingering on the book. If it was there, it was Kathe's copy, which she and I both saw get hit with the tea. Two witnesses saw it happen. Let Professor Brewer explain how his copy of such a rare book could also have the smell of elderberries. They sniffed, they detected, they confronted, and he confessed."

Kathe looked at me. "And you don't care for elderberry tea,"

I smiled. "I might still develop a fondness for it."

From what Joel was later able to piece together, Brewer feared that Emery planned to use Goodwife Wilson to claim that the chapbooks were outright forgeries, bound with the sermons to provide dating, and were not actual writings of Whittier. Brewer's position was also that the chapbooks themselves were frauds, but that Tewksbury-Wise-Forman used actual Whittier poems, cuttings from newspapers lost over time. In other words, Brewer was heroically trying to protect the legitimacy of lost poems that Emery was going to discredit.

He claimed that Emery had been badgering him over the telephone before he finally decided that a face-to-face meeting was the only way to resolve their differences. He claims that he traveled to Dayton to propose a collaborative article arguing both sides. Emery accused him of undermining his work. Brewer claims that Emery became enraged and attacked him. He says that the two struggled and that he fired the fatal shot in self-defense. He says that he brought a gun to their interview because of the aggressive attitude Emery had taken in their prior conversations.

Brewer tells a good story, but I don't think it's going to get him off the hook. His bringing of a gun to the interview and his removal of Emery's copy of Baptist Miscellany and Emery's draft paper, combined with his flight back to Pittsburgh, tell a different story. Ironically, Emery's draft paper actually agreed with Brewer that the chapbooks, while they were indeed forgeries, contain legitimate writings of Whittier.

The tragedy, of course, is that the dispute over these chapbooks cost a life, possibly two.

After two years of numerous delays and motions, the trial of Emerson Brewer for the murder of William Emery took place in 2008. The District Attorney tried for First Degree Murder. The jury settled on Voluntary Manslaughter. Professor Brewer will spend the next decade in jail, his career over and his reputation in tatters. As a witness, I was not able to attend any other sessions except sentencing. I did attend that, with Kathe's copy of Whittier's poems in my purse. I bought it at the sell-out of the contents of her store as part of her estate. Kathe Koellner had died several months before, passing in her sleep on a cot in the alcove where she rested in the afternoons while the shop was closed for lunch. I'm glad she passed quietly among her beloved antiques but I believe, in my heart of hearts, that the murder and her inadvertent part in it, had weighed too heavily on her tired old heart. I hope, in her eternal rest, she has the opportunity to meet Whittier and tell the story of the chapbook and how her discovery brought Whittier's name once again to the forefront. I think they'd both enjoy that.

The Murdered Traveller

William Cullen Bryant

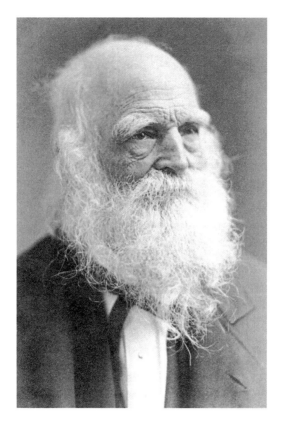

William Cullen Bryant Cabinet Card
*Bryant cemented his status as one of America's foremost literary figures with
"Thanatopsis," his meditation on death. Much like other fellow Fireside Poets
such as Whittier and Longfellow, his house has become a literary shrine*

WHEN spring, to woods and wastes around,
Brought bloom and joy again,
The murdered traveller's bones were found,
Far down a narrow glen.

The fragrant birch, above him, hung

Her tassels in the sky;
And many a vernal blossom sprung,
And nodded careless by.
The red-bird warbled, as he wrought
His hanging nest o'erhead,
And fearless, near the fatal spot,
Her young the partridge led.

But there was weeping far away,
And gentle eyes, for him,
With watching many an anxious day,
Were sorrowful and dim.

They little knew, who loved him so,
The fearful death he met,
When shouting o'er the desert snow,
Unarmed, and hard beset;--

Nor how, when round the frosty pole
The northern dawn was red,
The mountain wolf and wild-cat stole
To banquet on the dead;

Nor how, when strangers found his bones,
They dressed the hasty bier,
And marked his grave with nameless stones,
Unmoistened by a tear.

But long they looked, and feared, and wept,
Within his distant home;
And dreamed, and started as they slept,
For joy that he was come.

So long they looked--but never spied
His welcome step again,
Nor knew the fearful death he died
Far down that narrow glen.

The Death Clock
David Bernard

Whittier Statue, Whittier, California
"John Greenleaf Whittier," a statue by Christoph Rittershausen was dedicated on May 9, 1987, and placed on the Friends Ave side of Central Park in the city named after him. Photograph (2015) by jkelly is licensed under CC BY 4.0

I stepped out the front door of the Security Bank Building on the Cahuenga side to wait for my ride. The sun was overhead, the street was sweltering, and it was only early June. 1941 had been a lousy year so far and the weather was just icing on the cake at this point. People were already on edge with the specter of war already hanging over our heads. The war in Europe was going to draw us in. It wasn't a matter of if anymore, it was a matter of when – the Ruskies were killing off one group or another, the Krauts were attacking any country they took a shine to, and the Nips were trying to retake the Pacific. The heat was making waiting for the inevitable all the worse.

I saw the car as soon as it turned off Franklin onto Cahuenga. Hell, most of Los Angeles must have noticed the car. Hupmobile Skylarks were expensive and rare, and I'd be willing to bet the C-note hidden in my shoe that this was the only Skylark painted bright celery green. I still had no idea what Masterton wanted, but it obviously wasn't a low-profile job. The car idled and I assumed that meant the driver wasn't rushing out to open the door for me. I could live with that.

I slid into a back seat big enough to house a family of five, savoring the cool leather. The car took off and through the tinted windows, I watched as we rolled out of LA and out into the suburbs. The further we got from downtown, the bigger the houses and the greener the lawns. By the time we reached Whittier, the locals were spending more on lawn care in a month than I would earn in my lifetime.

When Arthur Brownell Masterton's personal assistant had called and invited me to his house, it was safe to assume it was not for a champagne brunch and croquet. With barely an hour's notice, I didn't have time to put on my good suit, but I did have my shoes shined in the lobby. That was as close to dressing to impress as you get on short notice.

When the scion of the Brownell Consolidated Industries fortune sends a private car to haul a hired gunsel like me out to his house, the best thing to do is wait for the car, find out how desperate Masterson really is, and hope it doesn't involve anything too illegal. If nothing else, it would be a lovely hour-long drive in the suburbs.

The skylark pulled into the driveway of Oak Knoll, the Masterton estate. Calling it a house was like calling the Silver Lake Reservoir a puddle. The garage alone was slightly larger than the fleabag Hobart Arms I called home, but Oak Knoll used a lot more stucco. I decided that I didn't like it. The color was some sort of yellow that looked closer to curdled milk than buttercup, making the burgundy brick trim look like open wounds. I liked the roof, but then again, you can't do much to mess up terra cotta tile, even with Brownell levels of cash. Factoring in the color of the car, I decided that Masterson was either colorblind or hated the neighbors. The car pulled up beneath a massive portico. I hopped out and paused to let my retinas recover from temporary celery blindness. The chauffeur had not said a word the entire trip.

I didn't know much about Arthur Masterson, and I wasn't given enough time to look into him. I knew he had two great passions in life: making money and collecting rarities about the poet on the East Coast they had named the city of Whittier after. When you have the kind of money he had, moving to Whittier just because it was named after a poet you liked is considered an eccentricity.

The door opened and a silent butler ushered me into a two story entry done in the southwest style. The room was silent except for a towering grandfather clock passing time. The back of the second floor had a walkway framed by a wrought iron railing which gave a close-up view of a chandelier larger than my office. The railing matched the chandelier's iron arms, naturally. The back wall itself was a row of French doors, with stained glass rising above it. I'd been in cathedrals that were less showy. It was all obscenely expensive but tasteful if passionless. Some designer got paid good money to make it look pretty for Masterson, but I could tell it was to impress high society guests. I was more impressed by the tantalizing aroma. Nothing smells like old money like a mansion owned by old money.

I felt out of place already, even with my freshly shined shoes. Although, in all fairness, I was wearing my best fedora and my least shiny jacket. The butler made a move to take my hat. I let him have it. Even if I left in a hurry, there was a thrift shop on Diego Ave that had several good looking replacements.

I kept the jacket. I wasn't wearing a shoulder holster since this was a high-class neighborhood, but I had tucked my M1908 Vest Pocket Colt in my pocket. It wasn't my first choice in a gunfight, but I wasn't expecting trouble while hobnobbing with the gentry.

More than once, some idiot thugs frisking me grabbed my real gun but missed the tiny little thing in a vest pocket. And I had found it convenient to be armed when the bad guys thought you weren't. Plus I would hate to break the crisp lines of my ensemble with a more practical gun on the chance a croquet game turned ugly.

I was ushered wordlessly into a library about the size of a small city block. It smelled of old books and good cigars. I took a deep breath and savored the bouquet. There was a good chance I'd hyperventilate before I got out of Oak Knoll. I wandered around the room. The books were all old and leather-bound, mostly by or about Whittier.

The door opened and a tall blonde in a short dress walked in. She had tanned legs that promised paradise and a figure that suggested the legs weren't exaggerating. Her dress was lavender silk, off one shoulder and tight in all the right places. She glided into the room and leaned against a marble pedestal with the head of an old guy that I assumed was Whittier. She looked faintly bemused.

"So," she said, "you're the private dick. Impress me with your detecting."

"If you're expecting me to look at you and give your life story, your old man hired the wrong guy. Sherlock Holmes lives in London." I replied from the safety of the far side of the room. Even a lamb knows when it's being lead to slaughter.

She reached into a pocket and pulled out a cigarette. Custom blend – I could see the gold ring around the paper that meant it was from Fernando of Beverly Hills. She probably paid more for those cigarettes than I spent on my jacket, even if I had bought it new. She lit the cigarette and looked at me. She exhaled. The scent of clove filled the room.

"Very good. You figured out I was the daughter, not the secretary. I'm Amanda."

"If the Fernando cigarette didn't prove it, the dress did. It probably cost more than what a secretary makes in a year, even Arthur Masterson's private secretary." I wasn't sure if I was a diversion or fresh meat. I hope to distract her either way.

"This little frock?" She twirled to show me the entire thing. It had no bad sides, but that had nothing to do with the dress. "Daddy's private secretary is a man named Rollins. And Rollins thinks this dress is scandalous. I like annoying him and I like this dress. You'd be amazed how quickly I can get it on and off when I need to." She fiddled with the button on the shoulder that I suspected was structurally significant.

"I'll remember that, should I ever need a dress." I have very few rules I live by, but I was certain sleeping with the client or the client's immediate family was definitely not encouraged in the unwritten code of private eyes.

"I'll tell Daddy you're here." She stubbed out the cigarette. I think she was trying to pout as she turned and walked out the door. The dress definitely had its merits.

I returned to wandering around the room. There was a massive oil painting on the wall of a farmhouse and a barn. The door opened again, and this time the view was not nearly as enticing. As he walked over to his desk, we were both assessing each other. Arthur Masterson was a big man, and I doubted any of it was fat. His carefully trimmed mustache was gray, and his hair was thinning and turning salt and pepper. He moved easily and had a feral glint in his eyes. I'm suspected he didn't lose often or gracefully.

He sat at the desk and motioned me to sit. He opened the folder in front of him. Even upside down and across the expanse of mahogany I could see it was a dossier on me.

I decided it was time to pump some life in this shindig. "If that file includes the time when I was eight and got pinched stealing peppermints from old man MacDougal's store, just be aware I was framed. Tommy Flaherty took them and tucked them in my school bag."

He looked up and snorted. "Mr. McAvoy, I sincerely doubt you ever carried a school bag." I smiled. He had me there.

"Kirk McAvoy. Private investigator. Former police officer, Boston. Former police officer, New York. Former police officer, Los Angeles. Apparently, you do not play well under supervision."

He read a few additional details from the file, none of which I was unaware of.

He shoved the folder away and gestured at it. "My assistant has never met a person, dead or alive, he couldn't compile a useless file on. I prefer my gut."

He stood up and went over to the painting had been looking at. I stayed seated. "Mr. McAvoy, how many times were you shot in the line of duty in your somewhat spotty police career?"

"None. Getting shot creates far too much paperwork."

"And how many times have you been shot since you went freelance?"

I had to stop and think about that one. "Are we talking grazes or just those requiring medical attention?"

He snorted again. I suspected that was his way of laughing. He finally turned toward me. "I saw you admiring the painting. Whittier's Birthplace in Massachusetts."

I decided to prove I was more than a pretty face. "Unless I'm mistaken, a J. Jiquel Lanoe oil. Based on the date, right before he returned to France."

That scored a raised eyebrow. "That is correct. And it was the last canvas he painting in America. I paid his travel expenses on the condition that he stop in Massachusetts and paint the birthplace."

I simply shrugged. "I met him once or twice before he took up painting." I had gotten Lanoe out of a blackmail jam when he was still a washed-up silent actor. So I knew far more about him than I wanted.

Masterson seemed to have made up his mind. "Mr. McAvoy, you don't know a damn thing about John Greenleaf Whittier, do you?"

I shook my head. "I was never much of a student of literature."

"Fortunately, I don't need a Whittier scholar." He pressed a button under his desk and I heard a solid click. Masterson stood up and walked back to the painting. He grabbed the shelf next to it and it pivoted away from the wall on hidden hinges. He gestured me to join him. I walked over. There was a door with a very expensive looking lock. Masterson fished a key out of his pocket and unlocked the door. He reached in and lights flickered to life. We entered the room.

If his library was that of wealthy Whittier enthusiast, this was the chamber of a very rich, very obsessed collector. He walked further in and turned around. The walls were covered in framed handwritten letters that I assumed were from Whittier. Old books were under glass domes, looking more like holy relics than books. Display cases were full of odd debris – all carefully labeled – a burnt chunk of wood labeled "1902 fire," a clump of gray hair, button hooks, pieces of cloth, moldy old newspapers – all junk which I guessed he paid a pretty penny for.

"This, Mr. McAvoy, is what I want you to find." He handed me a folder and gestured to a writing desk in the corner.

I sat and opened the folder and thumbed through the papers. "It's a clock. You want to find you a clock?"

Masterson stopped straightening picture frames that were already even. "A clock? Oh, Mr. McAvoy, this is no ordinary clock. This is an Elias Ingraham 8-Day, 4 Column, Black Mantle Clock. Originally purchased by Miss Sarah Gove in 1890 and placed on a desk in her formal parlor in Hampton Falls, New Hampshire."

I looked at the photos. It still looked like an old clock. "I'm going to guess that this clock has something to do with your pal Whittier here. Otherwise, you'd already own a dozen of them."

Masterson walked over to a clock-sized bare spot on a shelf and wiped the dust from it. He looked at the blank space almost lovingly. It was making me a little nervous, but I was certain that shooting your client in his secret vault, deranged or not, was also frowned upon in the unwritten code.

"You assume correctly. In 1892, Whittier was staying at Elmfield, the Gove home in Hampton Falls. He retired for the evening and headed to his room. As he went up the stairs, the clock chimed once."

"Correct me if I'm wrong, but aren't mantle clocks supposed to chime as part of their job?"

"Indeed, Mr. McAvoy. However, in this case, the clock hadn't chimed in years and wasn't kept wound anymore. It was strictly ornamental. When a broken clock chimed, it's was something the

Murder Among Friends > 67

people in the parlor remembered. Whittier suffered a stroke during the night, lingered another day and then died. The clock never chimed again." Masterson still had that gleam. I casually brushed against my pocket to make sure the Colt was still there.

Now I understood. "Whittier's death clock. You want me to locate it so you can buy it."

Masterson headed back toward the door. I followed. He carefully locked the room again and slid the bookcase into place. He gestured toward the desk. We sat down again. He leaned back in the chair.

"You're partly correct, Mr. McAvoy. I do you want you to find the – what did you call it? – "the death clock." However, I don't need to buy it. I already own it. The house was sold three years ago, and the new owner, Dr. Straw, quickly discovered that maintaining an old house was expensive on a small town doctor's salary. So I concocted some woeful tale about my recently deceased father and his fond memories of staying in the Gove house, and since my father was a clock collector, could I inquiring as to the availability of an "old broken clock" that he had had always wanted to have repaired. That is how I acquired a memento of my dear dead father."

"I don't recall seeing a clock in your collection." I had a sneaky suspicion where this conversation was going.

"I had it shipped by air mail. It was stolen from the terminal at Mines Field." He sat forward.

I stood up. "And this is where I come in. I assume the LA police were less than sympathetic?"

"Consider this a retainer. Find my clock and there will be another envelope." He nodded and pulled an envelope out of his pocket.

I tucked it in my jacket without counting it, which I thought was a particularly classy move on my part. It was not a thin envelope. Masterson stood up and walked me to the door.

"A Sergeant Nelson took my report, for all the good that will do you." He paused as his butler returned my hat. I thanked him. He nodded and slid away. It looked like old Jeeves had tried to clean it. I could have saved him the effort – there was a better chance of raising the dead than raising the nap on that fedora. Still, points for trying. Hadn't heard a word from the butler either. I wasn't sure if working for Masterson meant you took a vow of silence or if he only hired mutes.

"Mr. McAvoy, you were hired because you seem to have a knack for finding trouble yet somehow surviving. I don't particularly care whose skull you need to break to get my clock back, but if the police come looking for me because of something you did, I never met you."

"Mr. Masterson, I prefer when clients don't ask for details, it save me the trouble of making up something palatable." He opened the door. The motorized celery stalk was rolling up to the entrance. I adjusted my fedora.

He may or may not have nodded as the door shut quickly. I wasn't offended. I could overlook a lot of things with that envelope in my pocket. I had the Skylark drop me off in front of the bank near my apartment. No point in making the deposit at the bank in the lobby of my office and letting the landlord know how much rent money I had. I grabbed coffee and a sandwich at a diner and pretended to be plotting my next move.

I walked back down to Cahuenga. I knew Nelson at LAPD, and Masterson was not going to get any traction from him. He was an honest cop, but dumber than a box of hammers. A stolen clock was not going to be a priority in the middle of another mob war. And Nelson wasn't bright enough to recognize he had just brushed off one of the richest men in southern California.

As I approached the Security Bank Building, I decided my best bet was to retrieve my car and head down to Mines Field and see what sort of records the air shipping company had. It was late enough that the night shift would be working, and they were always just bored enough to be chatty.

I use a different entrance each time I head into the building. No point getting into routines that could get you killed. This time, I decided to take the entrance on the Hollywood side. As I opened the door, I noticed a cherry red Mercury convertible parked in front of the bank entrance. I checked my watch – it was nearly six o'clock. The bank had closed an hour before. In this neighborhood, it stuck out like a cherry red sore thumb. I patted the Colt in my pocket and wished I had something larger. I took the elevator to the fifth floor and the stairs for the last two floors to the rat hole I called an office.

I eased open the door to a dark, empty corridor. The white-collar mooks with real lives were long gone for the day. The only light still on was coming from my office. I pulled the gun out, hoping it had magically transformed into something a little less embarrassing, and carefully approached the door. The door was slightly ajar. I peered in and saw lavender silk. Of course.

I pushed the door open. Amanda Masterson wheeled around with the .357 Magnum I kept in my desk. The good news was she fired as she was still turning, meaning my filing cabinet took a fatal shot to the belly, as opposed to me. The bad news was that the landlord was definitely not returning my security deposit. The recoil knocked her across the room into me. I grabbed the gun out of her hand before she decided to take out any more of my furniture. She just looked at me, stunned. I let her go. Her hair smelled of jasmine. I am a trained observer. I tucked Colt back in my jacket and the .357 in my waistband and sat on the edge of the desk.

"You do realize that's going on your old man's bill." The mention of her father seemed to snap her out of the shock.

"My father can't know I was here." She looked a little panicked.

"Amanda, you just blew a hole in my file cabinet. And that drawer had my last good bottle of scotch, which is now leaking all over the floor."

"I-I'm sorry. I thought you were one of Vinnie's boys." She looked like she was about to cry.

I was still digesting her last statement. "Vinnie's boys? Please don't tell me you mean you mean "Vinnie the Axe?"

She nodded. And then just stood there. Vinnie the Axe was Vincenzo Vittobara, who acquired his charming nickname when during a mob hit, his gun jammed and he grabbed the fire axe off the wall and finished the job using a more hands-on approach. The word "gleeful" gets used a lot by witnesses describing the incident. It's rumored he kept the axe and I don't mean as a trophy.

I looked over at the wounded filing cabinet, bleeding scotch. It still looked better than I would if I wasn't very careful. I looked at Amanda. She was still standing there.

"All right Amanda Masterson, suppose you tell me how bad this situation really is. Let's start with why you're in my office?" I did not imagine any version of an answer that would warm the cockles of my heart.

She fidgeted. "I was looking for your file on Daddy's stupid clock."

I sighed. "I assume you noticed I don't have any files." She nodded and started playing with her necklace. "Files leave a paper trail. Paper trails can be used against you in the court of law. And, just to prove how bad a burglar you are, you got here before I did."

She tried to do that pouty face thing again. I remained unimpressed.

"Amanda, are you working for Vinnie the Axe?"

She shook her head. "No. And I'm not sleeping with him either if that was your next question. My boyfriend stole the clock and Vinnie stole it from him."

I looked longing at the evaporating puddle of scotch and wished I had a sponge or a straw. "Your boyfriend?"

"Timmy DiMarco." She started fiddling with her necklace again.

That surprised me. First, because I was pretty sure DiMarco was married to City Councilman Sullivan's daughter Lorna, and second, if Timmy DiMarco was any slimier, he'd leave a trail behind him.

I got up off the corner of the desk. I stashed my jacket and fedora on the hat rack and then moved behind my desk. I had just remembered a bottle of rye stashed in a drawer. I motioned for her to sit down. I pulled out the bottle, and being a gentleman, offered her the cleanest of the glasses. She sipped the rye, made a face, and then placed it quickly on the desk. Apparently not a good year for rotgut.

"So Amanda, let me see if I got this straight. Your boyfriend stole your father's clock." She just nodded. "Your boyfriend is the worst gambler in LA, possibly the entire west coast. I'm going to

Murder Among Friends > 71

guess that he lost a fortune at Vinnie's casino." She looked down and nodded again.

I continued to think out loud. "He lost so much, that even you can't bail him out without asking your father. Having met your father, he'd say no you did ask. So you and Timmy hatched up a scheme to grab the clock and ransom it back for enough cash to keep Timmy attached to his kneecaps."

She nodded and stood up and started pacing. Finally, she stopped in the middle of the room and started fiddling with the button of the shoulder of her dress. She had decided she needed to cooperate.

"Yes," she said quietly. "Somehow Vinnie got wind of the plan and decided to cut out the middle man."

That made me uneasy. Vinnie the Axe was not noted for his finesse and subtle was not a word used to describe his MO. Amanda Masterson just kept standing there, fiddling with that button on her dress. She had said how easy she could get out of that dress, and I still suspected that button was the key to the entire operation. Sure enough, she suddenly undid the button and the entire dress slid to the floor. It was all she was wearing.

"Mr. McAvoy, I need your help." She stood there, looking like alabaster in the glare of the office lights. "I'm willing to do anything to fix this problem." I swallowed hard and remembered the unwritten rule about sleeping with clients.

"First of all," I said, carefully remembering to breathe, "This rug hasn't been vacuumed since I've been here. I'd have that dress cleaned and disinfected as soon as you get out of here."

"Anything," she whispered. She stepped out of the crumpled dress and took several steps forward.

"Amanda, I think your willingness to do anything is what got you into this situation." This time her pout was much more believable. I was running out of resolve.

"I'll tell you what. I've been hired to find the clock, no questions asked. You keep Timmy DiMarco from doing anything to get himself or you killed. I won't mention where I found it or suggest how the thief figured out where and when the clock was arriving."

Her eyes suddenly filled with tears. She turned and went back to the dress. Her back was a mass of welts and bruises.

"Vinnie did that to you." It was not a question. Vinnie's people skills were as highly developed as his sense of personal hygiene.

She turned and nodded. "Timmy wouldn't tell him where he hid the clock, so he whipped me until Timmy couldn't stand it anymore. They drove off to get the clock and that's the last time I saw Timmy." The tears started rolling down her face. She was shaking but determined not to fall apart in front of me. Apparently, there was some her father's toughness in her. I got up and walked toward her.

I was planning on walking her to her car, but she misread my intent and threw herself at me, burying her face in my chest and weeping. I try to console her but wished she had put the dress back on first. When she cried herself out, I pulled back and nodded toward the crumpled silk on the floor. She rolled her eyes and pulled the dress up. Trying to regain her composure, she wiped the tears away and straightened the dress.

"I'll say this much for you, shamus. You just missed out on a once in a lifetime opportunity." She smiled, but her quavering voice gave her away.

I led her to the elevator. "Amanda, once I get the clock back, I'd be happy to get drinks and talk. I can think of at least three other ways to get that dress off."

"You'll never call. You know I'd take you up on the offer." The elevator doors groaned open. She kissed me on the cheek. The doors closed.

I walked back to my office. She was probably right. Plus I had a date with a bottle of rotgut rye and I needed to figure out how to keep me from getting killed by Vinnie's goons. I'd kill the bottle of rye personally.

I was halfway through the rye when the phone rang. I glanced at the clock – 10:30. One of my life philosophies is that nothing good ever came from a phone call after 8 PM. "I picked it up with dread.

"Kirk? Sol Fiedler." Sol was in the DA's office. Probably one of the few ADAs that wouldn't shoot me if given an excuse and the opportunity.

"Sol. You know about my philosophy about late night phone calls." I splashed a little more rye in the glass.

"Your track record is fine. Are you going to be there for a while?"

I glanced at the bottle. "Yeah, until this bottle of rye evaporates."

"Rye? What happen to that bottle of Old Smuggler you had stashed?"

I glanced at the mangled filing cabinet and sighed. "Work related accident. Long story."

Sol paused. "Alright. I'll be there in 10 minutes." I hung up the phone. I capped the rye. I had a feeling I was going to need it later. Sol popping by for a visit this late made me more than a little uneasy.

Sol Fiedler was legendary for his wardrobe and his promptness. Ten minutes later, I heard the elevator doors begrudgingly open. Sol walked in the office dressed like he stepped out a Brooks Brothers magazine ad, with a bottle in his hand. He glanced at the filing cabinet and looked at me.

"Work related accident?" He grinned and handed me the bottle. It was Old Crow bourbon. A step up from the rye but a far cry from my late bottle of Old Smuggler. I opened the bottle.

"I'd offer you a snort, but I don't want to hear the lecture about the kosher thing."

"Rumor has it you're working for Old Man Masterson out in Whittier." Sol sat down and picked an imaginary bit of lint off his cuff. Whatever was bothering him, it was serious.

"Word gets out fast. He has an item he wants me to track down." I sipped the bourbon. It burned but in a good way.

"You wouldn't happen to have seen his daughter lately?"

"Sol, if was anyone else but you, I'd scream client confidentiality. But yes, she was here earlier. She is also interested in making sure her father retrieves the item."

I don't think Sol had blinked. He glanced around the room and I knew what ever was eating him was about to become my problem as well.

"Patrolman spotted a body in the tar pits tonight. It was Timmy DiMarco."

I took a more generous hit of the bourbon. That complicated things.

"Timmy DiMarco owed Vinnie the Axe a great deal of money," I said. "Seems like an inefficient way to recoup your profits."

"Give me a glass. Bourbon is kosher." Sol glanced at the filing cabinet. He took a sip and made the same face that Amanda Masterson had made.

"This is nasty stuff. I've busted up moonshine rings with better quality." We sat there quietly, drinking bourbon. Some of us more enthusiastically than others.

Finally, he looked at me. "DiMarco's wife is claiming Amanda Masterson offed her husband because he was going to break it off with her. Can you vouch for her whereabouts?" That was what was bothering him. Sol never liked sending pretty little blondes to the electric chair. He'd done it, but never felt good about it. He put down the barely touched glass.

"Amanda was already here when I got back about 6 and was out of here in a half hour." I looked at his glass and wondered if I could pour the leftovers back in the bottle after he left.

Sol looked at his watch. "That puts her in the clear. DiMarco's watch stopped at 6:35. From here to La Brea is 30 minutes by car with Hollywood traffic at that time of the day, and that's a good day."

I put the bourbon down. "From what I saw, I think Amanda Masterson loved the creep. I'd put my money on the wife setting up Amanda because Timmy wanted out of the marriage."

"Unfortunately, the widow DiMarco was at Rodeo Drive spending like a drunken sailor."

I reached for the glass and then paused. "That's interesting. If DiMarco was into Vinnie the Axe so deep that Vinnie tried to see if he could breathe tar, where is Lorna DiMarco getting the money?"

Sol blinked. "That is an excellent question. Rumor has it that her old man cut her off when she married DiMarco. If he's broke, and she's cut off from Daddy, there seems to be some serious money unaccounted for in Lorna's purse." Sol reached for his glass, then thought better of it.

"Sol, I had a bad idea where Lorna got the money and his last name is 'the Axe.'" I sat back.

"Care to elaborate on where the hell you came up with that?" He crossed his legs, looked at his watch, and flicked another microscopic piece of lint off his suit.

I would have preferred to straighten this out by myself, but having the DA's office involved might mean Mother McAvoy's darling son could avoid buying the farm. "Timmy DiMarco has been losing badly at the Marina Club – so badly that even Amanda Masterson's allowance couldn't cover it this time. So the two of them hatch a plan. She knew her father had a delivery arriving at Mines Field, an old clock for his collection. Timmy goes to the airfield, retrieves the package. The plan was to ransom it back to Masterson for enough to cover the gambling debt. Only our friend Mr. Vittobara, with or without his axe, found out about it and decided to recoup his money without Mr. DiMarco. As far as I can tell, the only two people who knew what the plan was – Amanda Masterson and Timmy DiMarco. Now, who else could possibly have known about it?"

"Lorna DiMarco. Especially if her genius husband did something stupid like hiding the stolen clock in his own house." Sol picked up the bourbon.

"I think it's time to visit the Marina Club and see if Vinnie feels like chatting." I stood up and started putting on my holster

"It makes sense. Mr. DiMarco wants to dump Mrs. DiMarco for Miss Masterson. Mrs. DiMarco approaches Mr. Vittobara with a deal. She'll give Vinnie the clock and he can negotiate his own deal to recoup his losses. In return, she wants to be a grieving widow instead of a bitter divorcée."

"Sol," I started, formulating a really bad plan. "I have an idea, but you're not going to like it." I grabbed my coat and fedora.

Twenty minutes later, we were pulling into the Marina Club, Vinnie's "private social club." Sol still didn't like the plan, but he hadn't come up with a better one that didn't involve repairing bullet holes in his Brooks Brothers, So, he would go into the club and talk to Vinnie about Timmy DiMarco. Vinnie would be polite, offer an alibi, and the visit would be over unless Sol decided to play the roulette wheel that officially didn't exist. Sol was basically distracting Vinnie while I did the really stupid part of the plan.

I got out of the car down the block and walked toward the Casa Marina parking lot. Sol continued on and drove up to the valet, a very large man who did not look happy or comfortable to be wearing a monkey suit. Not that I blamed him. It didn't fit well, and barely hid the cannon he had holstered on his hip. Sol was ushered in, and while the gorilla was dealing with Sol, I slipped into the lot. No one in their right mind would bother a car parked at Vinnie Vittobara's place, so security was basically the gunsel at the door looking for idiots like me.

I crouched low as I moved past the cars, only half of which were city-owned vehicles. Being Vinnie, he had his own parking spot near the back door. What I didn't expect was the man mountain in a chauffeur cap sitting on the fender of Vinnie's Packard 180. Unfortunately, knowing Vinnie, it made sense to keep his driver near the car. If the Feds raided the place, or a competitor showed up with Tommy guns, the ape in the chauffeur suit would have the engine revved and ready when Vinnie came running.

I pulled my gun and grabbed it by the barrel. It wasn't a blackjack, but any port in a storm. I pulled my fedora down low to hide my face, undid my tie and untucked my shirt. Keeping my gun hand out of his line of sight, I began staggering toward the building. He saw me but didn't seem too worried. Apparently, drunks in the parking lot were fairly common.

I staggered toward him. "Shay pal, where'd they hide the little boy' room? That cute lil' waitresh gave me the wrong door." As drunken slurring went, it wasn't bad, but it wouldn't get me into Juilliard either.

I was close enough now that the second he turned to point to the door, I slammed the gun butt into his neck right below the ear. He went down hard and silently along the car. And surprise, the tires were splattered with tar. Stepping over King Kong, I popped the trunk. As suspected, a small, wooden shipping crate. Vinnie was just paranoid enough to keep it nearby, but not where anyone could grab it, like in an illegal casino. I'd bet the driver wasn't told he was also a guard.

The lid had been jimmied open, but not nailed shut all the way. I forced it open – there was Masterson's clock. I pulled it out of the crate and start to reseal it. If I was lucky, Vinnie would check the trunk and see the crate was still there and not realize there was a problem until he lifted the crate and realized it was a clock-free weight. I had an inspiration. I grabbed a couple of bricks from the flowerbed and tucked them in the box and forced the lid down hard. Now no one would know the clock was gone until they opened the crate. I grabbed the driver's wallet and watch to make it look like a robbery. Hopefully, that would be another little misdirection to buy me some time. I changed the time on the watch and smashed it so that it looked like it broke in the "robbery" and that it took place after Sol's visit. I grabbed the bills out of the wallet and then tossed the watch and wallet in the shrubbery toward the entrance. In a perfect world, it would appear that a drunk guest robbed Vinnie's driver, then dumped the evidence before going back into the casino.

I closed the trunk and hightailed it back toward the back gate with the clock. Sol was waiting. We drove back to my office. Sol would go to Judge Mason in the morning and see if tar on the car was enough for a warrant. It probably wasn't, knowing Vinnie's extensive clientele list. But maybe it would rattle him that the DA already figured it out who offed DiMarco. Rattled gangsters get nervous. Nervous gangsters made mistakes. And all Sol needed was one mistake.

I, on the other hand, had the clock, stolen from Masterson and then stolen again from Vinnie the Axe. Nobody knew I had it but Sol. Amanda Masterson would figure it out pretty quickly, but as soon as she found out about Timmy DiMarco, I doubted she'd even remember the clock.

Sol dropped me off in front of the Security Bank Building. The ride back had been quiet. I think Sol was thinking about how to arrest Vinnie for DiMarco's murder. I was more concerned with what to do with the thing until morning. I may have covered my tracks, but a little healthy paranoia hadn't killed me yet.

I glanced up at my office. The light was on. I may have left it on - I'd done it before. Tonight, I was going to assume the worst. I walked to the back of the building. After making sure the coast was clear, I went to my car. I wrapped the clock in a blanket and placed it on the floorboard. And then I drove. The roads in Los Angeles are never deserted, but by 2 AM, traffic is light enough that even a nervous private investigator could spot a tail. Finally, drove up to Griffith Park and sat there for the rest of the night, napping on and off. I watched the sunrise over the new observatory.

About 6 AM, I decided to drive down to El Monte. There was a small diner there. I knew the owner and I could park where I could watch the traffic and my car. And it was halfway to Whittier. By 8 AM, I was fed, regrouped, and ready to visit Masterson and unload the clock on him. If there had been a barbershop open that early, I might have even gotten a shave to look presentable. I decided the grizzled look would have to do and headed south for the last 20 minutes of the drive.

I drove up to Oak Knoll. There was a black sedan parked in front that I recognized, and it was not a happy reunion feeling. It had been washed and the tar scraped off the wheels, but it was Vinnie's Packard. Based on the bruise behind his ear, it was being watched by the same gorilla that I coldcocked last night. I left my fedora on the seat, just in case he remembered the hat, parked and got out. I walked toward him like I knew who he was. By the time I got up to him, my survival instinct had figured out my plan and was strenuously objecting.

I got up in his face. "Hey, where the hell you been?"

He looked confused. "I've been right here."

"Boss called from inside the house. The old man pulled a gun and shot him in the leg. Says he's bleeding pretty bad, but you didn't answer when he called."

Kong looked at me suspiciously. "I didn't hear no gun."

I looked at him. "And you didn't hear the boss yelling either. He had to call the office. That's why you're in trouble." I gestured toward the house. "Come on, before we both get in trouble."

He turned toward the house and I nailed him in the back of the head again, this time with a sap. He went down hard again. I just happen to have a pair of genuine LAPD issue handcuffs and I was not afraid to use them. I dragged the unluckiest hood in the city into the landscaping, just in case someone actually did show up looking for him. As I came out of the shrubs, a familiar cherry red Mercury convertible rolled into the yard. Amanda Masterson got out of the car and ran into the house carrying a small gun. Suddenly it dawned on me. My vest pocket Colt was not in my pocket, where I had put it after Amanda's little visit yesterday. Great, thanks to me getting distracted, she was now an armed basket case. I headed toward the house.

She had left the front door wide open. I pulled my gun and cautiously entered the house. The butler was crumpled in the corner. I checked for a pulse. He had one – and a gash where someone had pistol whipped him, and it was certainly not Amanda with that tiny little gun. The library door was slightly ajar. The voices coming from inside were Amanda and someone I didn't recognize. And Amanda sounded hysterical.

I approached the door. Amanda was screaming at Vinnie, accusing him of killing her Timmy. Vinnie seemed unusually calm in his denials. I eased the door open just enough to see Vinnie's back was to the door. His stance was off, so I risked opening the door a hair wider. He had a gun pulled, but he wasn't aiming it as Masterson, sitting at his desk in the back of the room at his desk. I gambled and opened the door another fraction of an inch.

The wooden crate was open and the bricks were scattered on the floor. Apparently, Vinnie never checked the crate before bringing the clock to Masterson. Normally, I'd have found that hilarious, but Vinnie was now aiming his gun at Amanda, who was pointing my poor little Colt at Vinnie. Masterson had what looked like a shotgun aimed at Vinnie – Mexican Standoff.

I pulled my .357 and dropped to one knee and desperately tried to come up with a plan that didn't involve someone bleeding all over Masterson's fancy carpet. Masterson's eyes flickered in my direction for a split second. To his credit. He didn't react to my arrival. Or, he didn't see me and had only noticed the door was slightly ajar. Either way, all eyes were to Amanda Masterson as she kept screaming at Vinnie.

Amanda looked like hell. Her eyes were red-rimmed, her hair matted, and most telling, there were tar stains on her hands. I knew then that she had been down at the morgue to see Timmy DiMarco's corpse. I also knew Vinnie was not leaving that room alive. Vinnie the Axe wasn't stupid. He knew he had two guns aimed at him. Technically, he had three aimed at him, but he didn't know about me. So, he was talking in soothing tones to Amanda trying to get her to lower her gun. The problem was, Vinnie was not a sweet talker.

Tears streamed down her face. Without warning, she fired the Colt. She hit him in the belly. I watched in horror as Vinnie fired back, the bullet passing through her and hitting bust of Whittier. It ricocheted out into the room. Masterson fired the shotgun and Vinnie dropped like a rock. I ran into the room. What was left of Vinnie wasn't going anywhere. Amanda was already gone by the time I reached her – Vinnie was a crack shot.

Suddenly I realized Masterson hadn't said a word. I ran to the desk. Masterson had caught the ricochet off Whittier squarely in the chest. He flopped back in his chair. I looked at him and he shook his head no. He knew he wasn't going to make it. He was fighting for every breath.

He looked up at me. "The clock?"

I nodded. The fire in his eyes was already going out. "L-let me see it."

I ran out to the car and picked up the clock. I carried it over to where he could see it. For the first time, he looked content.

He looked at it. "Finally."

The clock chimed one. The sound cut through the silence. Masterson looked up in wonder.

"What do you know? The legend's true."

Masterson's eyes rolled back in his head and the rasping breaths stopped. I left the clock on the desk. Maybe the clock chimed with death in the room, or maybe I flicked the hammer. It didn't matter to Masterson anymore. I wiped the clock down. I doubted the locals would contact the FBI for fingerprints, but why look for trouble?

I had to step over Vinnie and Amanda to reach the phone and call in an anonymous tip to the Whittier cops. By the time they got here, I'd be long gone. It would be obvious to the boys in blue that Vinnie, with a rap sheet thicker than the LA Phonebook, had tried to rob the house, and he and Masterson had shot it out with poor Amanda getting caught in the crossfire. It was not my finest resolution to a case.

I walked out, pausing long enough to grab a handful of those fancy Beverly Hills cigarettes from a case on the table. I lit one as I drove away. Expensive or not, it left a bitter taste in my mouth.

Miss Larcom Meets the Neighbors

Susan Oleksiw

John Greenleaf Whittier Home, Amesbury, Massachusetts
The Poet's home from 1836 until his death in 1892 was built circa 1811 and expanded several times in the 80 years it was owned by the Whittier family. The Whittier Home Association was established in 1898 to preserve the house

The driver of the coach carrying Miss Lucy Larcom to Amesbury seemed adept at finding every rut and bump in the road, but the lady was willing to admit that her joints were perhaps more sensitive now that she was in her fifties. Only her loyal affection for Mr. Whittier, who had championed her poems and essays over the years, could overcome her dislike of travel and the distance from her home in Beverly.

Lucy gripped the open window and counted the houses until the Whittier home. It wouldn't be long now. From her perch in the carriage, she had the pleasure of viewing men and women going about their afternoon business. A young woman in a yellow cotton dress hurried down a path to a house with a fine porch nearly hidden under an abundance of wisteria. As the carriage reached the corner of the property, where the fence turned, a man in a well-cut brown coat could be seen walking briskly across the lane. At the next house, a woman in a window drew the draperies. And beyond that house, a man carrying a green jacket—understandable, with the heat, but still—walked across the back yard. Despite the bucolic scene, life seemed busy here.

The sight of John Greenleaf Whittier standing on the steps of his clapboard home lifted Lucy Larcom's heart. Seeing her mentor looking hale and hearty, despite his years, cheered her. In a few strides, he reached the carriage door as the driver pulled to a halt. Lucy climbed down, arrangements were made, and the guest was soon ensconced in the parlor.

"This evening we shall enjoy a walk," Mr. Whittier said as he lowered himself into a red-upholstered chair. Now in his seventies but never robust in health, he seemed more careful in his movements. "My neighbors are eager to meet thee again," he said, "so a soiree has been organized for tomorrow evening. Thee shall be entertained with poetry and music and lively discussion."

Mr. Whittier was an excellent host, as Miss Larcom knew, and they set off for their stroll soon after a light supper. Since he was now spending winters nearer Beverly, at the home of his cousins in Danvers, some of the discussion revolved around arrangements for literary gatherings there. At the house Lucy had first noticed for its abundant wisteria, Whittier stopped and turned.

"The young lady visiting here hails also from Danvers," he said. "Ann Beston has come to visit her father's brother and his family." He paused. "She has expressed an interest in composing poetry."

"Then she should do well if she has the talent," Lucy said. She appreciated the advantages that had come her way, thanks to Whittier's support.

"Ah," he said, nodding his head with its full head of hair. He kept his mutton chops well trimmed. "Yes, if she has the talent."

"I surmise there's some question there." Lucy smiled as she said this. Whittier's kindness to the young was well known, and he was infinitely patient with those whose talent was less than what he would have liked to see.

"This is her fourth visit this summer," he said, "and I have yet to read a line by her hand. She cares more for arranging parties and managing the guest list, including those for my own soirees."

"Perhaps she'll tire of the effort to write."

"I think, Lucy, she prefers the poetry of romance and the effect of casting her beautiful eyes on young men." With a knowing nod to his companion, they resumed their stroll.

The next evening's gathering was a lively affair. Ann Beston did indeed have beautiful green eyes, and the young men of the neighborhood vied with each other to draw her attention. She smiled at one and all, but especially at the young man Lucy had seen on her first day, in the brown coat. That was Mr. William Kenley, a schoolteacher new to the area. The man in the green coat was Mr. Ephraim Winter, a widower with two daughters, who was accompanied by his oldest daughter. The rest of the circle comprised Lillian and Thomas Beston, Ann's aunt and uncle, an editor for the Essex Transcript, two young men pursuing writing careers, and Mr. Whittier's cousin and his wife.

"Ephraim thinks his younger one, Lisa, too young for this sort of evening," Whittier told Lucy in a whisper. "But she has attained sixteen years."

The discussion ranged widely, from the recent elections to the newest publications. Whittier contributed but always made certain others did too, and Lucy was delighted with the comments and questions. This was what she had missed during her quiet hours maintaining her writing career in Beverly, and the reason she had been willing to undertake an arduous journey. She went to bed pleasantly exhausted.

In the morning, the teenage girl assigned to attend her arrived with early tea. She deposited the cup and saucer, and Lucy offered her a smile but quickly retracted it when she saw the girl's swollen red eyes.

"Whatever is wrong?" Lucy asked.

"Oh, Miss. There's been a death. Such an awful thing to happen." The girl began tearing up. "Dear Mr. Kenley is gone."

Lucy sat up swiftly, pulling the sheets up to her chest. "What has happened?"

"He musta fallen, Miss, right off the horse and been crushed under its hoofs." She began sniffling and pulled a balled-up handkerchief from a hidden pocket.

Lucy hurried down to breakfast and didn't have to ask anyone if what she'd heard was true. Two other houseguests, an older cousin and his wife who visited Whittier often, were quick to confirm the story.

"Skull broken," the cousin said, then turned to his wife. "My dear, so sorry to bring up the image again."

"When did this happen?"

"Late last night," his wife said. "He took it into his head to go out for a ride, and, foolish man, no one was about to help him when the horse bolted." She waved her hand in distress and then thought better of giving way to emotion. "Tea, Miss Larcom?"

Breakfast was a solemn affair as the cousins commiserated and Lucy tried to imagine just what young Kenley had been thinking to go off for a ride so late at night. "Was this his normal practice?" she asked out of the blue. The cousins looked at her. Mr. Whittier arrived in the dining room at this moment and took his place at the table. He greeted the others and then turned to Lucy.

"Thomas Beston has given him the run of the stables," Whittier said. "He admired the young man. And, of course, his niece admired him too." He enjoyed seeing young love blossom, but his smile turned to sorrow. "I fear she shall be broken up by this development."

"Were they that serious?" Lucy asked.

"Oh, I do think so. She has made four trips here, and young Mr. Kenley had taken time from his own duties to be in attendance." He heaped scrambled eggs on his plate and examined the platter of ham before selecting a slice.

"How late was it when he went out?" Lucy asked.

"It must have been near midnight," Whittier said. "I was laboring over a particularly difficult passage and looked out and spied William pass by in his brown coat. Moonlight was quite adequate to see by."

"Did you see anyone else?" she asked.

He shook his head. "I saw him enter the yard and later cross the lane to the stable."

"You knew it was him?"

"I saw his figure from a distance."

"Most interesting," Lucy said. "Does he have family nearby?"

"No, none at all." Whittier poured cream into his morning tea. "I do believe he is entirely on his own."

"Interesting." Lucy gazed out the window as she considered this.

"How so, Miss Larcom?" The cousin's wife had taken herself in hand and was now curious.

"William Kenley is an attractive figure, and he seems to have earned a good position as a teacher, but he has been taken up by the community without anyone knowing who he is," Lucy said.

"All true," Whittier said.

"That is a testament to your principles of egalitarianism, certainly," Lucy said. "But do all your neighbors agree with this?"

The cousins glanced at each other. The wife opened her mouth, glanced at her husband and Whittier, and shut her eyes before speaking. "It is perhaps unkind but I did hear a sour note, if I may put it like that, from Mr. Winter."

"Ephraim didn't agree with our including William?" Whittier's eyebrows rose almost a good inch, but then he had a long visage.

"Not entirely, Cousin," she said.

"I think after breakfast I shall take a walk," Lucy said. "It's invigorating to be in a new environment, don't you think?" Everyone nodded agreement.

Despite the early hour, at least for visiting, Lucy had no lack of people to talk to. Everyone in the little neighborhood, it seemed, was equally appalled and fascinated by the midnight death of the young schoolteacher. He was universally regarded as good-natured, handsome, hardworking, but, unfortunately, a little shallow. Lucy found the last detail intriguing and tried to find a way to pursue it. She approached a coterie of ladies near a shop.

They knew who she was, a guest of Whittier's, and welcomed her into their circle of conversation.

"Well, he does like the ladies," one woman said, "especially Ann Beston. But her uncle and her father would never allow her to become involved with him, no matter how often she sees him."

"She must be heartbroken," Lucy said. "They seemed quite close."

"She's been coming up here all through the summer," another one said. "And we can see what for." She looked around the circle and the other women knowingly nodded. "But she has plenty of suitors, so I doubt he'll be missed for long."

On her way back to the Whittier house, Lucy stopped at the gate to the Beston home just as Ann Beston emerged, wearing a light blue dress with lace at the neck and wrists, and carrying a basket on her arm. She strolled down the steps and greeted Lucy with warmth and energy.

"Such a tragedy," Ann said. "I so enjoyed Mr. Kenley's company and now the remainder of the summer will be quite dull."

Not sure what to say to this, Lucy murmured her condolences.

"Of course, it's worse for my friend, Lisa." Ann tipped her head to indicate the next house, the home of Ephraim Winter and his family. She was the only near neighbor whom Lucy hadn't met yet.

"How so?"

"Well, that is something of a secret." Ann resettled the basket on her arm.

"Even though Mr. Kenley is dead?" Lucy had never experienced the lightness of life that belonged to the likes of Ann Beston. After her father's death when she was only eight years old, she had gone to work in the Lowell mills, earning a few extra coins by her writing. That had opened the door to a better future, but she had never forgotten how hard life could be. Now in her fifties, any youth she had ever known long gone, she found the new crop of young ladies sometimes foolish and often tiresome. She vowed to think more kindly of Ann Beston in the future, but at the moment she wanted to know why the girl thought as she did.

"Well, I did give my word," Ann said, arching her eyebrow.

"Admirable, Miss Beston. Admirable. And I for one will always encourage you on the path to virtue. I trust you gave it in a worthy cause." Lucy lowered her chin and gave the girl her best schoolmarm look.

"True love, Miss Larcom. In the cause of true love." And with that and a Cheshire cat smile, Ann gave a shake of her curls and set off on her errands.

"Curiouser and curiouser," Lucy thought as she watched the girl walk down the road. She continued her stroll, but as the traffic changed from men and women on their daily rounds to those heading home for dinner, the main meal of the day, Lucy concluded she could learn more at Whittier's house. Minutes later she joined her host in the parlor.

"Thank you for asking," she said to him after he inquired about her morning walk. "Most informative. I feel quite inspired."

Whittier found this amusing. "Does that mean thee may compose a poem about thy visit here?"

"Quite possibly," Lucy said. "But, tell me, Mr. Whittier, where do you find inspiration? You described your work at your desk late at night. I don't believe I have seen your desk. Will you show it to me?"

"My goodness, Lucy," Whittier said. "Thee art quite the curious one. It would be my pleasure."

Whittier rose and led the way to the second floor, where a desk was placed near a window. The furnishings were modest, and the chairs upholstered in quiet beiges and creams, with a red shawl tossed over one and an orange blanket lying on another. From his window, he could look out onto the lane and the houses beyond. The road curved, and in some cases obscured yards and other structures such as stables and sheds.

"And from here you saw Mr. Kenley leave for his ride?" Lucy said, moving close to the window. She rested her fingers lightly on the mullions and leaned forward, her nose almost touching the glass panes.

"Well, not leave exactly," Whittier said, "but out to the stable."

"I see," Lucy said, but in fact, she didn't. The sight lines were not as they should be to reveal all that Whittier thought he had seen. "Tell me again how you recognized him?"

"That brown coat of his," Whittier said.

"Ah, yes, the brown coat." Lucy stepped away from the window. "I think I shall take one more turn around the neighborhood before dinner. Do I have time?"

Whittier frowned, then looked confused. "Yes, of course. Dinner is served at two o'clock." He bowed and led the way from the room.

Lucy stepped outside and gazed up and down the street. Everyone had welcomed her unreservedly, and she considered the warmth a reflection of her friendship with John Greenleaf Whittier and his reputation as a leading poet and essayist of the time. He had led valiant efforts against slavery and other injustices, his life fully informed by his Quaker beliefs. But she was not Whittier, and she did not live in Amesbury. As often as she visited, she was always a visitor, an outsider. She did not want to trade on Whittier's reputation, but then again, she did not want to walk away from what she considered a serious crime, the murder of a young man late at night. Lucy stepped onto the walk and headed down the street.

The door to the Winter home was opened on the second knock. Before her stood another teenage girl wearing a stained white apron over her plain blue dress. Lucy had apparently interrupted dinner preparations. She asked to see Lisa Winter.

"Oh, Miss, she ain't feeling good. Napping, she is."

Behind the servant, Lucy saw a staircase and glimpsed the hem of a black skirt high up on the stairs. She crouched down, to get a better look at the woman, and called out.

"Miss Lisa Winter?"

The young woman descended the stairs and sent the serving girl away. Dressed in a black skirt and white blouse with a black vest, she came as close to wearing mourning as she decently could without proclaiming herself. She led the way into the parlor and drew the pocket doors closed behind them. Lucy was invited to sit and chose a chair facing the tall windows. Lisa sat opposite, as Lucy knew she would.

Lucy began by offering condolences and her concern was rewarded by a flow of tears from eyes already sore and red from hours of crying. "Your grief is raw," she said.

The girl crushed a handkerchief in her hand, stiffened, and tried to speak. She managed to say a few words. "He was a good friend to me."

"I can see that." Lucy stopped to admire her surroundings, the furnishings of a well-to-do home, despite its remoteness from Boston or Lowell or Lawrence. The Oriental rug and newly upholstered chairs, the fine glass lamp shades and the gold-trimmed mirror, the artwork on the walls and the vases filled with flowers. "But I think he was more than a friend."

The girl gasped.

"I saw you watching him," Lucy said. Immediately the girl turned to the window, as Lucy suspected she would. "On my first day here, you watched him leave this house and safely cross the lane to the next, to Miss Beston's."

"How –?"

"I saw you draw the draperies."

"Oh." Lisa sagged in her chair, the training of almost sixteen years collapsing in an instant of grief.

"She was your cover, wasn't she? If anyone noticed how often Mr. Kenley came to visit this area, the obvious explanation was the beautiful and vivacious Miss Beston." Lucy watched the sorrow in Lisa's eyes deepen. "But Miss Beston was not deceived. She noticed that Mr. Kenley was different with you, and she offered to help you see each other secretly. She's a romantic and she likes to manage things, particularly other people's lives."

"She was kind to us." Lisa's plea for understanding was palpable.

"She helped you keep the news of your liaison with Mr. Kenley secret from everyone, including your father."

"He would never have approved. He called him a penniless teacher, less than a scribbler." Lucy bridled at the insult to her profession.

"But your father did find out, didn't he?"

Lisa's eyes widened. "Oh, no! He can't have." She rose from her chair. "You must go at once." She hurried to the doors, slid them open, and ran back upstairs.

Resigned, Lucy left. She strolled the short distance to the Whittier house and entered, surprised to see through the open parlor door a man in a neat gray suit standing in the center of the room. Mr. Whittier sat in a chair and looked up at him. Lucy approached, and Whittier waved her in and introduced her.

"Jonathan Coles is the town constable. Jonathan came to call after hearing about my late night observations of the road," Whittier said. "It seems that servants not only talk but also enthusiastically. Here it is, not even twenty-four hours later, and we have an official investigation. In answer to the question, Jonathan, yes, I'm certain I did see a brown coat at that time."

Mr. Coles wrote this down in a small notebook he carried, frowning perhaps at the small space for all he had to write, or perhaps at the labor it took to do so. "Anything else? It is fortuitous that you were awake and near a window at that hour, Mr. Whittier."

"Indeed, Mr. Coles," Lucy said, breaking in. "Mr. Whittier is most fastidious about his work. I can vouch for that."

Mr. Coles paused, looking over at her. "This name of yours," he said. "Do you also write poetry?"

Lucy allowed as how she did. He smiled, happy now that he had placed her. But she wouldn't be dismissed so easily.

"Do I surmise that there is some question about how Mr. Kenley died?" she asked.

Mr. Coles looked to Mr. Whittier to save him, but Mr. Whittier looked to Mr. Coles to answer. He too was loyal to his friends. The great poet lifted an eyebrow in query.

"Yes, ma'am. It seems that the damage to Mr. Kenley's skull couldn't have come from a horse, and we've looked at the Beston horses and not a one has any blood or, hmm, tissue on its hoofs. So, we're thinking something else must have occurred."

"Quite wise, Mr. Coles, quite wise," Lucy said. "And what kind of wound did Mr. Kenley sustain?"

"Not a pleasant thing to discuss with a lady," Mr. Coles said.

"Thee need not be concerned, Jonathan. Lucy is made of stout stuff." The poet nodded approvingly and Lucy thought of how she had filled out over the years so she was now as sturdy as most men her age.

"Well, ma'am, he took a blow to his forehead and it, ahm, crushed his skull in and broke his nose."

"That's quite severe. So you are looking for someone wearing a brown coat, or another man who might have followed Mr. Kenley to the stable?" Lucy clasped her hands in her lap and sat forward on the edge of her chair, in the same manner she had used to bring difficult school supervisors into line during her years of teaching. "And Mr. Whittier has apprised you of his affliction, has he?"

"Ah, what affliction would that be?"

"Ah, yes, that!" Whittier slapped the chair arm in agreement. "I forget."

"Mr. Whittier is color blind, Mr. Coles. Most coats will appear to be brown, no matter the color—red or green or yellow. They're all brown to Mr. Whittier." She smiled and lifted her chin, signaling it was time for him to agree with her.

"Is that so, Sir?" Mr. Coles turned to the poet.

"Indeed, sir. And thee can thank friend Lucy for saving thee from filing an erroneous report."

Mr. Coles looked down at his notes and began scratching things out. "I see."

"Perhaps, Mr. Coles, you might want to look at men's coats to find some evidence of a fight," Lucy said. "Surely any man who strikes another will himself be splattered with blood. And this man must know Mr. Kenley in order to come close enough to attack him face to face."

"Ah, quite so." Mr. Coles looked more confused than ever.

"And as a duly appointed officer in Amesbury, you could go door to door, beginning with this house—"

"Oh, no, ma'am, the impertinence—"

"And moving on to our neighbors and farther along, the Winters and the Bestons." Lucy again waited for his agreement.

"Quite right, Lucy," Whittier said. "We are not above standing equal before the law though it may be inconvenient or embarrassing." He stood. "This is our duty."

Mr. Coles gave the poet a hangdog look as if he wanted anything but to search the Whittier home. "Sir, have you such a coat?"

"No, of course not."

"I'll take your word for it."

"That is not fulfilling thy duty, Jonathan. Come, we'll search together." Whittier led the way from the room, and then into all the other rooms where clothing might be kept. At the end, he accompanied the constable to the next house. And so taken was the poet with this new duty that he continued on to the Winter house. But here his pleasure in the duty of the law abandoned him. Lucy felt bad for her mentor, knowing that his disappointment in his fellow man would be painful to bear. Two hours after Mr. Coles first arrived at the Whittier home, Lucy opened the door to the returning poet, long in the face and slow of step.

"I do not know how thee knew, Lucy," Whittier said. "Thee were correct. Look for a coat, thee said. And there it was, piled into a basket for the laundry. The front of Mr. Winter's coat was covered in blood. The cloth is green, I'm told." He leaned back in his chair and closed his eyes.

"Did you speak to his daughter, Lisa?"

"Mr. Coles did notice her all in black, eyes red and sore from crying," the poet said. "He gathered all the pieces together, as did I. She and Mr. Kenley planned to make their escape last night. She had her baggage ready to go." He pulled out a large white handkerchief, dabbing at the perspiration beading his forehead and chin.

"Mr. Winter will pay a high price for thwarting his daughter's happiness," Lucy said. "And all because Mr. Kenley had only himself and his own good character to put forward. No family and no other prospects."

Whittier's large hands hung over the end of the chair arms, flaccid as though the energy of a hopeful life had gone out of them. "He shalt pay a high price for forgetting the most important lessons of a loving God."

The Cricket in the Wall
Kristi Petersen Schoonover

Whittier Pine, Center Harbor, New Hampshire
Situated between Lake Winnipesaukee and Squam Lake, a massive pine tree stood atop of Sunset Hill that was a favorite resting spot for Whittier, who was summering at a nearby camp. Here he composed "Summer by the Lakeside," "The Wood Giant" and several other poems immortalizing the Granite State. The tree was over 400 years old when it was struck by lightning in 1950 and needed to be cut down. Library of Congress Prints and Photographs Division.

I understand, now, the thing that happened to me.

I'd bought the five-mile-long overgrown Cloud Island and lodge on Lake Winnipesaukee despite its problems. The exterior was shagged with mold, the rock paths were weed-choked, the roof was shy a few shingles, and the wraparound porch, as well as the front door, demanded paint jobs. The main hall—a once grand affair in dark-stained knotty pine—sported worn sapphire outdoor carpet and reeked of rose perfume and mildew. The décor was a visual cacophony of peacock feathers in flea market vases, faux Tiffany lamps, and yellowed, water-stained lace curtains.

The restoration cost years and hundreds of thousands.

It also cost my life.

It was Fourth of July weekend. The original owners bragged the lodge had been frequented by Whittier, so I named it "Cricket's Wail" after a line in his poem "Summer by the Lakeside." The repairs to the exterior of Cricket's Wail had been finished two years before, but there was still some work in progress inside. My fiancé, Russell, insisted we add an additional revolving wall into a secret room off the grand hall— he'd said what mansion shouldn't have a secret room?

Russell and I had decided to get married out in the gardens overlooking the silvering bay on Independence Day, and my usual staff had been there since early May making preparations for the wedding.

On that day instead, though, as I stood in my wedding gown on the balcony, overlooking the gardens with dismay—they were fast flooding, the few plastic chairs we'd arranged for the reception overturning and colliding—my head seized with a painful flurry of tiny white lights.

The world went black.

When I awakened, the house was dark and cold. I screamed for help until my throat burned, but no one heard; everyone, I thought, was just sleeping soundly. I had only to wait, and not for long; the first creep of dawn had already begun.

I saw into the grand hall. The windows were boarded up. The chandeliers were bearded in spider webs, moss laced the wallpaper, and my Great Camp-style furniture was covered in stained drop cloths. The portrait of Whittier over the stairs was cloaked under a black drape. Where was I? Outside? No . . . no. I'm inside. Thin, crooked twigs branched in front of my face; on further examination, I realized they weren't twigs at all, but bones . . . my bones, not those of a Halloween decoration! How long had I been here that my lovely fingers were gone? Was this a dream? Wake yourself! Wake yourself, you just got married!

That first night came, and I understood: I was dead.

I was dead. I probably had been for many years. My body had been crammed inside the formerly unfinished revolving wall, and . . . and somehow, my view of the grand hall was through a mirror that had been mounted on it. I couldn't have moved if I wanted to. I could feel several objects at my feet; my toe bones I could move just enough to hear the ding against metal, the scrape against wood, the scratch against glass. What the hell is all of that?

Someone did come back: Miles. I'd known him since I was thirteen, as he'd come to work for my parents as their handyman while he was in high school. He'd been the essence of what I thought a man should be, in control and far stronger and sexier than the heartthrobs that looked back at me from my bedroom's posters. My parents found out and fired him, but I never forgot him, and I found him a few years later—grizzled and rawboned—when it was my turn to own something grand enough to need a gardener, a painter, a repairman . . . and a lover. He'd been only too happy to work for me, at least until I met Russell, and I learned what it was like to be in the hands of someone gentle, someone who didn't treat me like something he owned.

I screamed and screamed but he didn't hear me.

So it's been every night since. He takes a long walk through every hall and every room, probably to repair a window or perform one of many other tasks, I imagine, to keep nature from taking over. Always I scream for help. Always he never hears me.

What is worst of all is the preternatural quiet. There's the occasional skittering of a mouse or cry of a bird, but they are distant. It's only my thoughts that are loud, thoughts that, as long as I'm trapped in here, will not rest until I answer the question: what happened to me?

* * * * *

I'll admit there are pieces of the last twenty-four hours of my life that I don't remember, but each day there isn't much else to do.

The day before the wedding, an oppressive pigeon-colored sky sobbed a steady rain; deafening thunder resonated inside me, an unusually cold July wind sliced through my bones, and the water taxi pitched so much that it was a battle not to get sick.

"This isn't a good day to be out here!" yelled Miles from his post at the helm.

"You remember what tomorrow is, right?" I tightened my rain hat.

"I haven't forgotten!" All things considered, he'd taken our breakup well. He said he wasn't going to leave, and since he was all I'd ever really known as a caretaker and didn't want to look for a replacement, I didn't ask him to.

Russell, who was youthful but with sad ice-blue eyes, was an artist who painted the insides of wealthy New Yorkers' apartments to make ends meet. We'd met four years ago at a party at a mutual friend's home in the Village. There was weed. There was alcohol. There were deep conversations about the sharp discipline of pain—he'd been injured in a car wreck and limped, albeit painfully, with a cane, which made his day job a challenge—and there was electric sex on a makeshift bed of fur coats. He'd wanted us just to live together, but I needed commitment. He kept saying it was more important to be free, to do things without being tethered, but then, just after he'd met my parents and our first summer on Cloud Island, he'd changed his mind. I became his benefactor so he could focus on his art, which paid off; he'd been working, often late into the evenings, on new pieces for a show he managed to secure. Bright things were ahead.

The boat smacked a hard swell, and two empty bottles of Jack Daniels rolled across the floor and bounced against Miles's large brown duffel bag that I hadn't seen since our together days.

I took note of his scowl. "Planning on staying tonight?"

"The storm's gonna get a lot worse!" Miles said. "I'll get your guests in the morning!"

After we broke up, he'd never stayed on the island overnight, no matter the weather. "I'm expecting you to help with the setup tomorrow, then!"

He smirked. "That might not happen!"

"It will!" I said, although as the island loomed closer I was losing confidence. Waves white-capped against the rocky spines of its shore; the trees of its dark wood huddled like plotting giants, the swollen sky strobed with lightning, and Cricket's Wail's freshly painted turret—red with chocolate trim—thrust above the forest like a terrifying dragon. "For God's sake, just make sure we get there in one piece!"

When at last we reached the dock, the boat jockeyed so much he actually had trouble securing the rope around a piling. He was still spry, though, and he hefted my bags out and set them on the planks, climbed his way up, and offered me his hand, which was a familiar comfort until it lingered too long. I wrested my hand away and shoved both in the pockets of my raincoat. After a tense moment, he bore two of my bags with a grunt.

"Get the third one now, too, Miles. That's got stuff in it I need immediately."

He turned, and I spied a full whiskey bottle in each pocket of his oilskin. He nodded in the direction of the house. "Go on. I'll take care of it."

I trekked to the house. Cold dollops of rain kissed my neck and sent a violent shiver down my spine.

The damp had embraced the grand hall despite the fire that Vicki—the poli-sci major at a nearby college I hired every summer to clean and change the sheets for guests—was tending in the study's fireplace to my right. "Hey, Miss Grandjean." She flipped her long honey hair over her shoulder, rested the heavy poker against the mantle, and billowed the flames. "How was your ride?"

"Bumpy." I unbuttoned my coat and hung it on the antique coat rack adjacent to the study's entrance.

She stood up and turned to face me. She'd changed since the last time I'd seen her—last August when she was heading back to school. She'd always been underdeveloped, thin, and somewhat tomboyish, but now she was fuller-figured and lithe. She was even wearing a necklace, and an elegant one at that: the jewel was an amethyst, cut in the shape of a ladybug, the legs of which were studded with tiny diamonds. Then I noticed the hems of her jeans were caked with mud, so much so I could see smears of it on the study's oak floor. "You're making a mess. You should change those."

She seized the poker again, jabbed it in between a couple of burning logs. "What?"

"Your pants. You're not going to have time to clean this whole floor again tomorrow before people get here. I need you for other things."

She turned and looked at me. A crack of thunder shook the walls.

"Where's Russell?" I asked.

She glanced toward the front door. "He was—outside, last I saw him."

It was pouring. "Doing what?"

"Um . . . setting up the plastic chairs for tomorrow? Or moving them, maybe?"

"In this?"

Miles, who'd been lagging behind me, finally arrived. "You want your bags upstairs?"

"Yes, and—Miles is staying the night," I told Vicki.

"I'll take the Northland Room." Miles moved toward the stairs.

"Wait!" Vicki cried. "The sheets aren't done in there."

I frowned. "Why not? What do I pay you for?"

"Um . . ." she looked uncomfortable. "I was . . . getting wood for the fire."

"You know what, that's fine." Miles was terse. "Is the Eastern Room available and ready?"

The door flew open and Russell brushed water off the navy blue pea coat I'd bought him last fall. "Man, this is going to be one wet wedding!" He attempted to rest his cane against the wall, but the bottom was so slick with mud it fell on the floor, its heavy brass eagle head banging loudly on the wood. "Marcia? You're here!"

I went to him for a kiss. Out of the corner of my eye, I noted Vicki had turned around to watch us, but she was still, poker in hand. "Vicki? Don't you have something to do?"

Russell pulled away a little.

She nodded and motioned to Miles. She alighted on the stairs with all the spring in her step of a confident girl and took the poker with her.

* * * * *

Dinner that night was a strange affair. The four of us sat in the windowless dining room, under the glare of several hunting trophies.

The tension was thick as the stroganoff Vicki had made—she'd offered since my regular cook was bringing the caterers with him early in the morning. At that point, though, the storming had only gotten more intense, and we were beginning to face the reality that our caterers and the pastor—let alone the guests—wouldn't be able to make it the next day.

Miles, who'd been drinking his dinner, filled up another glass with whiskey. "It's too damn dangerous," he said. "I'm not taking my life in my hands."

Russell swallowed his food. "Haven't you had enough, Miles?"

I'd never told Russell about Miles. Miles was drunk, and he'd certainly acted this way before, but Russell had never asked. I could see that perhaps this was ratcheting to disaster.

"You're not my mother," Miles grunted.

The only sound for a few moments was the scraping of forks on the china.

"Well, even if no one's here, we should go ahead with it." Russell took a sip of Bordeaux.

I nearly choked on mine. "We have planned this to the nth degree, Russell. Now I don't like being made to wait either, but I've worked on this and I'm not about to throw it all away. Miles is right. The storms are supposed to continue through Monday and already the shoreline's flooding. We're rescheduling everything for September."

"Timing is really important, Marsh. We can get married tomorrow, go on our honeymoon, and then have a party—same food, cake, and all if you like—for everyone here at the house when we return. By then the weather will be better." He raised his glass. "I have wanted this for so long, too. Let's not let anything get in the way."

"My family does things a certain way, Russell, and so do I. We can't tell them we got married without them."

"Exactly."

Outside, the wind howled. I could hear the windows in the adjoining study shiver in their frames. Vicki's fire emitted a loud pop. The situation seemed, indeed, hopeless. But it was in moments like this that I realized Russell was what I wanted, and everything I wanted. Clever and gentle and artistic and calm, intellectual, and humble. We wouldn't have to tell anyone we'd already been married. Would it matter?

I was just about to agree when I realized there was no one to perform the ceremony.

Russell grinned.

"You didn't know Miles is a justice of the peace?" Vicki blurted.

Miles frowned. "How's that any of your business?"

"You married a couple of my friends last year." Vicki played with the jewel on her necklace, leaned conspiratorially over her plate at me. "It was totally weird to find out he worked for you."

"If you think I'm going to perform your ceremony tomorrow, you're mistaken." Miles pushed back his chair, seized his glass and bottle, and retreated upstairs, his heavy footfalls and slam of the door to the Eastern room rattling the deer antler chandelier above our heads.

Russell cleared his throat. "What the hell was that all about?"

"Nothing." I rose from my seat. "He just needs to be spoken to." I left my napkin on the table and went to tell Miles he had no choice.

* * * * *

There is a hole where that night used to be. The next thing I remember is the following morning's ceremony on the porch, the shock of its anticlimax, and going to my room to change. That's when I stood on the balcony and the world went black.

When I awakened, the house was dark and cold.

As long as I'm trapped in here, my thoughts will not rest until I answer the question: what happened to me? Yet no matter how many times I replay the most significant moments of the last twenty-four hours of my life hoping the details of that evening will come back, they never do.

It has stayed that way until now.

The door groans open and, finally, a mighty thwack. Two figures stand in the kinetic lightning and a rain as driving as that on my wedding day.

I scream—I'm in the wall! I'm in the wall!—but a bolt of thunder drowns my cries.

"Jesus, honey!" a man shouts over the din. "This is one helluva creepy wedding gift! We should've waited until tomorrow."

"Don't be ridiculous." That's a woman's voice—and it sounds familiar, but I can't quite place it. She reaches behind the door and toggles the ancient light switch, and to my delight, a golden, gray-tinged glow floods the dingy corners. "They turned on the electricity on time, so we're good."

They step into the grand hall, and the strapping bear of a man shakes excess water off his coat and closes the door, thrusting against it with his hip to get it firmly closed. "I guess you're right. It's not like we'll make it back in that boat tonight. When they said this place was prone to 'sudden squalls' they weren't joking."

"Apparently sometimes they last for days." The slight woman—I will call her Bird—pulls the drop cloth off the coat tree. Dust welters into the air, and she coughs.

Bear smirks. "Couldn't your parents have just given us the cash?"

She waves her hand in front of her face. "No. The lady who owned this place was super-rich, they got it with everything else she owned, and they've been saving it for me." She shrugs out of her coat. "Unless you have any objection, we're going to clean it up and get rid of it."

"No objections here."

No! Let me out first! Let me out!

Bear reaches out and touches Bird's arm. "You hear that?"

Bird takes off her rain hat, shakes her long hair free. "What?"

"Thought I heard something from the wall." He points directly at me.

She gazes, too, and I see that, in the dim light, she also looks slightly familiar. "Probably just mice."

No, no! It's me! I'm here! Let me out!

Bird hesitates for a moment as though, yes, she has heard me, but it leads to nothing. "Or some other animal. The place has been closed up for years."

Yes, and I've been here the whole time! Please, please!

Bear looks at me again. "You know—"

A crash of thunder, the worst yet, makes them both jump.

Bird wanders into the study behind me; I can't see her, but I can still hear her. "I'm totally agreeing with you. This room is really creepy."

For God's sake, I'm right here!

I start to feel that familiar burn in the back of my throat.

"Jesus." Bear freezes.

"What?"

"I just—I keep thinking I'm hearing something. Coming out of that wall."

Bird comes back into the room and comes near to my wall, sets her hands on her hips. Then she sets her ear against it.

I scream and scream: help help help!

She jolts away, and I think again, maybe she hears! No; she furrows her brow in the mirror, and I notice a gleam at the base of her throat.

"We may just have to get an exterminator, although honestly, I don't know if any of those people would do a call out here on short notice." Bird goes to the door and grabs her bag. "I'm beat. Want to check out the upstairs? Pick a room to crash in? It might be a little dusty, but I'm sure it's doable."

No! No! Don't leave me!

"Sure." Bear hefts his pack over his shoulder. As they tread up the stairs, dust puffs from the carpet. "I'm shocked this place is in any decent shape at all."

"My parents took care of it until we got married." The way she says married, the way she alights on the stairs. Have I seen you before?

"So nobody's been here in a year?" Bear is halfway up the stairs, but he gazes uncomfortably in my direction yet again. His pack brushes against the black drape over Whittier's portrait; it slides nearly off, and the heavy art wobbles on its nail. Both he and Bird dive for it.

"Careful!" Bird says. "Damn thing would break your foot if it fell on it."

He tips it so it's straight again. "Related to you?"

She shrugs. "I have no idea."

They shut off the lights and the room plunges into the usual devastating darkness, although the storm is receding, and soon there is the sad shine of the moon streaming through the cracks in the boarded-up windows.

All's quiet except for the sound of crickets, which doesn't last long; the silence is rocked by the portrait of Whittier banging against the wall, rumbling like a low tympani—and something else. It's coming from the Northland Room, which backs the wall behind Whittier: the lilting moans and husky gasps of Bird and Bear, making love.

It's a sound I've heard before, but when? When?

The night before the wedding.

A rumbling—which I thought was thunder until it went on too long—woke me. I padded down the hall, the soft tremors of the boards under my feet increasing as I got closer to the disturbance: Whittier's portrait banging against the staircase wall. Another sound, from the Northland Room behind it, sighed above the din.

My breath stopped short, and I crept forward to press my ear against the door.

I heard the moans and gasps of Vicki and Russell in the grand release of lovemaking, and when it was done, there were whispers about a baby, what his or her name would be, that Vicki hoped it would be born on Valentine's Day.

No. Nonononono how come I didn't see this? What did I miss?

I fled downstairs to fetch something to calm my nerves. The study was pitch, save for the intermittent seizure of lightning, but I easily navigated to the decanter and glasses. I knocked back a shot, calming as the liquid warmth coated my throat and spread to my limbs.

You took forever to find Russell and you're not letting him go! He belongs to you! Just marry him before he knows you're aware.

Then fire her and demand he never see her again or else you'll divorce him and leave him with nothing.

He'll concede. He'll have to go back to work if he doesn't.

"Sorry, was I keeping you up?"

Startled, I snapped around and squinted into the ink of the room. In a lightning flash, I saw a dark form: Miles. He'd been sitting on the leather sofa.

He reached over and turned on the lamp, slurred at me: "Oh, no, something else was." He patted the empty seat next to him. "Come on, come sit."

"I . . . I have a big day tomorrow. I need to get my beauty sleep."

"Sit!"

Another crash of thunder.

"No," I said.

"We always used to talk."

"You were always mostly sober."

"Because you left me, Marcia!" He slammed the rocks glass on the tree trunk coffee table. "You weren't supposed to. We were supposed to be together."

"I don't love you that way, Miles. I'm marrying Russell." Fear was fast rising in my throat.

"He doesn't love you."

"That's not true! He just was tempted. That's all." I set my glass down on the small bar. "Now good night."

"I can still refuse to perform the ceremony tomorrow." Still came out shtill.

I stopped at the threshold of the grand hall and pivoted to stare at him. In the shudder of lightning, he looked twisted, like a man I didn't know. "If you do, I will do what I have to do to get rid of you. You love me so much? You'll never see me again. Ever."

Everything was ruined in the span of twenty minutes.

For the first time since I've been trapped in this wall, instead of screaming in frustration, I weep, and I swear I feel the very walls of my tomb weeping with me, through the night to the dawn, through to the moment Bird and Bear awaken, through to when Bear tells Bird that he couldn't sleep because he could hear the whatever it is that's in the damn walls and I'm going to find out and he rushes out to the shed to get a sledgehammer.

* * * * *

"Bobby, you will totally not go putting a hole in this wall!" Bird blocks the antique mirror, her arms spread wide. I see it, around her neck: that necklace, the one Vicki wore: an unusual amethyst, cut in the shape of a ladybug, the legs of which are studded with tiny diamonds. The way she says married and totally and that confident spring in her step and her . . . her long, honey hair!

That's why she looks familiar; it's why I think I've seen her before. Her mother and father . . . her mother and father are Vicki and Russell!

I scream.

"Don't you hear that?"

"Stop it!"

"Get out of the way, Angie. I can hear it!"

"It's mice!"

"It's screaming!"

There's a still moment, and I see a shift in Angie's eyes, and she concedes. "At least let me take down this mirror. It's probably worth a mint."

"Hurry up!" Bobby rests the sledgehammer on his shoulder.

The world goes dark, and I panic because I'm about to get—boomshake, boomshake, and splinters rain and dust halts my screaming for them to stop, stop, you'll hit me, but Bobby doesn't stop; he is relentless.

The wall in front of me crumbles. My soul escapes, and I'm light and wispy as a zephyr. At first, I cannot control my movements, and I burst up and circle above the terrified couple, who clutch each other at the horror that now lies at their feet: my bones. Me, or what is left of me, scattered like a child's pick-up sticks.

It is my skull that is the most shocking thing of all: it's smashed in.

I understand, now, the thing that happened to me, but it doesn't make sense until the objects that had been sealed at my feet spill from the wall, too. Near my scattered toe bones: Vicki's fireplace poker. Russell's cane. Miles' whiskey bottle.

Each is encrusted in blood.

There is also something else.

There is another skeleton.

"I knew you were still here!"

I look up, and it's Miles. He is as I always see him. I think that he is talking to Bobby and Angie, but the only response either exhibits is a shiver when he passes through them. "Miles?"

"They killed me, too. Told the world we were lovers and ran off. Been wandering ever since, looking for you. If it hadn't been for them taking that wall down, I'd have missed you again." He reaches me and grasps my hands. "I told you we were supposed to be together."

This time when I scream, I am sure that at last, everyone can hear me.

Antiques
Gregory L. Norris

The original c.1840 bridge connecting Orr's and Great Island beginning to fade into the fog, as photographed c.1901.
In the shipbuilding communities around Harpswell, and the neighboring islands, there was a legend about a ghost ship that appears out of the fog, and heads toward shore, regardless of the wind. Under full sail with no hands, the ship then disappears back into the fog before it can run aground. The ship's appearance foretells death will strike Harpswell. Whittier immortalized the legend as "The Dead Ship of Harpswell" after a Maine schoolteacher wrote him, bemoaning that the local folklore was fading away. *Library of Congress Prints and Photographs Division.*

Someone had attached plastic streamers to the handlebars of Vivee Driscoll's wheelchair—gaudy neon yellow and electric blue ones, just like those in the colorized version of her cinema classic, Girl on a Bike, Marni saw when she entered the room. A glance at the wall and an original movie poster from the film almost mirrored the scene before her: a much younger Vivee, tearing down a hill on her bicycle, a crazy, youthful smile on her face. Film noir heavies in trench coats, club-wielding coppers, and an escaped gorilla were in hot pursuit of that Vivee Driscoll. The present day model was a tiny china doll with a head of thinning white hair, confined to a wheelchair and dozing in the shaft of sunlight spilling through the window of Room 209 in the east wing of Whittier Hill Retirement Community.

A flotilla of Mylar balloons drifted in the corner, some already losing their oomph. A bouquet of long-stemmed red roses fared better. There were birthday cards along the sill, atop the heating unit, the deck shuffled and reshuffled whenever a nurse or visitor shifted the curtains, Marni imagined. She moved quietly, carefully, past the dozing birthday girl and reached for the latest card tumbled over, righting it. At one bookend of the cards was Vivee's Emmy, which she'd taken home in the 1970s for an ABC movie-of-the-week based on John Greenleaf Whittier's eerie poem of the same name, The Dead Ship of Harpswell. Marni had watched a grainy copy of the flick online weeks earlier when she took the volunteer position.

"Oh, it's you, thank goodness," Vivee said, straightening in her chair.

Marni smiled. "Who else were you expecting?"

"That pain in the rump," Vivee sighed. "The one with the mustache. Always staring at me. The one that looks like him." She waved a hand at the wall. "That gorilla."

Marni snickered. "You know that's only a poster."

Vivee's eyes widened. "Not that, the man in the monkey suit. Actor...oh, what was his name? Albert or some such nonsense. Like him, always gaping at me when he visits. Like he's a fancy jeweler and I'm the Hope Diamond. I've got half a mind to tell him to take a picture—it'll last longer!"

"Sure he wasn't a dream, Vivee?"

Vivee sighed. "Who do you think I am?"

"You're the Vivee Driscoll, star of the big and little screens. And it's almost time to celebrate your one-hundredth birthday, my dear."

Marni reached for Vivee's sweater, a lilac button-down, and draped it around her shoulders.

"A century old," Vivee sighed. "It's official. I'm an antique!"

* * * * *

Marni wheeled Vivee to the elevator, and from there down to Happy Days Ahead, where the event awaited its star. She'd always disliked the name of the function room—the days ahead were short and likely to be ones filled with discomfort. It wasn't like there were prospects to be had among them, however, many or few. No Hollywood agent was going to call up or come racing down the corridor, dodging wheelchairs and oxygen tanks, with a lucrative contract for some new film deal thrust ahead of him. Vivee Driscoll had last acted before the camera's twenty years earlier—a cameo in a sitcom. A novelty. An ending.

A different kind of cast party awaited them in Happy Days Ahead. The small crowd broke into applause at their entrance, and a few camera phones flashed for pictures.

There were more balloons and a big sheet cake, which displayed a recent photograph of Vivee, photocopied across edible rice paper. A parade of partygoers in wheelchairs wore hats, as did the half-dozen staff members and a mix of strangers—likely the representatives from the Vivee Driscoll Fan Club, who'd helped to organize the party.

"There better be ice cream," Vivee groused.

"Coffee ice cream, just like you requested," Marni said.

* * * * *

Marni made a pass through the lobby. The reception desk, at that moment, sat unmanned. At first, Marni didn't think Kathy's absence odd. Reception didn't link up to a prison—Kathy was entitled to leave for bathroom breaks and to enjoy a slice of birthday cake at Vivee's celebration like anyone else on staff.

Then Marni passed the sign-in book for visitors laid atop the marble table, located just inside the front entrance, and an invisible finger stroked her spine. The book sat out of alignment. The top page was gone, torn out according to the jagged leaflet still attached, marking the vandalism.

"Kathy?" she called.

No one answered.

Marni reached for her phone on instinct and found her pocket empty. The party—she'd dialed down to the kitchen for an update, and then had returned it to her bag, presently locked safely away with the other volunteers' totes and purse's in the nurse's lounge.

She instead reached across the reception area desk and picked the phone from its cradle. She called upstairs.

"Hi, is Kathy up there with you?"

"No, sorry," the nurse answered.

She hung up, scooted around the desk, and entered Whittier Hill's security area. There, the facility's cameras eyed and recorded. Kathy lay sprawled before the bank of monitors and, for a terrible second, Marni wasn't sure that the other woman was breathing.

"Oh my God," Marni gasped.

She knelt beside Kathy. The receptionist groaned and opened her eyes as movement on one of the monitors drew Marni's gaze back up. The image shouldn't have seemed out of place—Vivee Driscoll, still in her party hat and lilac sweater—except for that particular screen, whose camera was aimed at the back patio. The streamers on the wheelchair's handlebar whipped madly about in the early spring breeze.

And then a second figure passed across the patio. A man. She only saw him briefly as he wheeled Vivee Driscoll away and out of sight.

The man had a mustache.

Kathy attempted to sit up. Marni rose from beside her and hastened toward the exit to the back patio.

"I'm sending help, Kathy," Marni promised.

Across the lobby, past the Happy Days Ahead room, where the party continued, its guests oblivious that its star was being kidnapped, she reached the vestibule leading to the back patio. Marni punched the button that released the double doors to the outside. The doors unsealed. Marni readied to push through them, then paused. She reached up and pulled the fire alarm. The building came alive around her in shrill whoops that signaled danger.

She hurried outside in search of Vivee Driscoll and her abductor.

*****

Whittier Hill was located in the town of Bradford's rural west, a green belt that had mostly managed to escape the greedy developers and strip malls of the east. As she pedaled farther down the single-lane road, the irony struck her—how life could alter so quickly and without warning.

Marni hit the brakes. The bike screeched to a stop across the asphalt. The tall oaks on either side of the road, still without their spring leaves, seemed to leer down at her. They were the trees of nightmares, like those lining the shadow-cloaked estuary in The Dead Ship of Harpswell. Any second, she expected them to make a grab at her with their skeletal limbs.

The red van. She'd caught sight of it as it was turning out of the parking lot, headed right. Right led deeper into the west, where not a lot of anything was located. Her car keys were upstairs, along with her phone. As Whittier Hill shrieked itself to action courtesy of the fire alarm, she remembered that Hector Padillo, one of the kitchen workers, rode a bike to work every day. He kept it in the gated area behind the dumpsters.

The van had turned right, and right again. Two or three turns later, with the afternoon growing dark and the trees closing in, it struck her that Marni had become Vivee's character from the classic movie she'd starred in so many years earlier, the girl on a bike.

Vivee had said she'd had a visitor, a man with a mustache who'd gawked at her like she was the Hope Diamond. No mere senile fantasy on the centenarian's part, Marni had seen Vivee's kidnapper, and he'd sported a mustache.

A chill cut through the heat that coated Marni's skin. She glanced around, down. The road had ended at a row of lichen-covered boulders, the remains of an old farmer's wall. The red van had eluded her effort to catch up to it, seemingly by vanishing into thin air.

The police. She had to tell them what had happened, what she'd seen. By now, Whittier Hill would have sounded the all-clear, at least in regards to fire. Kathy would have given a report—she'd been attacked. And they likely knew that Vivee was missing.

She turned the bike around and started back in the direction of the nursing home, and an awful thought crept in. What if she never found her way out of the woods and home to civilization? Just as Marni killed that notion, she noticed the stretch of meadow, likely all that was left of the farmer's field whose boundary was marked by the wall of boulders. A gap in the lichen-encrusted rocks was big enough for a vehicle the size of a van to slip through.

Marni's heart galloped. She traveled off the road, onto the grass. Farther in, she saw that fresh tracks had torn up the greening sod. A trail appeared at the wood line and ran between the trees.

This is it, Marni thought. This is where he took Vivee Driscoll!

She pedaled the bike onto the trail and pressed deeper into the darkening forest.

* * * * *

A lone light appeared, golden-white, a beacon that drew her toward it. The day's relative warmth had waned, and Marni's sweat had cooled. The light represented a house, a mystery, and danger. The man who'd kidnapped Vivee had likely knocked out Kathy to abduct the former actress, for whatever diabolical reason.

The house materialized in the last of the dying daylight. At first, Marni wasn't sure what she was looking at because house and forest were one. Then she neared enough to understand the structure was no simple house.

It was a manor, the kind of place with wings and parlors, libraries and drawing rooms. She'd come out upon the manor's rear. A series of decks and an elaborate portico graced this part of the grand estate—the only visible house in all directions, Marni also noted. Another set of fresh tracks led in the direction of a garage the size of a barn. Marni peered through the first window she came upon. A boxy shape lurked in the garage's shadows. She knew it was the van.

Vivee was somewhere inside that vast house.

Peeking around the corner of the garage, she absorbed what she could: the manor faced a long, rolling driveway connected to pavement but no visible nearby help in the form of neighbors. Abandoning the bike, she scurried over to the portico and its door. The frosted glass pane prevented a clear view of the inside of the house. She tested the door's knob. It was locked.

Steeling herself, Marni moved toward a set of French doors, the source of the only light in the house. Diaphanous ripple-fold curtains made it difficult to see inside, though not impossible.

"Anything you want, anything you need," she heard a man say, his voice muffled by the door glass. "Anything at all. You only have to ask, Vivee."

"It's Ms. Driscoll to you," Vivee fired back. "And so far, you haven't delivered on my one request."

"Ice cream? It's coming, my treasure."

Marni heard Vivee sigh. "Your treasure? I think your mother wears combat boots."

After that, silence.

Marni reached for the doorknob and turned, again to the same results. She knocked. "Vivee?"

Breathless seconds later, the door opened. Gossamer curtains billowed out. Vivee in her wheelchair filled the gap. She was still clad in her party outfit and lilac sweater.

"Oh, thank my lucky stars!" Vivee exclaimed.

Marni hurried in and embraced the other woman. "I followed you all the way here from Whittier Hill," she said, her voice barely louder than a whisper. "I'm going to get you home."

Home. That last word sat heavy on her tongue. Whittier Hill wasn't home in the word's truest meaning—it was a way station between Home and Afterlife. Then Marni absorbed the room about them in quick order: its vaulted ceiling and overhead light, which was nothing short of a chandelier, the four-post bed and luxurious fainting couch worthy of the finest diva of the silver screen. Fresh clothes were draped over the tufted back cushions of an easy chair upholstered in merlot-colored velvet—a nightgown perfect for a woman of Vivee's height and age. The room boasted vases filled with pink roses. One of those vases, Marni saw, was Waterford. Another was cranberry glass, a beautiful antique with plenty of dimples. Everything about the room was exquisite, from its antique furniture to the framed botanical watercolors and sterling silver candlesticks on the mahogany sideboard.

"Marni?" Vivee said, shattering the spell.

Marni closed the French doors and hurried back. "I'm here. Did he hurt you?"

"Hurt me?" Vivee huffed. "No, but he's boring me to tears!"

Marni stifled a laugh. "Vivee, what's going on here?"

"Something to do with him being a collector."

"Of what?"

"Priceless antiques. He said he wants to add me to his collection. I thought he was taking me out for ice cream—the damned lout tried to pass himself off as the leader of my fan club. You know, The Vivee Driscoll Society. But I saw right through him, I can tell you!"

"An antique collector?" Marni asked.

She stole another glance around the room. The place was palatial, and fitting for a woman of Vivee's past celebrity. But it was also a prison—a maniac who'd broken the law had taken Vivee here against her will.

"Time to get you back," Marni said.

Vivee clapped her hands together. "Good. The only antiques I want to be surrounded by are the rest of the old ladies at Whittier Hill!"

Marni moved to take Vivee's wheelchair by the handlebars. Then the approach of footsteps reached them through the bedroom's closed door.

"Hide, my dear," Vivee whispered.

Marni hurried behind the tufted seat and its overlay of high-thread nightwear. Her heart attempted to jump into her throat as the next few seconds tolled and the footsteps caught up to the door.

"Rocky Road," the man said.

"Blech," said Vivee. "But it'll have to do, I suppose."

Marni chanced a look around the corner of the chair, afraid to breathe. The man carried a silver tray upon which sat a crystal bowl filled with ice cream, a cherry on top.

"Do you have any other requests?" he asked.

"Well, as kind as your offer is, I'd like to return to Whittier Hill."

The man laughed. "You're too good to waste away in a place like that."

"So you say," Vivee said. "But I've already lived my life and had my kicks. I'm ready to coast along now."

"Coast?" the man parroted.

"Yes, to the top deck of Charon's ferry over the River Styx—or The Dead Ship of Harpswell. Whatever next script awaits. I'm tired, and, frankly, Rocky Road plays hell with my bridgework."

The man rolled over a tray table, adjusted its height, and presented Vivee with the bowl, a silver spoon, and a cloth napkin. "Nonsense. You're one of a kind, an object of rare beauty. Tomorrow, you'll have Neapolitan, my treasure."

He turned toward the door, and Marni caught her first clear look at him—blue eyes, a man in his fifties with a shock of neat, dark hair that seemed to jump away from his skull. A toupee, Marni realized.

"Please, for the love of all that's holy," Vivee attempted, hands clasped in prayer for mercy.

The man smiled. "I remember that scene—Canadian Holiday, wasn't it?"

Vivee waved him away.

"If you need help changing into your nightie…"

"You should get so lucky!"

The man smiled. "You're a treasure."

"Stop saying that," she said, and then downed a spoonful of ice cream.

"I'll check back in when you're done."

He closed the door. Marni heard a lock turn from the other side.

"Albert," Vivee sighed. "That one's nuttier than this ice cream."

Marni remembered to breathe and scurried out of hiding, back to Vivee. "Albert?" she whispered.

Vivee looked up from the bowl. "Yes, dear. You remember me telling you about him. That was the name of the gorilla in Girl on a Bike. Only Albert was a man in a monkey suit, not a real ape. He was such a bore, as I recall, but harmless."

Marni remembered the receptionist, knocked out and carried into the security room. "No, he's not harmless, Vivee. Time to make our escape."

She tried the door and found it locked, as she feared. That only left the French doors, but after Marni stepped out into the brisk night, motion sensors that hadn't been active in the late afternoon switched on, alerted to her movements. Marni hastened back inside the room.

"That's not the smartest way out or the most direct anyway."

"Then how are we supposed to toodle away from this crazy Popsicle stand?" asked Vivee.

*****

Marni examined the candlestick—a big, old piece, weighty. Given the largesse and elegance that surrounded them, it could have been authentic Revere silver. The thought of what she planned to do with it sickened her, but it was the best scenario for their escape.

"Get ready," Marni said.

Vivee flashed a thumbs-up, then began to scream.

"Help! Help, Albert—help!"

Footsteps sounded in the terrible silence that followed the former actress's brilliant performance. Marni shot a glance at Vivee and tightened her grip on the candlestick. The great Vivee Driscoll, emerged from retirement one last time for a final curtain call, had, perhaps, given the greatest running of lines of her career. The look on Vivee's face mixed fear and triumph. But the applause Marni wanted to offer would have to wait.

The lock turned and the door flew open.

"Vivee, what's wro-?" the man started.

Marni swung. He was taller than she'd judged, and the head of the candlestick bounced off his toupee. As he turned toward her, shock and rage both showing in his expression, she hit him again. This time, he went down.

"Take that, Albert!" Vivee said.

Marni tossed the candlestick and hurried to the wheelchair. She angled it around the man's body and out through the open door. Marni attempted to shut the door but the man's twitching, socked feet blocked the threshold. She swept them both inside the room with a kick. The door shut. Marni found the deadbolt and turned it, locking him in.

The actress clapped her hands together. "Well done!"

Marni flashed what she imagined was a maniac's smile. "Thanks, but we're not back to Whittier Hill yet! Did you see a landline phone?"

Vivee pointed down the long hallway with its rosewood wainscoting, elegant sconces, and birthday cake decorative molding. "I think so. In that big room."

Marni pushed. The hallway whisked by, offering brief glimpses of shadowy rooms filled with phantoms. The vast space Vivee indicated sat mostly dark, too, save for the glow of the outside motion sensor lights outside another set of French doors, which chose the next second to again go dark.

Gasping, Marni felt along the wall. She found the light switch, and a golden effulgence rained down on what she assumed was an art gallery, judging by the exquisite, oversized oil paintings in gilt frames and statuary. The marble floor boasted expensive Persian rugs. Dust cloths that transformed the artwork beneath into ghosts covered several of the statues.

A chill stroked Marni's spine, one she'd barely kept ahead of since departing Whittier Hill in pursuit of Vivee and her abductor. She started to shake in its aftermath and willed her nerves to steady.

"The phone," Marni said through chattering teeth. "Where did you see it?"

"Over there."

Vivee pointed at an antique table, upon which sat a beautiful object crafted of detailed filigree metal, silver in color.

"That Grand Emperor phone," said Vivee.

Marni blinked. At first, she didn't realize the object with its handset and jeweled rotary was the landline phone Vivee meant. Another priceless antique, that phone wouldn't get them the help they needed.

"I say we go, just go," Vivee said. "Through that set of doors, and out into the night!"

Marni nodded. But en route, she noticed the kind of cord running along the wall that only could have belonged to a phone system.

"One sec, I promise," she said and left to follow the cord's direction. One of those cloaked ghost-statues blocked her at the next corner. Marni grabbed the dustsheet and pulled. The sheet slipped free.

Standing underneath was a statue of a man—a regal, elderly gent dressed smartly in a tweed suit, with a monocle fixed over one eye. More than simply a statue, the details were stunningly lifelike. A mannequin? Even more than that, Marni thought.

Fear slithered over her flesh. She moved to the next statue and drew off its dust cover. Beneath was a silver-haired woman dressed in a colorful pantsuit and cameo broach. Like the man with the monocle, the details were beyond precise.

"Dear God," Marni gasped.

Albert had done this before.

Right as the first knocks hammered the prison bedroom behind them—proof that Vivee's kidnapper had recovered—Marni recognized the wires for what they were.

"Security system," she whispered.

It wouldn't be long before Albert turned away from the one locked door and backtracked into the house through the French doors leading out to the deck. Any second, she expected the motion sensor lights to activate, a warning that he was coming. The full horror of what the antique collector was capable of loomed around them in the macabre gallery of preserved centenarians.

The door panes were linked to the wires. Marni rolled Vivee outside, onto the small courtyard. Then, she pitched the antique phone through the glass. Thunder boomed. Alarms followed, shrieking across the new night.

And then they were running down the driveway, their escape set to the pulsing whoop of Albert's security alarm. The two women raced down the slope of the driveway, toward the street.

It struck Marni that they were recreating the classic chase scene from Girl on a Bike, seventy years after the fact. Streamers flew behind Vivee Driscoll as she prevailed against the villains and rode her way into history.

They reached the road, a dark stretch leading in an uncertain direction. Marni tipped a glance over her shoulder and saw the outline of the villain in pursuit.

"The gorilla," she said and pushed Vivee's wheelchair faster.

Ahead of them, the headlights of a car appeared. To Marni's relief, electric blue strobed from its light strip as it approached.

"Bravo!" Vivee Driscoll said and began to clap.

The Murderer's Request
Lucy Larcom

Lucy Larcom, c.1889
Larcom's A New England Girlhood was such a popular book that the author's likeness from the front of the publication has become the de facto official portrait for subsequent projects needing her image.

Bury me not where, so solemnly waving,
    The sentinel yew guards my forefathers' sleep;
They would start in their shrouds with a voice of wild raving,
    And scare me with curses low muttered and deep;
And their glances of vengeance would glare through the gloom—
Oh! bury me not near my forefathers' tomb!

Bury me not where the breezes are sighing
    O'er those whom I loved in my innocent days,
For their eyes, that beamed love and forgiveness when dying,
    Would haunt me, for aye, with their seraph-like gaze.
And I would not pollute the sweet spot where they are,
With an ingrate's vile ashes: oh! lay me not there!

Bury me not where in myriad numbers
    The city crowds throng the low halls of the dead;
For with echoes of scorn they would wake from their slumbers
    And bid me arise from that last narrow bed;
And with skeleton fingers would point me away;
Oh! bury me not where those ghastly hosts lay!

Bury me not in the shadowy wildwood,
    'Mongst wild birds and flowers the tree and the stream;
Ah! they were my guiltless companions in childhood—
    But never again may return that bright dream;
For the birds and the stream from my presence would flee;
And all verdure and beauty would vanish near me.

Bury ye me on some storm-rifted mountain
    O'erhanging the depths of a yawning abyss,
Where the song of the zephyr, the gush of the fountain,
    Are changed for the whirlwind, and vile reptile's hiss;
Mid whose pestilent vapors no mortal may come;
And no being, save One, view my desolate home.

Yet, can ye not find within Nature's dominion,
    A nook where that Eye's piercing ray may not see,
Let me fly to that spot, on some demon's dark pinion,
    Far, far from the glory so hateful to me.
Though the horrors of Erebus blacken the air,
Yet to me it were Paradise! Bury me there!

Cane Fishing

Rock Neelly

The Old Country Bridge, c.1900
Spanning the East Meadow River, also known as Country Brook, a bridge existed at this location prior to 1665, when a road was laid out from Holt's Rocks (Rocks Village) to the bridge. In 1685, the road was continued, following a footpath from the bridge to the main road. The name of the bridge remained unchanged after being immortalized by Whittier, although the bridge itself was repeatedly replaced and upgraded until the 1960s when nearby I-495 construction rerouted the old roads and rendered both the road and bridge obsolete. Whittier-Land: A Handbook of North Essex (1904).

Death comes to visit at inopportune moments. And indeed it came as an uninvited caller on a warm, spring day with a five-year-old boy as its witness. A boy who first saw the evil of man and behavior that can only be explained by our connection to Cain, our murderous ancestor.

It was a rare day that Jonathan Junior accompanied his father into town. Most times, the family business would be done in Amesbury, but the cordwainer there had been ill and did not have any shoes, let alone bridles, completed, necessitating a trip into Haverhill. Thus, today, a Saturday, John G. was happy to walk in his father's shadow along the main street of Haverhill, Massachusetts despite a chill early morning wind rolling along the Merrimack River. His father, a Quaker, wore his black Sunday suit and proceeded down the boardwalk next to Jonathan's uncle. Both men looked severe in their dark suits, long beards and wide brimmed hats. Jonathan himself was attired in his meeting clothes as well. He wore a black vest with a cream colored shirt under. His pants were knee-length with leggings that roughly matched his shirt. His boots were brown and rough. His hat was much like his father's, except it was new and made of straw. It had a chin strap of rawhide to keep the hat tight to his head as he walked.

It was two weeks past Easter. The year was 1812. The town was now home to 3,000 residents. Salem was roughly 30 miles east, still carrying the heavy weight of the witch trials now 125 years in the past. Those witch trials had never been the topic of conversation at the Whittier home, but Jonathan knew of them because the sons of the working men at his father's farm related the frightening tales at the bonfires the menfolk often lit and stood around when the work day was done. His older sister Mary sometimes tried to scare him with witchlike taunts as he performed his chores. Once his father had caught her and had caned her wrists as punishment. Both children were well aware that the word "witches" was not spoken aloud at the Whittier home.

Their community of Haverhill was a growing place. It was beginning to overrun the small village of Bradford across the river. Jonathan knew Bradford was home to a small co-educational school called Bradford Academy. He also knew that his father and uncle did not approve of the education of women, and he was not surprised that each time they passed a gap in the buildings that gave a view across the river to where the tower of the school proudly rose above the trees, they lowered their eyes to the ground. Jonathan had seen the school once on a trip into Bradford. He remembered all of the books neatly on shelves through the window of the brick building as they passed by. He still wished he could go in and flip through the pages. His father owned five books, all Quaker religious tracts. His uncle also owned a handful of books too, and one of those was Jonathan's favorite, a book of poetry by Robert Burns. Jonathan knew that the Bible was supposed to be everyone's favorite book, but the words of Burns made his mind go wild with the mental images of Scotland and what his uncle called the "old country."

Jonathan remembered the words above the doors of the academy. "Surgo ut Prosim" was etched into the stone there. He knew his letters and even their sounds, but he did not know what these words meant and admitted to himself that he had never heard them spoken. Somehow that made these particular words magical. But, he thought to himself, the word "magical" was another not to be spoken in the Whittier household if one wanted to avoid the switch. Nonetheless, he had memorized the order of the letters.

Suddenly his father's gruff voice ordered him to move along and catch up to the men. He jumped with his father's stern admonition, realizing he had slowed down while daydreaming about the academy. He broke into a run as he closed the distance until he was again at the expected, respectful distance of five strides.

After the two men had finished purchasing a new bridle for the plow horse at the livery, Jonathan's father nodded he would be going to the general store on his own. Jonathan was disappointed. Although he had never purchased anything in the store, seeing the goods which had been shipped in all the way from Boston was tremendously exciting for the boy.

He had turned five on December 17, and was long-legged for his age, but was gaunt. His frame, and his temperament for that matter, were more like his uncle than his father. His father was blocky, thick at the shoulders, with a full face and a prominent chin even under his heavy beard. But Jonathan, like his uncle, was thin and quick to smile. However, he had learned not to do so around his father.

After the disappointment of not going to the general store had passed, Jonathan was somewhat relieved to be in the company of his uncle. Uncle Moses was a kind soul and often explained all manner of things to his nephew. His father seldom did more than give orders, except when offering the daily ministries after the dinner hour. After his father departed toward the town center, Uncle Moses motioned for the boy to walk beside him, not in keeping the customary subordinate distance his father preferred.

"Thee must walk beside me," said the man, as he turned to the west toward Main Street and the route home. Jonathan hurried to catch up and noticed his uncle smile and shorten his gate to allow the boy to keep pace. As the two left the city, the mud which had clung to their boots became less prominent and the lane became dusty and pleasant. The streets in town seemed always to be muddy, especially in spring.

"Perhaps, as this is nearly the first fine, sunny day of spring, the two of us can finish our chores with care and speed. Then I shall take thee fishing. It would be nice if we were to provide the farm a nourishing dinner. Would it not, lad?"

Jonathan agreed and the two of them hurried home to the barn and gave a hired man, Joseph Boyer, the new set of reins. Then Uncle Moses moved to the orchard where he pared away limbs broken in the winter storms. The apple trees' leaves were tender, but the limbs cut away by his uncle's saw were brittle and in some cases still held the dead, crisp leaves of last fall. The boy struggled at times with the heavier limbs, but with the promise of afternoon fishing, he did not lag in his labors. Before noon the two were done.

Jonathan Jr. stopped at the edge of the full acre of strawberry plants that were just now starting to the promise of fruit. "Uncle Moses, what does 'Surgo ut Prosim' mean?"

Uncle Moses smiled. "It is a Christian promise. Not one specifically Quaker, but a good one nonetheless. It means 'I rise that I might serve.'"

The boy raised his eyebrows.

The man clarified. "It means that every day that thee rise in the morning that thee should serve the Lord."

Then the two went and washed up for lunch. After taking sup with his mother Abigail, his sister Mary, and his baby sister Elizabeth, the two grabbed the cane poles and headed further northwest toward the marshes along Country Brook and the woods past them.

"We shall need some bait if we are to provide the fish with enough temptation that they should end up on our hooks, John G.," his uncle said, using a nickname he only used when the two of them were alone together.

"Should I go back for a shovel? We will need worms, will we not?" asked the boy.

"No, thee need not go back. See what is contained in this pack?" The bearded man unfolded a gray net from the rucksack.

"A net? Are we not fishing with our cane poles and hooks today, Uncle Moses?"

"Yes," said his uncle, smiling. "But it is a warm day. The minnows will be at play in the stream along Samuel Duggers' farm. Thee and I shall seine some stripers. That is why I carry this bucket."

The boy paused in the meandering game path through the trees. "It was my belief the bucket was for all the fish we will catch."

Uncle Moses roared with laughter. "We should be so blessed. Let us set our goals at a more modest level."

The two began to walk again until they were in deep shade. The track was again muddy as this part of the forest seldom saw sunlight. Jonathan followed in his uncle's steps; wet grass along the game trail moistened his leggings. "May I ask thee a question, Uncle Moses?"

"Of course, boy. What are your thoughts?"

"Father said I was never to go toward the Duggers' homestead. He said they were not Godly people and consumed hard cider. They are to be given wide berth, Father said."

Uncle Moses stopped in midstride. "John G., my brother is less than Godly himself. Only the Lord himself can judge if a man is Godly or not. It is not ours to judge a man's sins. We are all sinners in his eyes, thee and I included."

The boy pursed his lips, thinking. "Then Father is wrong?"

Uncle Moses laughed again. "No, boy. We just do not have the information to make a determination, and it is not ours to make in the first place." He paused. "But thee shall not speak of this conversation to your father. Do thee understand?"

The gangly boy nodded, smiling to himself that his uncle and father disagreed on something. It was a chink in his father's armor, perhaps the first of which he was aware.

When they reached the creek, John saw his uncle had indeed been correct. The minnows, stripers between two and three inches long, danced in the shallows of the sand bar. As the two approached, the minnows sliced through the shining, flowing water crossing the sandy shallows to a deep hole cut into the bank. Beyond the creek, the small boy could just see the roof of the Dugger farmhouse. Smoke curled from the fireplace and two horses stomped in the stable as if they had been denied their oats.

Uncle Moses indicated that John G. should follow his lead. Both stopped short of the stream, leaving their boots and stockings on the bank. Then Uncle Moses took off the rest of his clothing, motioning for the boy to do so as well. They hung their clothing on a mulberry bush that was just beginning to bud leaves. It would be mid-summer before fruit would be on these limbs. The last thing the two placed upon the bush's limbs were their broad-brimmed hats. John G. hung his by its leather strap.

Both Whittier males were nearly icicle-white in their nudity, but the sun was warm and John G., despite his embarrassment at being naked, actually laughed out loud. His uncle nodded his head and laughed as well. John G. allowed himself a broad smile, showing his teeth in a broad grin.

With John G. in the shallower water and his uncle in the deeper, the two pulled the net tight through the water, using two long sticks of about four feet long to anchor it in the water. The stream was so cold that once the water was above his thighs and along his belly, his grin changed to chattering teeth. As the two progressed through the deep cut into the bank, the minnows raced out in front of them, back into the shallows of the sand bank. Uncle Moses called for the boy to raise the bottom of the seine, and he did so with great effort. As the water fell away, the two emerged shaking with cold from the depths. They could see perhaps as many as three dozen stripers languishing in the folds of the nets.

Together they carried the writhing net to the bank. "Go and fill the bucket with water from the hole. Bring it to me, boy," instructed his uncle. John G. did so, his teeth chattering so badly that he could not speak. Returning with the bucket, he saw his uncle, upon his knees, taking gasping minnows into his hands. As John G. arrived with the bucket, his uncle released five or six into the bucket.

"Get thee busy helping me, boy."

John G. nodded his assent and reached down for a minnow. He had never held one before, and the tiny fish wriggled free, falling back onto the sand bar. The boy pressed down with excessive vigor and his uncle frowned. "Thee have killed that animal needlessly, boy. Take more care."

John G. looked down into his hand at the broken minnow and saw the light fading from the striper's eyes as it died. He was not aware of killing a thing before and it shocked him. The Quaker teachings were already greatly ingrained from his father's daily ministries and from attending worship twice a week. The taking of life was a tenet the boy understood to be perhaps the most important of his Lord's teaching.

Uncle Moses seemed to understand the boy's sudden halting behavior. "Thee did not intend it, John G. Throw the lifeless thing back into the water that its flesh might feed another. It is the way of the animal world. It is too often the way of those who do not follow the Quaker way as well. It is good thee should understand that."

After that, the boy's hands were gentle in gathering the minnows into the bucket. And as they worked to get the remaining elusive fish into the bucket, the sun warmed their flesh. Their lips were no longer blue and John G.'s teeth no longer chattered. Soon they had been in the sun long enough to dry out and redress. The boy shook his hair with one hand as they now headed along the trail away from the Duggers' farmstead toward the confluence of the Merrimack River. The result caused a wide pool to form. It was perhaps fifty yards wide, its banks covered in willows and was difficult to fish without a boat. John G. at his height would have great difficulty casting with the cane pole, so it was with some relief he noticed that his uncle turned downstream to an open meadow past the pool. Here his uncle walked carefully, keeping the water in the bucket level as he carried the waterlogged net and rucksack over his shoulder. Each carried one cane pole. John G. recognized where they were headed—a smaller backwater in the river, just a wrinkle where the water pooled lazily. Tufts of white from the cottonwood trees graced the surface of the water.

The pool was perhaps a three hundred yards long and perhaps a hundred yards wide, running to the north and south. On the west bank not far away, the farmers at Holt's Rocks had started a gravesite, called the Greenside Cemetery. John G. could see the headstones as they approached the water from the eastern side. He was glad they were not fishing on the side of the lake where dead people were buried. He did not like to think about dead people.

By now it was mid-afternoon, not the best time to fish, but God was beneficent in his gifts. The shad in the deep water of the pool seemed to not have eaten a minnow throughout the entire winter. John G. had caught a fish before, but never several in quick succession like today and he was joyous in his celebrations. Soon he and his uncle had nine fish, all big enough to clean and eat for dinner back at the farm.

Uncle Moses called a halt to the fishing, saying that John G. must leave some for next time. He then slit the fish from gill to tail, pulling guts from the fish and rinsing them in the chilled waters of the Merrimack. After gutting each one, he placed the shad in the bucket covering their catch with a kerchief.

Afterward, the shadows were long as the two began the hike back to the farm. John G. hoped they would arrive home before his father and the fish could be grilling on the fire as his father approached on the road from town. He was proud he had caught dinner for the entire family and had enough for the working men and their families as well.

Uncle Moses carried the pail heavy with shad, their deep green crested fins now faded in death. John G. followed but was tired of walking. It had been a long, but good day for the little boy. He would be glad to get back to the farm and his mother and two sisters, so it was with some dismay and more than a little shock when he heard his uncle's question.

"John G., where is your hat?"

He reached behind him, reaching for the leather thong which he used for a chin strap but also to let the hat rest off his shoulders. It was not there.

He flushed, trying to think where he had last worn the hat. He remembered and was embarrassed to speak, so he did not.

"Where is it, boy?"

He turned his chin down as he spoke. His uncle had stopped walking and was facing him. John G. said, "I must have left it in the mulberry bush, hanging on a limb back where we got the minnows."

The boy saw the irritation on his uncle's face. It was a look he knew from his father's face, but he did not like seeing it in his uncle's. He was ashamed.

Uncle Moses looked down at the fish in the bucket. "You will have to go back for it. If you come home without your new summer hat, thee and I will be both get the cane before the sun has set."

"Why cannot we go together, Uncle?"

The man raised his eyebrows in consternation. "Because I did not forget my hat, boy. And because only I can carry this pail filled with so many fish. Now get thee down the trail to the Duggers' farm. It is not far. I will get this bucket of fish to Abigail, your mother. Hurry along, John G. I am not mad. Go get your hat and dinner will be on the fire when you arrive home."

With that, his uncle turned his back and strode down the path away from him. The boy knew there was no option but to head the other direction, back into the woods and back to the stream where the Dugger farm was visible beyond. Back to where he had left his hat hanging in the bush.

The trail was not hard to find or follow, but the shadows were now deep and the boy hurried along, forcing himself not to run pell-mell back home without retrieving his hat. Keeping his fear in check was in his head, but his heart seemed to not understand the message. He could hear his heart beating through his vest and shirt. He felt cold sweat on his arms and his back as he walked quickly down the game trail which seemed longer, narrower and much more menacing than when he had followed his uncle.

As John G. approached the stream, the water was striped with dark purple streaks with the sun now perhaps less than an hour from setting. The boy reached the mulberry bush and saw his hat had fallen onto the sand below the thin sagging limb where he had left it.

As he crawled into the underbrush to reach the hat, a wild scramble seemed to occur on the far bank. He stared up at movement in the foliage where tree roots were exposed by erosion. The boy stifled a scream and placed his hands over his mouth in terror. He froze in place and squatted in the semi-darkness, shielded from view by the mulberry bush's foliage.

On the far bank, he recognized Samuel Duggers, a man nearly his uncle's age. The flabby-faced, florid man staggered down the sandy slope. He wore ragged coveralls and boots. His shirt was a filthy white and was blotted with green splotches of color. His hands too were covered in the slime. Duggers' eyes were wild. He called out to the approaching night, but his utterance was not words. It was animalistic. Primal.

The boy froze in place. Somehow he knew if he were to be discovered something terrible would happen to him. So he squatted there in the gathering gloom and watched the farmer, now actually spinning around at the water's edge in a crazed and maniacal manner. The man bellowed into the night, then vaulted down the steep bank, falling into the water. There he knelt and scrubbed the sticky greenish fluid from his arms, shirt, and even from his face.

As John G. watched in horror and with a complete lack of comprehension, the man howled again, this time at the moon which was just appearing above the skyline of the trees. It was now truly dusk. What was this madness he was witness to?

And then the boy saw her.

She had to be a witch. Her face, that horrifying face surely confirmed it. She was covered in the same shade of slime. Her dress, her bodice, and her white cap all were covered. But she did not move. Her face was frozen; her eyes focused on him. He knew she must see him. But she made no indication of John G.'s location to her husband. Yes, he realized, it was Mrs. Duggers. He had seen her once at his father's farm. His father once purchased a calf from the man and the woman had been there as well. She sat without speaking during the transaction in the wagon. What was her name? Sarah. Yes, Sarah Duggers.

The man staggered up the bank and began shouting at the woman. "You finally did it, didn't you, Sarah? You finally pushed me too far. There is only a certain distance a man will be pushed and you crossed that line, woman. And now you and me, because of your wicked tongue, are damned for all time. This is your fault. Don't try to blame me. You just couldn't hold your tongue. You've damned both of us for all time. Damned us for all time."

As the crazed or drunken man reached the summit, he crossed to the prone woman, the slime on her now showing black in the oncoming evening. Then the man grabbed the woman's frame and lifted her in his arms. He wailed once again. The boy took the moment to grab his hat and run across the clearing into the cover of the trees. He heard a call in the night behind him but did not look to see if it was because he had been seen. No, it filled him with terror. So he ran. John G. knew Samuel Duggers must be coming after him in the night.

The boy ran all the way to the farm, racing inside the farm's gate. His father and mother met him on the path just inside. They evidently had been discussing whether to send the men off into the woods to find him.

"Where have you been, boy? Thee have put fear into your mother. That is not a Godly thing, son. Why have thee been for so long?"

With Uncle Moses approaching, Jonathan Jr. told all there his tale. That he had seen Samuel and Sarah Duggers both covered in green slime. That she was obviously a witch, so green was her face. So still her eyes. Duggers himself was an animal of some kind. Part wolf, part man. He told them the neighbor had howled at the moon, had shouted at the witch, and had washed the green slime off of his clothes in the stream.

After his tale, told in an excited voice with hardly a breath taken, his father's face turned a deep color, so deep that it was visibly flushed even in the light of the cooking fire. There the cooking fish were now forgotten, their tails now curling with char.

John Sr. grabbed the boy roughly by the shoulder and dragged him, shrieking, into the barn. Taking the youngster over his knee, he whipped the boy with the new bridle purchased in town that very day. The flailing blows with his right hand were violent and steady. His left held the boy still under the blows. After six lashes lacerated the boy's buttocks, Uncle Moses blocked a seventh blow. "It is enough. He is but five."

Jonathan Jr. collapsed on the floor of the barn. He now longer cried, but simply whimpered as his uncle carried his listless form into the house.

*****

It was at the dinner after worship eight days later (Jonathan Junior had been too ill the day after the beating to travel to Amesbury), that the boy overheard Uncle Moses say Samuel Duggers had sold his plow to Taylor Osborne, a farmer whose property was near Great Pond. A week or two later, Elliot Walcott told Jonathan Sr. he had purchased both of Duggers' plow horses from the farmer. It was Walcott's understanding the Duggers planned to move west toward Salem or perhaps even further west into the frontier country. Uncle Moses asked if Walcott had seen Sarah Duggers when he purchased the animals. Walcott wrinkled his nose as if he thought the question queer. "No," was all he answered.

Not long after, Uncle Moses reported to the family at dinner that he had taken a walk out to the Duggers' place and had found the place abandoned. The buckboard was there, but the meager furnishings were gone from the house. There were no personal effects left in the house, except for two women's dresses. Both were familiar to Uncle Moses as belonging to Sarah Duggers. No one had seen either of the childless couple before they left town.

*****

It was late May. The first of the season's strawberries were ready to be picked. On this day each year, the children of the hired men, the womenfolk and the two older Whittier children were given baskets and sent among the rows to gather. It was a warm day and the work was hard as each bent to pull strawberries free and put them in buckets.

John Sr. was at the bushel baskets, readying the harvest for a trip to town to the market. Many of the citizens of Haverhill did not have strawberries planted and these delicacies brought top dollar among those who could afford to pay. John Sr. was excited to be able to pay bills and put money in the bank for the next month or so as the fruit ripened each week.

Mary, John G.'s sister, was older and filled her bucket first. She brought it and emptied it into the bushel basket manned by her father. He eyed her labors, tousled the bangs which extended below her white cap and then ushered her back into the field. Several of the field hands' children emptied their buckets before John Jr. moved to the head of the line. He moved to dump his bucket when his father grabbed his arm with anger.

"Most of these strawberries are green, boy! What are thee thinking?"

John G. looked at his father, his face one of surprise. The gaze was misinterpreted as insolence. His father cuffed him roughly across the face. The slap was audible across the field. Everyone froze. Uncle Moses and Abigail his mother dropped their buckets and ran toward the father and son, but did not arrive until the boy had unsuccessfully attempted to twist away from the man who slapped him. His left arm dangled in the vice-like grip of his father. Blood dripped from his nose, tears rolled down his cheeks.

Uncle Moses grabbed his brother's shoulders. "I beseech thee, stop. Do not forget your Quaker beliefs. What could the boy have done to deserve such brutality?"

"Look at the contents of his bucket."

Uncle Moses peered down at the bucket full of green strawberries. He reached down and pulled John G.'s face over the lip of the bucket. "What is the meaning of this?"

The boy did not respond and only cried.

Abigail arrived, her eyes lowered and took the boy by the hand, pulling him to his feet. She dusted him off and led him away out of the eyesight of his father who still burned with the shame of a landowner embarrassed by his son in front of his hired men.

It was not until evening when his mother discovered the cause of the unripe fruit in her son's bucket. She placed 30 strawberries on the dining room table, asking her son to place the red strawberries in the bucket. The five-year-old could not do so. He could no more tell the difference between red and green than could a blind man.

His father did not apologize to him for the beating, but Jonathan Jr. could tell by the tension in the family that his father's violence and the subsequent explanation of why it had happened was a source of conflict between both his father, mother, and uncle.

Lying in his bed that night, he heard his uncle come into the house. It was later than he normally arrived in from checking on the animals and closing up the barn. Uncle Moses slammed the door with great force as he arrived. John G. heard his father exclaim, "I may have crossed a line today with my son, but it is still my roof thee live under. Thee need to keep that in mind."

Uncle Moses uttered a word that John G. had never heard before. His father stood and bellowed, "Thee shall not curse in my home. No matter that thee are my brother."

Uncle Moses said, "I do not curse at the beating thee gave your son today. I curse at the one thee gave him in the spring. I have just returned from talking to the men at the cabins. Jonas has just returned from town after taking in the strawberries. Everyone in Haverhill is talking about the body some boys found today. They were out by the Duggers' place. One of their coon dogs came back with a human arm. They found a corpse, mostly skeleton and but definitely female."

John G.'s father stood but did not speak.

"The constable seems to believe it is most likely Sarah Duggers. The dress was nearly rotted away, but some in the town claim to recognize the fabric."

The boy by now had risen from the bed, crept down the stairs, and peeked around the corner at the two men in his life. His father shrugged. "The boy's tale was too incredible. A witch covered in slime."

Uncle William cocked his head. "Think thee of today's revelations. Red and green."

"Red and green?"

"Yes, red and green. My brother, thee have much penance to ask for from our lord."

"Blood, green blood," was his father's response, finally understanding. His voice sounded hollow as the logs popped an accent.

"Blood" was his brother's accusation.

Neither man saw the boy standing in the doorway. They did not know that he did not understand. They did not know he returned to his bed and cried himself to sleep.

A Memorable Murder

Celia Thaxter

Graves of Anethe Matea and Karen Anne Christensen, Portsmouth, New Hampshire.
The 1873 Smuttynose murders captured the attention of the nation. The case continues to fascinate the public and has been the subject of, among other things, crime books, ballads, and novels. Celia Thaxter, on neighboring Appledore Island, knew the victims' families and wrote an account for Atlantic Monthly that humanized the victims beyond the salacious headlines. Courtesy of J. W. Ocker.

At the Isles of Shoals, on the 5th of March in the year 1873, occurred one of the most monstrous tragedies ever enacted on this planet. The sickening details of the double murder are well known; the newspapers teemed with them for months: but the pathos of the story is not realized; the world does not know how gentle a life these poor people led, how innocently happy were their quiet days. They were all Norwegians. The more I see of the natives of this far-off land, the more I admire the fine qualities which seem to characterize them as a race. Gentle, faithful, intelligent, God-fearing human beings, they daily use such courtesy toward each other and all who come in contact with them, as puts our ruder Yankee manners to shame. The men and women living on this lonely island were like the sweet, honest, simple folk we read of in Bjornson's charming Norwegian stories, full of kindly thoughts and ways. The murdered Anethe might have been the Eli of Bjornson's beautiful Arne or the Ragnhild of Boyesen's lovely romance. They rejoiced to find a home just such as they desired in this peaceful place; the women took such pleasure in the little house which they kept so neat and bright, in their flock of hens, their little dog Ringe, and all their humble belongings! The Norwegians are an exceptionally affectionate people; family ties are very strong and precious among them. Let me tell the story of their sorrow as simply as may be.

Louis Wagner murdered Anethe and Karen Christensen at midnight on the 5th of March, two years ago this spring. The whole affair shows the calmness of a practiced hand; there was no malice in the deed, no heat; it was one of the coolest instances of deliberation ever chronicled in the annals of crime. He admits that these people had shown him nothing but kindness. He says in so many words, "They were my best friends." They looked upon him as a brother. Yet he did not hesitate to murder them. The island called Smutty-Nose by human perversity (since in old times it bore the pleasanter title of Haley's Island) was selected to be the scene of this disaster. Long ago I lived two years upon it, and know well its whitened ledges and grassy slopes, its low thickets of wild rose and bayberry, its sea-wall still intact, connecting it with the small island Malaga, opposite Appledore, and the ruined breakwater which links it with Cedar Island on the other side. A lonely cairn, erected by some long ago forgotten fishermen or sailors, stands upon the highest rock at the southeastern extremity; at its western end a few houses are scattered, small, rude dwellings, with the square old Haley house near; two or three fish houses are falling into decay about the water-side, and the ancient wharf drops stone by stone into the little cove, where every day the tide ebbs and flows and ebbs again with pleasant sound and freshness. Near the houses is a small graveyard, where a few of the natives sleep, and not far, the graves of the fourteen Spaniards lost in the wreck of the ship Sagunto in the year 1813. I used to think it was a pleasant place, that low, rocky, and grassy island, though so wild and lonely.

From the little town of Laurvig, near Christiania, in Norway, came John and Maren Hontvet to this country, and five years ago took up their abode in this desolate spot, in one of the cottages facing the cove and Appledore. And there they lived through the long winters and the lovely summers, John making a comfortable living by fishing, Maren, his wife, keeping as bright and tidy and sweet a little home for him as a man could desire. The bit of garden they cultivated in the summer was a pleasure to them; they made their house as pretty as they could with paint and paper and gay pictures, and Maren had a shelf for her plants at the window; and John was always so good to her, so kind and thoughtful of her comfort and of what would please her, she was entirely happy. Sometimes she was a little lonely, perhaps, when he was tossing afar off on the sea, setting or hauling his trawls, or had sailed to Portsmouth to sell his fish. So that she was doubly glad when the news came that some of her people were coming over from Norway to live with her. And first, in the month of May 1871, came her sister Karen, who stayed only a short time with Maren, and then came to Appledore, where she lived in service two years, till within a fortnight of her death. The first time I saw Maren, she brought her sister to us, and I was charmed with the little woman's beautiful behavior; she was so gentle, courteous, decorous, she left on my mind a most delightful impression. Her face struck me as remarkably good and intelligent, and her gray eyes were full of light.

Karen was a rather sad-looking woman, about twenty-nine years old; she had lost a lover in Norway long since, and in her heart she fretted and mourned for this continually: she could not speak a word of English at first, but went patiently about her work and soon learned enough, and proved herself an excellent servant, doing faithfully and thoroughly everything she undertook, as is the way of her people generally. Her personal neatness was most attractive. She wore gowns made of cloth woven by herself in

Norway, a coarse blue stuff, always neat and clean, and often I used to watch her as she sat by the fire spinning at a spinning-wheel brought from her own country; she made such a pretty picture, with her blue gown and fresh white apron, and the nice, clear white muslin bow with which she was in the habit of fastening her linen collar, that she was very agreeable to look upon. She had a pensive way of letting her head droop a little sideways as she spun, and while the low wheel hummed monotonously, she would sit crooning sweet, sad old Norwegian airs by the hour together, perfectly unconscious that she was affording such pleasure to a pair of appreciative eyes. On the 12th of October, 1872, in the second year of her stay with us, her brother, Ivan Christensen, and his wife, Anethe Mathea, came over from their Norse land in an evil day, and joined Maren and John at their island, living in the same house with them.

Ivan and Anethe had been married only since Christmas of the preceding year. Ivan was tall, light-haired, rather quiet and grave. Anethe was young, fair, and merry, with thick, bright sunny hair, which was so long it reached, when unbraided, nearly to her knees; blue-eyed, with brilliant teeth and clear, fresh complexion, beautiful, and beloved beyond expression by her young husband, Ivan. Mathew Hontvet, John's brother, had also joined the little circle a year before, and now Maren's happiness was complete. Delighted to welcome them all, she made all things pleasant for them, and she told me only a few days ago, "I never was so happy in my life as when we were all living there together." So they abode in peace and quiet, with not an evil thought in their minds, kind and considerate toward each other, the men devoted to their women and the women repaying them with interest, till out of the perfectly cloudless sky one day a blot descended, without a whisper of warning, and brought ruin and desolation into that peaceful home.

Louis Wagner, who had been in this country seven years, appeared at the Shoals two years before the date of the murder. He lived about the islands during that time. He was born in Ueckermunde, a small town of lower Pomerania, in Northern Prussia. Very little is known about him, though there were vague rumors that his past life had not been without difficulties, and he had boasted foolishly among his mates that "not many had done what he had done and got off in safety;" but people did not trouble themselves about him or his past, all having enough to do to earn their bread and keep the wolf from the door. Maren describes him as tall, powerful, dark, with a peculiarly quiet manner. She says she never saw him drunk--he seemed always anxious to keep his wits about him: he would linger on the outskirts of a drunken brawl, listening to and absorbing everything, but never mixing himself up in any disturbance. He was always lurking in corners, lingering, looking, listening, and he would look no man straight in the eyes. She spoke, however, of having once heard him disputing with some sailors, at a table, about some point of navigation; she did not understand it, but all were against Louis, and, waxing warm, all strove to show him he was in the wrong. As he rose and left the table she heard him mutter to himself with an oath, "I know I'm wrong, but I'll never give in!" During the winter preceding the one in which his hideous deed was committed, he lived at Star Island and fished alone, in a wherry; but he made very little money, and came often over to the Hontvets, where Maren gave him food when he was suffering from want, and where he received always a welcome and the utmost kindness. In the following June, he joined Hontvet in his business of fishing and took up his abode as one of the family at Smutty-Nose. During the summer he was "crippled," as he said, by the rheumatism, and they were all very good to him, and sheltered, fed, nursed, and waited upon him the greater part of the season. He remained with them five weeks after Ivan and Anethe arrived, so that he grew to know Anethe as well as Maren, and was looked upon as a brother by all of them, as I have said before. Nothing occurred to show his true character, and in November he left the island and the kind people whose hospitality he was to repay so fearfully, and going to Portsmouth he took passage in another fishing schooner, the Addison Gilbert, which was presently wrecked off the coast, and he was again thrown out of employment. Very recklessly he said to Waldemar Ingebertsen, to Charles Jonsen, and even to John Hontvet himself, at different times, that "he must have money if he murdered for it." He loafed about Portsmouth eight weeks, doing nothing. Meanwhile, Karen left our service in February, intending to go to Boston and work at a sewing machine, for she was not strong and thought she should like it better than housework, but before going she lingered awhile with her sister Maren-fatal delay for her! Maren told me that during this time Karen went to Portsmouth and had her teeth removed, meaning to provide herself with a new set. At the Jonsens', where Louis was staying, one day she spoke to Mrs. Jonsen of her mouth, that it was so sensitive since the teeth had been taken out; and Mrs. Jonsen asked her how long she must wait before the new set could be put in. Karen replied that it would be three months. Louis Wagner was walking up and down at the other end of the room with his arms folded, his favorite attitude. Mrs. Jonsen's daughter passed near him and heard him mutter, "Three months! What is the use! In three months you will be dead!" He did not know the girl was so near and turning, he confronted her. He knew she must have heard what he said, and he glared at her like a wild man.

On the fifth day of March 1873, John Hontvet, his brother Mathew, and Ivan Christensen set sail in John's little schooner, the Clara Bella, to draw their trawls. At that time four of the islands were inhabited: one family on White Island, at the lighthouse; the workmen who were building the new hotel on Star Island, and one or two households beside; the Hontvet family at Smutty-Nose; and on Appledore, the household at the large house, and on the southern side, opposite Smutty-Nose, a little cottage, where lived Jorge Edvardt Ingebertsen, his wife and children, and several men who fished with him. Smutty-Nose is not in sight of the large house at Appledore, so we were in ignorance of all that happened on that dreadful night, longer than the other inhabitants of the Shoals.

John, Ivan, and Mathew went to draw their trawls, which had been set some miles to the eastward of the islands. They intended to be back to dinner, and then to go on to Portsmouth with their fish, and bait the trawls afresh, ready to bring back to set again next day. But the wind was strong and fair for Portsmouth and ahead for the island; it would have been a long beat home against it; so they went on to Portsmouth, without touching at the island to leave one man to guard the women, as had been their custom. This was the first night in all the years Maren had lived there that the house was without a man to protect it. But John, always thoughtful for her, asked Emil Ingebertsen, whom he met on the fishing-grounds, to go over from Appledore and tell her that they had gone on to Portsmouth with the favoring wind, but that they hoped to be back that night. And he would have been back had the bait he expected from Boston arrived on the train in which it was due. How curiously everything adjusted itself to favor the bringing about of this horrible catastrophe! The bait did not arrive till the half past twelve train, and they were obliged to work the whole night getting their trawls ready, thus leaving the way perfectly clear for Louis Wagner's awful work.

The three women left alone watched and waited in vain for the schooner to return, and kept the dinner hot for the men, and patiently wondered why they did not come. In vain they searched the wide horizon for that returning sail. Ah me, what pathos is in that longing look of women's eyes for far-off sails! that gaze so eager, so steadfast, that it would almost seem as if it must conjure up the ghostly shape of glimmering canvas from the mysterious distances of sea and sky, and draw it unerringly home by the mere force of intense wistfulness! And those gentle eyes, that were never to see the light of another sun, looked anxiously across the heaving sea till twilight fell, and then John's messenger, Emil, arrived-- Emil Ingebertsen, courteous and gentle as a youthful knight--and reassured them with his explanation, which having given, he departed, leaving them in a much more cheerful state of mind. So the three sisters, with only the little dog Ringe for a protector, sat by the fire chatting together cheerfully. They fully expected the schooner back again that night from Portsmouth, but they were not ill at ease while they waited. Of what should they be afraid? They had not an enemy in the world! No shadow crept to the fireside to warn them what was at hand, no portent of death chilled the air as they talked their pleasant talk and made their little plans in utter unconsciousness. Karen was to have gone to Portsmouth with the fishermen that day; she was already dressed to go. Various little commissions were given her, errands to do for the two sisters she was to leave behind. Maren wanted some buttons, and "I'll give you one for a pattern; I'll put it in your purse," she said to Karen, "and then when you open your purse you'll be sure to remember it." (That little button, of a peculiar pattern, was found in Wagner's possession afterward.) They sat up till ten o'clock, talking together. The night was bright and calm; it was a comfort to miss the bitter winds that had raved about the little dwelling all the long, rough winter. Already it was spring; this calm was the first token of its coming. It was the 6th of March; in a few weeks the weather would soften, the grass grow green, and Anethe would see the first flowers in this strange country, so far from her home where she had left father and mother, kith and kin, for love of Ivan. The delicious days of summer at hand would transform the work of the toiling fishermen to pleasure, and all things would bloom and smile about the poor people on the lonely rock! Alas, it was not to be.

At ten o'clock they went to bed. It was cold and "lonesome" upstairs, so Maren put some chairs by the side of the lounge, laid a mattress upon it, and made up a bed for Karen in the kitchen, where she presently fell asleep. Maren and Anethe slept in the next room. So safe they felt themselves, they did not pull down a curtain, nor even try to fasten the house-door. They went to their rest in absolute security and perfect trust. It was the first still night of the new year; a young moon stole softly down toward the west, a gentle wind breathed through the quiet dark, and the waves whispered gently about the island, helping to lull those innocent souls to yet more peaceful slumber. Ah, where were the gales of March that might have plowed that tranquil sea to foam, and cut off the fatal path of Louis Wagner to that happy home! But nature seemed to pause and wait for him. I remember looking abroad over the waves that night and rejoicing over "the first calm night of the year!" It was so still, so bright! The hope of all the light and beauty a few weeks would bring forth stirred me to sudden joy. There should be spring again after the long winter weariness.

"Can trouble live in April days,
Or sadness in the summer moons?"

I thought, as I watched the clear sky, grown less hard than it had been for weeks, and sparkling with stars. But before another sunset, it seemed to me that beauty had fled out of the world, and that goodness, innocence, mercy, gentleness, were a mere mockery of empty words.

Here let us leave the poor women, asleep on the lonely rock, with no help near them in heaven or upon earth, and follow the fishermen to Portsmouth, where they arrived about four o'clock that afternoon. One of the first men whom they saw as they neared the town was Louis Wagner; to him, they threw the rope from the schooner, and he helped draw her into the wharf. Greetings passed between them; he spoke to Mathew Hontvet, and as he looked at Ivan Christensen, the men noticed a flush pass over Louis's face. He asked were they going out again that night? Three times before they parted he asked that question; he saw that all the three men belonging to the island had come away together; he began to realize his opportunity. They answered him that if their bait came by the train in which they expected it, they hoped to get back that night, but if it was late they should be obliged to stay till morning, baiting their trawls; and they asked him to come and help them. It is a long and tedious business, the baiting of trawls; often more than a thousand hooks are to be manipulated, and lines and hooks coiled, clear of tangles, into tubs, all ready for throwing overboard when the fishing-grounds are reached. Louis gave them a half promise that he would help them, but they did not see him again after leaving the wharf. The three fishermen were hungry, not having touched at their island, where Maren always provided them with a supply of food to take with them; they asked each other if either had brought any money with which to buy bread, and it came out that everyone had left his pocketbook at home. Louis, standing by, heard all this. He asked John, then, if he had made fishing pay. John answered that he had cleared about six hundred dollars.

The men parted, the honest three about their business; but Louis, what became of him with his evil thoughts? At about half past seven he went into a liquor shop and had a glass of something; not enough to make him unsteady, -- he was too wise for that. He was not seen again in Portsmouth by any human creature that night. He must have gone, after that, directly down to the river, that beautiful, broad river, the Piscataqua, upon whose southern bank the quaint old city of Portsmouth dreams its quiet days away; and there he found a boat ready to his hand, a dory belonging to a man by the name of David Burke, who had that day furnished it with new thole-pins. When it was picked up afterward off the mouth of the river, Louis's anxious oars had eaten half-way through the substance of these pins, which are always made of the hardest, toughest wood that can be found. A terrible piece of rowing must that have been, in one night! Twelve miles from the city to the Shoals, – three to the light-houses, where the river meets the open sea, nine more to the islands; nine back again to Newcastle next morning! He took that boat, and with the favoring tide dropped down the rapid river where the swift current is so strong that oars are scarcely needed, except to keep the boat steady. Truly all nature seemed to play into his hands; this first relenting night of earliest spring favored him with its stillness, the tide was fair, the wind was fair, the little moon gave him just enough light, without betraying him to any curious eyes, as he glided down the three miles between the river banks, in haste to reach the sea. Doubtless, the light west wind played about him as delicately as if he had been the most human of God's creatures; nothing breathed remonstrance in his ear, nothing whispered in the whispering water that rippled about his inexorable keel, steering straight for the Shoals through the quiet darkness. The snow lay thick and white upon the land in the moonlight; lamps twinkled here and there from dwellings on either side; in Eliot and Newcastle, in Portsmouth and Kittery, roofs, chimneys, and gables showed faintly in the vague light; the leafless trees clustered dark in hollows or lifted their tracery of bare boughs in higher spaces against the wintry sky. His eyes must have looked on it all, whether he saw the peaceful picture or not. Beneath many a humble roof, honest folk were settling into their untroubled rest, as "this planned piece of deliberate wickedness" was stealing silently by with his heart full of darkness, blacker than the black tide that swirled beneath his boat and bore him fiercely on. At the river's mouth stood the sentinel light-houses, sending their great spokes of light afar into the night, like the arms of a wide humanity stretching into the darkness helping hands to bring all who needed succor safely home. He passed them, first the tower at Fort Point, then the taller one at Whale's Back, steadfastly holding aloft their warning fires. There was no signal from the warning bell as he rowed by, though a danger more subtle, more deadly, than fog, or hurricane, or pelting storm was passing swift beneath it. Unchallenged by anything in earth or heaven, he kept on his way and gained the great outer ocean, doubtless pulling strong and steadily, for he had no time to lose, and the longest night was all too short for an undertaking such as this. Nine miles from the light-houses to the islands! Slowly he makes his way; it seems to take an eternity of time. And now he is midway between the islands and the coast. That little toy of a boat with its one occupant in the midst of the awful, black, heaving sea! The vast dim ocean whispers with a thousand waves; against the boat's side the ripples lightly tap, and pass and are lost; the air is full of fine, mysterious voices of winds and waters. Has he no fear, alone there on the midnight sea with such a purpose in his heart? The moonlight sends a long, golden track across the waves; it touches his dark face and figure, it glitters on his dripping oars. On his right hand Boone Island light shows like a setting star on the horizon, low on his left the two beacons twinkle off Newburyport, at the mouth of the Merrimack River; all the lighthouses stand watching along the coast, wheeling their long, slender shafts of radiance as if pointing at this black atom creeping over the face of the planet with such colossal evil in his heart. Before him glitters the Shoals' light at White Island, and helps to guide him to his prey. Alas, my friendly lighthouse, that you should serve so terrible a purpose! Steadily the oars click in the rowlocks; stroke after stroke of the broad blades draws him away from the lessening line of land, over the wavering floor of the ocean, nearer the lonely rocks. Slowly the coast-lights fade, and now the rote of the sea among the lonely ledges of the Shoals salutes his attentive ear. A little longer and he nears Appledore, the first island, and now he passes by the snow-covered, ice-bound rock, with the long buildings showing clear in the moonlight. He must have looked at them as he went past. I wonder we who slept beneath the roofs that glimmered to his eyes in the uncertain light did not feel, through the thick veil of sleep, what fearful thing passed by! But we slumbered peacefully as the unhappy women whose doom every click of those oars in the rowlocks, like the ticking of some dreadful clock, was bringing nearer and nearer. Between the islands he passes; they are full of chilly gleams and glooms. There is no scene more weird than these snow-covered rocks in winter, more shudderful and strange: the moonlight touching them with mystic glimmer, the black water breaking about them and the vast shadowy spaces of the sea stretching to the horizon on every side, full of vague sounds, of half-lights and shadows, of fear, and of mystery. The island he seeks lies before him, lone and still; there is no gleam in any window, there is no help near, nothing upon which the women can call for succor. He does not land in the cove where all boats put in, he rows round to the south side and draws his boat up on the rocks. His red returning footsteps are found here next day, staining the snow. He makes his way to the house he knows so well.

All is silent: nothing moves, nothing sounds but the hushed voices of the sea. His hand is on the latch, he enters stealthily, there is nothing to resist him. The little dog, Ringe, begins to bark sharp and loud, and Karen rouses, crying, "John, is that you?" thinking the expected fishermen had returned. Louis seizes a chair and strikes at her in the dark; the clock on a shelf above her head falls down with the jarring of the blow and stops at exactly seven minutes to one. Maren in the next room, waked suddenly from her sound sleep, trying in vain to make out the meaning of it all, cries, "What's the matter?" Karen answers, "John scared me!" Maren springs from her bed and tries to open her chamber door; Louis has fastened it on the other side by pushing a stick through the latch. With her heart leaping with terror the poor child shakes the door with all her might, in vain. Utterly confounded and bewildered, she hears Karen screaming, "John kills me! John kills me!" She hears the sound of repeated blows and shrieks, till at last her sister falls heavily against the door, which gives way, and

Maren rushes out. She catches dimly a glimpse of a tall figure outlined against the southern window; she seizes poor Karen and drags her with the strength of frenzy within the bedroom. This unknown terror, this fierce, dumb monster who never utters a sound to betray himself through the whole, pursues her with blows, strikes her three times with a chair, either blow with fury sufficient to kill her, had it been light enough for him to see how to direct it; but she gets her sister inside and the door shut, and holds it against him with all her might and Karen's failing strength. What a little heroine was this poor child, struggling with the force of desperation to save herself and her sisters!

All this time Anethe lay dumb, not daring to move or breathe, roused from the deep sleep of youth and health by this nameless, formless terror. Maren, while she strives to hold the door at which Louis rattles again and again, calls to her in anguish, "Anethe, Anethe! Get out of the window! run! hide!" The poor girl, almost paralyzed with fear, tries to obey, puts her bare feet out of the low window, and stands outside in the freezing snow, with one light garment over her cowering figure, shrinking in the cold winter wind, the clear moonlight touching her white face and bright hair and fair young shoulders. "Scream! scream!" shouts frantic Maren. "Somebody at Star Island may hear!" but Anethe answers with the calmness of despair, "I cannot make a sound," Maren screams, herself, but the feeble sound avails nothing. "Run! run!" she cries to Anethe; but again Anethe answers, "I cannot move."

Louis has left off trying to force the door; he listens. Are the women trying to escape? He goes out-of-doors. Maren flies to the window; he comes round the corner of the house and confronts Anethe where she stands in the snow. The moonlight shines full in his face; she shrieks loudly and distinctly, "Louis, Louis!" Ah, he is discovered, he is recognized! Quick as thought he goes back to the front door, at the side of which stands an ax, left there by Maren, who had used it the day before to cut the ice from the well. He returns to Anethe standing shuddering there. It is no matter that she is beautiful, young, and helpless to resist, that she has been kind to him, that she never did a human creature harm, that she stretches her gentle hands out to him in agonized entreaty, crying piteously, "Oh, Louis, Louis, Louis!" He raises the axe and brings it down on her bright head in one tremendous blow, and she sinks without a sound and lies in a heap, with her warm blood reddening the snow. Then he deals her blow after blow, almost within reach of Maren's hands, as she stands at the window. Distracted, Maren strives to rouse poor Karen, who kneels with her head on the side of the bed; with desperate entreaty she tries to get her up and away, but Karen moans, "I can not, I cannot." She is too far gone; and then Maren knows she cannot save her, and that she must flee herself or die. So, while Louis again enters the house, she seizes a skirt and wraps round her shoulders, and makes her way out of the open window, over Anethe's murdered body, barefooted, flying away, anywhere, breathless, shaking with terror.

Where can she go? Her little dog, frightened into silence, follows her,--pressing so close to her feet that she falls over him more than once. Looking back she sees Louis has lit a lamp and is seeking for her. She flies to the cove; if she can but find his boat and row away in it and get help! It is not there; there is no boat in which she can get away. She hears Karen's wild screams, -he is killing her! Oh, where can she go? Is there any place on that little island where he will not find her? She thinks she will creep into one of the empty old houses by the water; but no, she reflects, if I hide there, Ringe will bark and betray me the moment Louis comes to look for me. And Ringe saved her life, for next day Louis's bloody tracks were found all about those old buildings where he had sought her. She flies, with Karen's awful cries in her ears, away over rocks and snow to the farthest limit she can gain. The moon has set; it is about two o'clock in the morning, and oh, so cold! She shivers and shudders from head to feet, but her agony of terror is so great she is hardly conscious of bodily sensation. And welcome is the freezing snow, the jagged ice and iron rocks that tear her unprotected feet, the bitter brine that beats against the shore, the winter winds that make her shrink and tremble; "they are not so unkind as man's ingratitude!" Falling often, rising, struggling on with feverish haste, she makes her way to the very edge of the water; down almost into the sea she creeps, between two rocks, upon her hands and knees, and crouches, face downward, with

Ringe nestled close beneath her breast, not daring to move through the long hours that must pass before the sun will rise again. She is so near the ocean she can almost reach the water with her hand. Had the wind breathed the least roughly the waves must have washed over her. There let us leave her and go back to Louis Wagner. Maren heard her sister Karen's shrieks as she fled. The poor girl had crept into an unoccupied room in a distant part of the house, striving to hide herself. He could not kill her with blows, blundering in the darkness, so he wound a handkerchief about her throat and strangled her. But now he seeks anxiously for Maren. Has she escaped? What terror is in the thought! Escaped, to tell the tale, to accuse him as the murderer of her sisters. Hurriedly, with desperate anxiety, he seeks for her. His time was growing short; it was not in his programme that this brave little creature should give him so much trouble; he had not calculated on resistance from these weak and helpless women. Already it was morning, soon it would be daylight. He could not find her in or near the house; he went down to the empty and dilapidated houses about the cove and sought her everywhere. What a picture! That blood-stained butcher, with his dark face, crawling about those cellars, peering for that woman! He dared not spend any more time; he must go back for the money he hoped to find, his reward for this! All about the house he searches, in bureau drawers, in trunks and boxes: he finds fifteen dollars for his night's work! Several hundred were lying between some sheets folded at the bottom of a drawer in which he looked. But he cannot stop for more thorough investigation; a dreadful haste pursues him like a thousand fiends. He drags Anethe's stiffening body into the house and leaves it on the kitchen floor. If the thought crosses his mind to set fire to the house and burn up his two victims, he dares not do it: it will make a fatal bonfire to light his homeward way; besides, it is useless, for Maren has escaped to accuse him, and the time presses so horribly! But how cool a monster is he! After all this hard work he must have refreshment to support him in the long row back to the land; knife and fork, cup and plate, were found next morning on the table near where Anethe lay; fragments of food which was not cooked in the house, but brought from

Portsmouth, were scattered about. Tidy Maren had left neither dishes nor food when they went to bed. The handle of the teapot which she had left on the stove was stained and smeared with blood. Can the human mind conceive of such hideous nonchalance? Wagner sat down in that room and ate and drank! It is almost beyond belief! Then he went to the well with a basin and towels, tried to wash off the blood, and left towels and basin in the well. He knows he must be gone! It is certain death to linger. He takes his boat and rows away toward the dark coast and the twinkling lights; it is for dear life, now! What powerful strokes send the small skiff rushing over the water!

There is no longer any moon, the night is far spent; already the east changes, the stars fade; he rows like a madman to reach the land, but a blush of morning is stealing up the sky and sunrise is rosy over shore and sea, when panting, trembling, weary, a creature accursed, a blot on the face of the day, he lands at Newcastle--too late! Too late! In vain he casts the dory adrift; she will not float away; the flood tide bears her back to give her testimony against him, and afterward she is found at Jaffrey's Point, near the "Devil's Den," and the fact of her worn thole-pins noted. Wet, covered with ice from the spray which has flown from his eager oars, utterly exhausted, he creeps to a knoll and reconnoiters; he thinks he is unobserved, and crawls on towards Portsmouth. But he is seen and recognized by many persons, and his identity established beyond a doubt. He goes to the house of Mathew Jonsen, where he has been living, steals upstairs, changes his clothes, and appears before the family, anxious, frightened, agitated, telling Jonsen he never felt so badly in his life; that he has got into trouble and is afraid he shall be taken. He cannot eat at breakfast, says "farewell forever," goes away and is shaved, and takes the train to Boston, where he provides himself with new clothes, shoes, a complete outfit, but lingering, held by fate, he cannot fly, and before night the officer's hand is on his shoulder and he is arrested.

Meanwhile, poor shuddering Maren on the lonely island, by the water-side, waits till the sun is high in heaven before she dares come forth. She thinks he may be still on the island. She said to me, "I thought he must be there, dead or alive. I thought he might go crazy and kill himself after having done all that." At last, she steals out. The little dog frisks before her; it is so cold her feet cling to the rocks and snow at every step, till the skin is fairly torn off. Still and frosty is the bright morning, the water lies smiling and sparkling, the hammers of the workmen building the new hotel on Star Island sound through the quiet air. Being on the side of Smutty-Nose opposite Star, she waves her skirt, and screams to attract their attention; they hear her, turn and look, see a woman waving a signal of distress, and, surprising to relate, turn tranquilly to their work again. She realizes, at last, there is no hope in that direction; she must go round toward Appledore in sight of the dreadful house. Passing it afar off she gives one swift glance toward it, terrified lest in the broad sunshine she may see some horrid token of last night's work, but all is still and peaceful. She notices the curtains the three had left up when they went to bed; they are now drawn down; she knows whose hand has done this, and what it hides from the light of day. Sick at heart, she makes her painful way to the northern edge of Malaga, which is connected with Smutty-Nose by the old sea-wall. She is directly opposite Appledore and the little cottage where abide her friend and countryman, Jorge Edvardt Ingebertsen, and his wife and children. Only a quarter of a mile of the still ocean separates her from safety and comfort. She sees the children playing about the door; she calls and calls. Will no one ever hear her? Her torn feet torment her, she is sore with blows and perishing with cold. At last her voice reaches the ears of the children, who run and tell their father that someone is crying and calling; looking across, he sees the poor little figure waving her arms, takes his dory and paddles over, and with amazement recognizes Maren in her night-dress, with bare feet and streaming hair, with a cruel bruise upon her face, with wild eyes, distracted, half senseless with cold and terror. He cries, "Maren, Maren, who has done this? what is it? who is it?" and her only answer is "Louis, Louis, Louis!" as he takes her on board his boat and rows home with her as fast as he can. From her incoherent statement, he learns what has happened. Leaving her in the care of his family, he comes over across the hill to the great house on Appledore. As I sit at my desk I see him pass the window and wonder why the old man comes so fast and anxiously through the heavy snow.

Presently I see him going back again, accompanied by several of his own countrymen and others of our workmen, carrying guns. They are going to Smutty-Nose, and take arms, thinking it possible Wagner may yet be there. I call downstairs, "What has happened?" and am answered, "Some trouble at Smutty-Nose; we hardly understand." "Probably a drunken brawl of the reckless fishermen who may have landed there," I say to myself, and go on with my work. In another half-hour I see the men returning, reinforced by others, coming fast, confusedly; and suddenly a wail of anguish comes up from the women below. I cannot believe it when I hear them crying, "Karen is dead! Anethe is dead! Louis Wagner has murdered them both!" I run out into the servants' quarters; there are all the men assembled, an awe-stricken crowd. Old Ingebertsen comes forward and tells me the bare facts and how Maren lies at his house, half crazy, suffering with her torn and frozen feet. Then the men are dispatched to search Appledore, to find if by any chance the murderer might be concealed about the place, and I go over to Maren to see if I can do anything for her. I find the women and children with frightened faces at the little cottage; as I go into the room where Maren lies, she catches my hands, crying, "Oh, I so glad to see you! I so glad I save my life!" and with her dry lips, she tells me all the story as I have told it here. Poor little creature, holding me with those wild, glittering', dilated eyes, she cannot tell me rapidly enough the whole horrible tale. Upon her cheek is yet the blood-stain from the blow he struck her with a chair, and she shows me two more upon her shoulder, and her torn feet. I go back for arnica with which to bathe them. What a mockery seems to me the "jocund day" as I emerge into the sunshine, and looking across the space of blue, sparkling water, see the house wherein all that horror lies!

Oh brightly shines the morning sun and glitters on the white sails of the little vessel that comes dancing back from Portsmouth before the favoring wind, with the two husbands on board! How glad they are for the sweet morning and the fair wind that brings them home again! And Ivan sees in fancy Anethe's face all beautiful with welcoming smiles, and John knows how happy his good and faithful Maren will be to see him back again. Alas, how little they dream what lies before them! From Appledore, they are signaled to come ashore, and Ivan and Mathew, landing, hear a confused rumor of trouble from tongues that hardly can frame the words that must tell the dreadful truth. Ivan only understands that something is wrong. His one thought is for Anethe; he flies to Ingebertsen's cottage, she may be there; he rushes in like a maniac, crying, "Anethe, Anethe! Where is Anethe?" and broken-hearted Maren answers her brother, "Anethe is--at home." He does not wait for another word, but seizes the little boat and lands at the same time with John on Smutty-Nose; with headlong haste, they reach the house, other men accompanying them; ah, there are bloodstains all about the snow! Ivan is the first to burst open the door and enter. What words can tell it! There upon the floor, naked, stiff, and stark, is the woman he idolizes, for whose dear feet he could not make life's ways smooth and pleasant enough-- stone dead! Dead--horribly butchered! her bright hair stiff with blood, the fair head that had so often rested on his breast crushed! cloven, mangled with the brutal ax! Their eyes are blasted by the intolerable sight: both John and Ivan stagger out and fall, senseless, in the snow. Poor Ivan! his wife a thousand times adored, the dear girl he had brought from Norway, the good, sweet girl who loved him so, whom he could not cherish tenderly enough! And he was not there to protect her! There was no one there to save her!

"Did Heaven look on
And would not take their part!"

Poor fellow, what had he done that fate should deal him such a blow as this! Dumb, blind with anguish, he made no sign.

"What says the body when they spring
Some monstrous torture engine's whole
Strength on it? No more says the soul."

Some of his pitying comrades lead him away, like one stupefied, and take him back to Appledore. John knows his wife is safe. Though stricken with horror and consumed with wrath, he is not paralyzed like poor Ivan, who has been smitten with worse than death. They find Karen's body in another part of the house, covered with blows and black in the face, strangled. They find Louis's tracks,--all the tokens of his disastrous presence,--the contents of trunks and drawers scattered about in his hasty search for the money, and, all within the house and without, blood, blood everywhere.

When I reach the cottage with the arnica for Maren, they have returned from Smutty-Nose. John, her husband, is there. He is a young man of the true Norse type, blue-eyed, fair-haired, tall and well-made, with handsome teeth and bronzed beard. Perhaps he is a little quiet and undemonstrative generally, but at this moment he is superb, kindled from head to feet, a fire-brand of woe and wrath, with eyes that flash and cheeks that burn. I speak a few words to him,--what words can meet such an occasion as this! -- and having given directions about the use of the arnica, for Maren, I go away, for nothing more can be done for her, and every comfort she needs is hers. The outer room is full of men; they make way for me, and as I pass through I catch a glimpse of Ivan crouched with his arms thrown round his knees and his head bowed down between them, motionless, his attitude expressing such abandonment of despair as cannot be described. His whole person seems to shrink as if deprecating the blow that has fallen upon him.

All day the slaughtered women lie as they were found, for nothing can be touched till the officers of the law have seen the whole. And John goes back to Portsmouth to tell his tale to the proper authorities. What a different voyage from the one he had just taken, when happy and careless he was returning to the home he had left so full of peace and comfort! What a load he bears back with him, as he makes his tedious way across the miles that separate him from the means of vengeance he burns to reach! But at last he arrives, tells his story, the police at other cities are at once telegraphed, and the city marshal follows Wagner to Boston. At eight o'clock that evening comes the steamer Mayflower to the Shoals, with all the officers on board. They land and make investigations at Smutty-Nose, then come here to Appledore and examine Maren, and, when everything is done, steam back to Portsmouth, which they reach at three o'clock in the morning. After all are gone and his awful day's work is finished at last, poor John comes back to Maren, and kneeling by the side of her bed, he is utterly overpowered with what he has passed through; he is shaken with sobs as he cries, "Oh, Maren, Maren, it is too much, too much! I cannot bear it!" And Maren throws her arms about his neck, crying, "Oh, John, John, don't! I shall be crazy, I shall die if you go on like that." Poor innocent, unhappy people, who never wronged a fellow-creature in their lives!

But Ivan—what is their anguish to his! They dare not leave him alone lest he do himself an injury. He is perfectly mute and listless; he cannot weep, he can neither eat nor sleep. He sits like one in a horrid dream. "Oh, my poor, poor brother!" Maren cries in tones of deepest grief, when I speak his name to her next day. She herself cannot rest a moment till she hears that Louis is taken; at every sound her crazed imagination fancies he is coming back for her; she is fairly beside herself with terror and anxiety; but the night following that of the catastrophe brings us news that he is arrested, and there is stern rejoicing at the Shoals; but no vengeance taken on him can bring back those unoffending lives, or restore that gentle home. The dead are properly cared for; the blood is washed from Anethe's beautiful bright hair; she is clothed in her wedding dress, the blue dress in which she was married, poor child, that happy Christmas time in Norway, a little more than a year ago. They are carried across the sea to Portsmouth, the burial service is read over them, and they are hidden in the earth. After poor Ivan has seen the faces of his wife and sister still and pale in their coffins, their ghastly wounds concealed as much as possible, flowers upon them and the priest praying over them, his trance of misery is broken, the grasp of despair is loosened a little about his heart. Yet hardly does he notice whether the sun shines or no, or care whether he lives or dies. Slowly his senses steady themselves from the effects of a shock that nearly destroyed him, and merciful time, with imperceptible touch, softens day by day the outlines of that picture at the memory of which he will never cease to shudder while he lives.

Louis Wagner was captured in Boston on the evening of the next day after his atrocious deed, and Friday morning, followed by a hooting mob, he was taken to the Eastern depot. At every station along the route, crowds were assembled, and there were fierce cries for vengeance. At the depot in Portsmouth a dense crowd of thousands of both sexes had gathered, who assailed him with yells and curses and cries of "Tear him to pieces!" It was with difficulty he was at last safely imprisoned. Poor Maren was taken to Portsmouth from Appledore on that day. The story of Wagner's day in Boston, like every other detail of the affair, has been told by every newspaper in the country: his agitation and restlessness, noted by all who saw him; his curious, reckless talk. To one he says, "I have just killed two sailors;" to another, Jacob Toldtman, into whose shop he goes to buy shoes, "I have seen a woman lie as still as that boot," and so on. When he is caught he puts on a bold face and determines to brave it out; denies everything with tears and virtuous indignation. The men whom he has so fearfully wronged are confronted with him; his attitude is one of injured innocence; he surveys them more in sorrow than in anger, while John is on fire with wrath and indignation, and hurls maledictions at him; but Ivan, poor Ivan, hurt beyond all hope or help, is utterly mute; he does not utter one word. Of what use is it to curse the murderer of his wife? It will not bring her back; he has no heart for cursing, he is too completely broken. Maren told me the first time she was brought into Louis's presence, her heart leaped so fast she could hardly breathe. She entered the room softly with her husband and Mathew Jonsen's daughter. Louis was whittling a stick. He looked up and saw her face, and the color ebbed out of his, and rushed back and stood in one burning spot in his cheek, as he looked at her and she looked at him for a space, in silence. Then he drew about his evil mind the detestable garment of sanctimoniousness, and in sentimental accents, he murmured, "I'm glad Jesus loves me!" "The devil loves you!" cried John, with uncompromising veracity. "I know it wasn't nice," said decorous Maren, "but John couldn't help it; it was too much to bear!"

The next Saturday afternoon, when he was to be taken to Saco, hundreds of fishermen came to Portsmouth from all parts of the coast, determined on his destruction, and there was a fearful scene in the quiet streets of that peaceful city when he was being escorted to the train by the police and various officers of justice. Two thousand people had assembled, and such a furious, yelling crowd was never seen or heard in Portsmouth. The air was rent with cries for vengeance; showers of bricks and stones were thrown from all directions and wounded several of the officers who surrounded Wagner. His knees trembled under him, he shook like an aspen, and the officers found it necessary to drag him along, telling him he must keep up if he would save his life. Except that they feared to injure the innocent as well as the guilty, those men would have literally torn him to pieces. But at last he was put on board the cars in safety and carried away to prison. His demeanor throughout the term of his confinement, and during his trial and subsequent imprisonment, was a wonderful piece of acting. He really inspired people with doubt as to his guilt. I make an extract from The Portsmouth Chronicle, dated March 13, 1873: "Wagner still retains his amazing sang-froid, which is wonderful, even in a strong-nerved German. The sympathy of most of the visitors at his jail has certainly been won by his calmness and his general appearance, which is quite prepossessing." This little instance of his method of proceeding I must subjoin: A lady who had come to converse with him on the subject of his eternal salvation said, as she left him, "I hope you put your trust in the Lord," to which he sweetly answered, "I always did, ma'am, and I always shall."

A few weeks after all this had happened, I sat by the window one afternoon, and, looking up from my work, I saw someone passing slowly,--a young man who seemed so thin, so pale, so bent and ill, that I said, "Here is some stranger who is so very sick, he is probably come to try the effect of the air, even thus early." It was Ivan Christensen. I did not recognize him. He dragged one foot after the other wearily, and walked with the feeble motion of an old man. He entered the house; his errand was to ask for work. He could not bear to go away from the neighborhood of the place where Anethe had lived and where they had been so happy, and he could not bear to work at fishing on the south side of the island, within sight of that house. There was work enough for him here; a kind voice told him so, a kind hand was laid on his shoulder, and he was bidden come and welcome. The tears rushed into the poor fellow's eyes, he went hastily away, and that night sent over his chest of tools,--he was a carpenter by trade. Next day he took up his abode here and worked all summer. Every day I carefully observed him as I passed him by, regarding him with an inexpressible pity, of which he was perfectly unconscious, as he seemed to be of everything and everybody. He never raised his head when he answered my "Good morning," or "Good evening, Ivan." Though I often wished to speak, I never said more to him, for he seemed to me to be hurt too sorely to be touched by human hand. With his head sunk on his breast, and wearily dragging his limbs, he pushed the plane or drove the saw to and fro with a kind of dogged persistence, looking neither to the left nor right. Well might the weight of woe he carried bow him to the earth! By and by he spoke, himself, to other members of the household, saying, with a patient sorrow, he believed it was to have been, it had been so ordered, else why did all things so play into Louis's hands? All things were furnished him: the knowledge of the unprotected state of the women, a perfectly clear field in which to carry out his plans, just the right boat he wanted in which to make his voyage, fair tide, fair wind, calm sea, just moonlight enough; even the ax with which to kill Anethe stood ready to his hand at the house door. Alas, it was to have been! Last summer Ivan went back again to Norway--alone. Hardly is it probable that he will ever return to a land whose welcome to him fate made so horrible. His sister Maren and her husband still live blameless lives, with the little dog Ringe, in a new home they have made for themselves in Portsmouth, not far from the riverside; the merciful lapse of days and years takes them gently but surely away from the thought of that season of anguish; and though they can never forget it all, they have grown resigned and quiet again. And on the island other Norwegians have settled, voices of charming children sound sweetly in the solitude that echoed so awfully to the shrieks of Karen and Maren. But to the weirdness of the winter midnight something is added, a vision of two dim, reproachful shades who watch while an agonized ghost prowls eternally about the dilapidated houses at the beach's edge, close by the black, whispering water, seeking for the woman who has escaped him--escaped to bring upon him the death he deserves, whom he never, never, never can find, though his distracted spirit may search till man shall vanish from off the face of the earth, and time shall be no more.

The Mother's Revenge
John Greenleaf. Whittier

Hannah Duston statue, GAR Park, Haverhill, Massachusetts
Prior to the US Civil War, there were three versions of the story of Hannah Duston. Cotton Mather's *Deliverances* (1697), Whittier's *Legends of New England* (1831), and Mirick's *History of Haverhill* (1832), which was mostly written by Whittier. It is possible to tell which version was used by subsequent writers based on the details that vary between the three sources. Whittier's versions were not meant as history – they were literary adaptations of the local folklore accounts. Debate continues if the Duston incident should be considered heroism or homicide. *Courtesy of Scott T. Goudsward.*

Woman's attributes are generally considered of a milder and purer character than those of man. The virtues of meek affection, of fervent piety, of winning sympathy and of that "charity which forgiveth often," are more peculiarly her own. Her sphere of action is generally limited to the endearments of home—the quiet communion with her friends, and the angelic exercise of the kindly charities of existence. Yet, there have been astonishing manifestations of female fortitude and power in the ruder and sterner trials of humanity; manifestations of a courage rising almost to sublimity; the revelation of all those dark and terrible passions, which madden and distract the heart of manhood.

The perils which surrounded the earliest settlers of New-England were of the most terrible character. None but such a people as were our forefathers could have successfully sustained them. In the dangers and the hardihood of that perilous period, woman herself shared largely. It was not unfrequently her task to garrison the dwelling of her absent husband, and hold at bay the fierce savages in their hunt for blood. Many have left behind them a record of their sufferings and trials in the great wilderness, when in the bondage of the heathen, which are full of wonderful and romantic incidents, related however without ostentation, plainly and simply, as if the authors felt assured that they had only performed the task which Providence had set before them, and for which they could ask no tribute of admiration.

In 1698 the Indians made an attack upon the English settlement at Haverhill—now a beautiful village on the left bank of the Merrimack. They surrounded the house of one Duston, which was a little removed from the main body of the settlement. The wife of Duston was at that time in bed with an infant child in her arms. Seven young children were around her. On the first alarm Duston bade his children fly towards the Garrison-house, and then turned to save his wife and infant. By this time the savages were pressing close upon them. The heroic woman saw the utter impossibility of her escape—and she bade her husband fly to succor his children, and leave her to her fate. It was a moment of terrible trial for the husband—he hesitated between his affection and his duty—but the entreaties of his wife fixed his determination.

He turned away, and followed his children. A part of the Indians pursued him, but he held them at a distance by the frequent discharge of his rifle. The children fled towards the garrison, where their friends waited, with breathless anxiety, to receive them. More than once, during their flight, the savages gained upon them; but a shot from the rifle of Duston, followed, as it was, by the fall of one of their number, effectually checked their progress. The garrison was reached, and Duston and his children, exhausted with fatigue and terror, were literally dragged into its enclosure by their anxious neighbors.

Mrs. Duston, her servant girl and her infant were made prisoners by the Indians, and were compelled to proceed before them in their retreat towards their lurking-place. The charge of her infant necessarily impeded her progress; and the savages could ill brook delay when they knew the avenger of blood was following closely behind them. Finding that the wretched mother was unable to keep pace with her captors, the leader of the band approached her, and wrested the infant from her arms. The savage held it before him for a moment, contemplating, with a smile of grim fierceness the terrors of its mother, and then dashed it from him with all his powerful strength. Its head smote heavily on the trunk of an adjacent tree, and the dried leaves around were sprinkled with brains and blood.

"Go on!" said the Indian.

The wretched mother cast one look upon her dead infant, and another to Heaven, as she obeyed her savage conductor. She has often said, that at this moment, all was darkness and horror—that her very heart seemed to cease beating, and to lie cold and dead in her bosom, and that her limbs moved only as involuntary machinery. But when she gazed around her and saw the unfeeling savages, grinning at her and mocking her, and pointing to the mangled body of her infant with fiendish exultation, a new and terrible feeling came over her. It was the thirst of revenge; and from that moment her purpose was fixed. There was a thought of death at her heart—an insatiate longing for blood. An instantaneous change had been wrought in her very nature; the angel had become a demon,—and she followed her captors, with a stern determination to embrace the earliest opportunity for a bloody retribution.

The Indians followed the course of the Merrimack, until they had reached their canoes, a distance of seventy or eighty miles. They paddled to a small island, a little above the upper falls of the river. Here they kindled a fire; and fatigued by their long marches and sleepless nights, stretched themselves around it, without dreaming of the escape of their captives.

Their sleep was deep—deeper than any which the white man knows,—a sleep from which they were never to awaken. The two captives lay silent, until the hour of midnight; but the bereaved mother did not close her eyes. There was a gnawing of revenge at her heart, which precluded slumber. There was a spirit within her which defied the weakness of the body.

She rose up and walked around the sleepers, in order to test the soundness of their slumber. They stirred not limb or muscle. Placing a hatchet in the hands of her fellow captive, and bidding her stand ready to assist her, she grasped another in her own hands, and smote its ragged edge deeply into the skull of the nearest sleeper. A slight shudder and a feeble groan followed. The savage was dead. She passed on to the next. Blow followed blow, until ten out of twelve, the whole number of the savages, were stiffening in blood. One escaped with a dreadful wound. The last—a small boy—still slept amidst the scene of carnage. Mrs. Duston lifted her dripping hatchet above his head, but hesitated to strike the blow.

"It is a poor boy," she said, mentally, "a poor child, and perhaps he has a mother!" The thought of her own children rushed upon her mind, and she spared him. She was in the act of leaving the bloody spot, when, suddenly reflecting that the people of her settlement would not credit her story, unsupported by any proof save her own assertion, she returned and deliberately scalped her ten victims. With this fearful evidence of her prowess, she loosed one of the Indian canoes, and floated down the river to the falls, from which place she travelled through the wilderness to the residence of her husband.

Such is the simple and unvarnished story of a New-England woman. The curious historian, who may hereafter search among the dim records of our "twilight time"—who may gather from the uncertain responses of tradition, the wonderful history of the past—will find much, of a similar character, to call forth by turns, admiration and horror. And the time is coming, when all these traditions shall be treasured up as a sacred legacy—when the tale of the Indian inroad and the perils of the hunter—of the sublime courage and the dark superstitions of our ancestors, will be listened to with an interest unknown to the present generation,—and those who are to fill our places will pause hereafter by the Indian's burial-place, and on the site of the old battle-field, or the thrown-down garrison, with a feeling of awe and reverence, as if communing, face to face, with the spirits of that stern race, which has passed away forever.

Exposed For Murder
Judi Calhoun

Whittier's Grave, Amesbury, Massachusetts
Whittier is interred in the Society of Friends Cemetery, which was absorbed into the Union Cemetery. He rests in a family plot along with family members commemorated in "Snow Bound." The simple headstone is not hard to find – ample signage points the way to those making a literary pilgrimage.

I was naked, except for my striped slippers and my camouflage hunting hat. I was in the Union Cemetery, pointing my service revolver at the maintenance building door, as if the green door in the brick building were a criminal. Right at that moment, my body decided to wake up.

Sleepwalking again! Had anyone seen me?

I wracked my brain trying to remember what could have triggered this episode. I couldn't sleep. I took a sedative – my first mistake – that's the combination that guarantees somnambulism.

A foggy memory surfaced. My cell phone had gone off a little after 3:00 a.m. I reached over to answer it. There was a homicide. Immediately, I went into autopilot. Get dressed. Go into work. Only that's when the sedative finally kicked in. I must have fallen back into a deep sleep, but when the other side of my brain woke up, I went on this long stroll.

Sleepwalking wasn't a new thing for me––although, I'd never walked this far before. Generally, I woke up to find myself at the end of the driveway or the end of my street, in my own neighborhood––over six blocks from here. I couldn't get my mind around the idea that I'd walked naked for six whole blocks. I began to wonder––just how long had I been standing in this same exact spot? The bank clock said it was 4:05 a.m. For once in my life, if I had to sleepwalk, why couldn't I just remember to bring my damn cell phone, or clothes for that matter––and not my gun?

A short distance away came the sound of a vehicle, then the bright beams of the headlamps flashed; a panel truck was turning from Haverhill Road onto Spruce Avenue. I glanced around in a panic, looking for somewhere to hide. I made a mad dash and ducked behind the brick maintenance building.

Odd.

What was an ice cream truck doing out in the middle of the night? The rusty frame squeaked as the truck drove by slowly, heading off toward Bevan Avenue.

A chill ran through me as I watched the tail lights disappear into the distance. In a panic, I ran down Linden Avenue and slipped across the loop, passing the Macy-Colby House. Crossing Main Street, I reached Kendricks Court. I was happy to be in a dark residential neighborhood, as I moved along quickly through front yards.

The first morning light was starting to brighten the sky, as I scurried down someone's driveway. I slipped into the backyard, hoping maybe I could find an old tarp or barbecue cover––anything to cloak my naked ass. Laundry was hanging on a pulley line––two floral bras, five pairs of underwear, a black silky skirt, and a pink fuzzy bathrobe. Just my luck––women's stuff!

The elastic-waisted skirt fit me perfectly, but the pink robe was a little tight across my shoulders. How do women wear this stuff? I slipped my gun into the waistband of the skirt and managed to wrap the robe around me, tying the sash. I looked like a gun-toting drag queen. If I were in a city like Boston, nobody would give me a second glance. But Amesbury was a much smaller community, and here this kind of behavior would turn heads and set tongues to wagging.

Just like walking in my sleep, picking my way through the darkness was hazardous. Sure enough, the moment I turned to leave, I stubbed my toe on some kid's metal toy truck. In anger, I tossed it away. It was lighter than I thought. It went sailing, accidentally slamming against the side of the house. Blam!

Almost immediately, the porch lights came on. Instinct told me to hide––fast. It wouldn't be good for the police department's image to have a detective found naked in a residential neighborhood stealing laundry. I ducked behind some bushes along the back fence just before the back door opened.

A pudgy man wearing a wife beater and tightie-whities stepped out onto the back porch, holding a baseball bat in one hand and shining a flashlight around the yard with the other.

"Is it the raccoons?" came the nasal Fran Dresher voice from inside. "I told you to take care of that garbage. You never listen to me."

"Shut up, Mona!" the pudgy man yelled. "You're voice will wake up the dead. Go back to sleep."

"You don't have to be so insulting," she whined. "Maybe you should sleep on the sofa."

They were both yelling now, as he closed the door and turned off the porch lights.

Heart pounding loudly in my chest, I cautiously made my way down the other side of the house until I reached the sidewalk. I bolted out into the road and began running down Main Street. I heard a short whoop, followed by the sharp, quick, blast of a siren. A cruiser pulled up next to me.

"Hold it right there, buddy!"

Panting breathlessly, I turned around to face––my partner, Nathan MacAdams.

"Nice outfit, Hasson," he sniggered as he got out of the car. Taking in my entire wardrobe he bent over, laughing loudly, having a really good belly laugh at my expense.

"Yah, yah, go ahead, enjoy yourself. Get it out of your system," I grumbled. Opening the passenger side door, I slipped inside, adjusting my silky black skirt as I slid onto the leather seat, waiting for him to pull himself together.

"That was you I saw earlier running naked from the cemetery, right?" Nathan was still fighting to speak between fits of laughter as he got back behind the wheel. "Tommy owes me ten bucks."

Yeah, like Nathan needed the ten bucks. Nathan MacAdams loved police work. He'd work every shift if he could even though he didn't have to because he'd won five million in the Mega Bucks last year. He'd used it to help his family; he paid off his parents' and his sister's houses, and he set his brother up in business, installing security cameras and wall safes. Tommy Shannon, our tech guy in the office, called him "Lucky Nathan."

"So, when did you decide on a career as a drag queen?" asked Nathan, struggling not to bust out laughing again. I stared at the football player-sized man, giving him the evil eye, as he made a U-turn. If I had his money, I'd have been long gone. I'd have been living the high life on a yacht in Hawaii. Who was I kidding? I couldn't leave Massachusetts; not as long as Cameron, my ex-wife, was here. I wouldn't say this out loud to anyone, but I ache all over, just thinking about her. God, how I miss her!

I grabbed the radio microphone the moment I heard Carol's transmission. Our dispatcher, Carol Lynch, was all business. She was an older woman who didn't take any shit––but she sure gave a lot of it out, just on principle.

"This is Lieutenant Michael Hasson."

"Lieutenant, please advise Dispatch of your current welfare?"

"Alive, for now, Carol," I responded. "Status is with MacAdams."

"Be advised Lieutenant, that there's been a homicide at the Union Cemetery."

I couldn't believe what I was hearing. I made her repeat the call again. I suddenly felt cold inside. Hadn't I just been standing at the maintenance building's door with a gun, when the murder might have taken place?

"When did this happen?" I asked.

"9-1-1 call just came in."

"10-4. Look, I need to go home first, Carol. Tell Captain I'll be out of the vehicle for twenty minutes."

"No way," said Carol. "Captain's called an emergency meeting for all homicide investigation personnel. He'll fire me if I tell him you've stopped by your house first."

"Give me a break here, Carol. I need to get some clothes."

"Mike, you better get your skinny, naked butt over there right now––if you catch my drift."

That was Carol-code for my ass was in big trouble. "On our way." I clipped the microphone back into the holder.

Nathan was shaking his head. "You know Hasson, you really need to get laid."

"Yeah, tell me about it," I said, thinking about Cameron again––missing her. It had been two years since the divorce was finalized. I couldn't blame her for taking off; nobody should have to live with this sleepwalking bullshit.

"I can fix you up with someone," said Nathan, pulling me out of my memory. He was turning from Main Street onto Haverhill Road. As we passed the BP gas station at the corner, I saw that ice cream truck again, going the opposite way this time. I turned in my seat, looking over my shoulder, my eyes following the rusty panel truck.

"Have you ever seen that truck before?"

Nathan glanced into his rearview. "That's Scott Rickers, you know, the freak of nature who dresses up like a clown all the time––and I mean *all the time*."

"In an ice cream truck?"

"Yeah, it's something new. He doesn't sell much ice cream––but he scares the shit out of little kids." He shrugged. "Hell, he scares the shit out of me, too."

* * * * *

"I don't think pink is your color," said Captain Hurley, arms crossed over his broad chest. His eyes traveled from my camo hat to the belted fuzzy pink robe with visible dark chest hair sticking out from the V-neck, and down to my silky black skirt and striped slippers. "Don't tell me," he shook his head, holding up his hand. "I don't want to hear it. What you do on your own time is your business."

That was Captain Hurley, always messing with my head. He knew about my sleepwalking problem, but to him, it was more of a joke. He had no clue what it felt like to wake up, finding yourself somewhere other than safe in your own warm bed.

He pointed now at the victim; a man in his early fifties, awkwardly slumped up against a gravestone inscribed "*Here Whittier Lies.*" He looked like any run-of-the-mill drunk, sleeping one off, except for the blood that soaked his shirt-front, and puddled around him in the dirt.

I might not be an ME, but the cause of death was easy enough to determine––his heart exploded. Our vic took two rounds in the chest, double tapped––killing him instantly. From the size of the entry and exit wound, he must have been shot at close range with a larger caliber round.

There should have been a blood splatter pattern on the granite grave monument directly behind him. There was no sign of struggle, and that was the strange part; it appeared he was killed somewhere else, and then placed here.

"Do you smell that?" I asked, leaning closer and sniffing because the air surrounding our victim was fragrant... sweet, like candy––strawberry syrup, to be exact.

"A-yup," said Captain. "He's the best smelling corpse I've ever encountered."

"Do we know his name?"

"Ben Silverstein. Did you know him?"

Captain Hurley was original New England old school. Whenever we encountered someone of the Jewish faith he mistakenly assumed we were related, which meant he was unaware that what he was saying would probably be considered unacceptable.

I rolled my eyes. "Why do you ask me that every time our victim happens to be Jewish?"

"Well, you see, Hasson, it might be a big old world out there, but really, we are all just a community of backyards separated by fences. Everyone knows everybody's business. It's not a stretch to think that maybe you both attend the same church."

I shook my head. "I've told you before, I haven't been to Synagogue since my youngest brother's Bar Mitzvah."

"Oh, right," said Captain Hurley. "You did tell me. Well, Tommy told me that Ben Silverstein was a great asset to the *Amesbury News*––been there since 1981. He'd worked his way up from mailroom clerk to lead advertising salesman. A-yup," said Captain Hurley. "I figured he must have been killed somewhere else. We found his wallet, but no cell phone. We already bagged the Highpoint he was carrying concealed. The assailant must have caught him by surprise––that would explain why he hadn't used his gun."

I was thinking––if Ben Silverstein wasn't killed here, then there had to be some sign of a blood trail in the grass. "How much do you think he weighs?"

"Oh, maybe close to 270 pounds." Captain drew in his lower lip and crossed his arms over his Buddha-like chest. "A-yup," he drawled. "I thought the same thing, but we sprayed Luminal, and ran the black lights over everything." He shook his head. "No blood anywhere other than right here. It's like he was supernaturally dropped right on this gravestone. It's got me stumped, boys. By God, it's a genuine mystery." He glanced at his watch. "The ME's almost done here. You and Nathan take a ride over to the newspaper and talk with his boss, see what you can find out."

* * * * *

A tall woman with a pointed nose and short-cropped black hair pointed toward a brown desk in a room behind a glass wall. "That was his desk."

As I walked over, I glanced into the other office belonging to, *James Nixon, Editor*, according to the shiny brass plaque on the door. I was surprised at how spotlessly clean it was. I stopped dead in my tracks—he had a Colt .45 revolver sitting on his desk, the barrel lying across a large margarita glass. How easy would that be if this was our murder weapon? After all, it was a large caliber. I'd stake my job on it, that it was a .45 caliber round that killed our vic.

"We need to run ballistics on this weapon," I said to Nathan, who was busy being flirted with by a young intern.

"Already on it." Nathan turned fast, snapping on some nitrile gloves, and pulling out an evidence bag.

As well as being an Editor, James Nixon owned *The Margarita Grill*. Displayed in his office he had a few marksmanship ribbons and this giant painting—a portrait of himself—which was really too large for such a small office. What he didn't have were the certificates like Ben had, stating he'd won the state shooting championship—for five years in a row.

"Ben was an accomplished marksman," I said to Nathan. "He had exceptional talent. It's a shame someone took him out this way."

* * * * *

The ME's preliminary report confirmed the cause of death and the approximate time of death——around 3 a.m.

Impossible! How could I have gotten a call at the exact same time that the murder was taking place? And yet, it had been enough to rouse me from my sleep. As I ran the call back through my thoughts, I realized it wasn't Carol's voice I had heard on the other end of the line. Yet, it was familiar. I'd swear I'd heard that voice before.

Chills caught hold of me. Had the killer wanted me to be standing in front of the maintenance building at the exact same moment he was killing our victim? I snapped out of my deep pondering when Captain Hurley called me into his office.

"I want to show you something," he said, waving me over to his computer, while he put on his glasses. "This is the video footage from the cemetery. We could be looking right at our murderer here on this film."

The video feed was grainy and dark. I saw myself naked, walking up to the door of the maintenance building. The footage jumped, then suddenly there was another figure, dark and hooded——he moved in a jerking blur, so fast. His ghost-like face was close to mine as if he were talking to me, for what seemed like a full two minutes. I raised my gun and pointed it at the door as the ghost vanished—there one frame—gone the next. Just as suddenly, Ben Silverstein's dead body lay in front of me on the sidewalk outside the building. Blood spattered the cement and wooden door. Wait——who had cleaned it up before the police got there?

"What the hell!" I yelled in disbelief, stumbling back away from his desk. "I didn't kill him. Not with my caliber weapon!"

Hurley tapped the keyboard, zooming in on the gun in my hand.

"Yup," said Hurley. "Ballistics believes that the murder weapon was a large round. A .45 could be the murder weapon. Of course, without having the actual bullet we don't know for sure."

I moved in a daze and collapsed onto one of Hurley's client chairs, holding my head in my hands. Someone was trying to frame me.

"Why would I kill him?" I asked, now on my feet again, and pacing. "I have no motive. I don't even know the guy. When did I have time to move the body? And for that matter, I don't even own a .45 caliber."

"I know," said Hurley. "I had Nathan search your place."

"You did what?" I barked.

"We had no choice, Mike. When I saw the video footage, I just didn't know..."

"You didn't know what?" I snapped. "If I was killing random people in my sleep?"

"Look Mike, nobody else has seen this video footage. No one suspects you of this crime. It will have to be analyzed—there are inconsistencies in the playback and the time stamp. But, put yourself in my shoes. I've got to explain this somehow. I'm under a lot of pressure. If we don't find the killer soon, I'm going to have to take you in."

I nodded, resigned. "I fucking hate this disease."

Hurley slowly nodded. "Damn shame...nothing the doctors can do. But this is me... you gotta level with me, Mike--can you remember anything? Did you discharge your weapon? What about that man... or that ghost--what did he say to you?"

"Don't you think I want to remember?" I gritted my teeth. "I gotta tell you, Captain, seeing this video--I'm a little freaked out right now."

The Captain pulled a test kit from his desk drawer. "Just for our own peace of mind, I'm gonna swab your hands for gun residue. Then we'll both know for sure you didn't discharge your weapon. I'm going to have to take your weapon, Mike." He held out an evidence bag.

I unholstered my weapon and reluctantly slipped it into the bag. The Captain sealed it as I sat down, slumped back in the chair, and let out a heavy sigh. I figured it would go better for me if I just told Hurley everything I knew, about the phone calls and stuff that had been plaguing me for weeks.

* * * * *

Nathan and I found very little evidence in Ben Silverstein's apartment to help solve this crime. We left a few hours later with his mail, a Colt .45 revolver, and his computer to give to our tech guy, Tommy Shannon.

Then we headed to the *Amesbury News* to again interview the staff and talk with the editor. Most of Ben's coworkers thought Ben was a nice guy. Many of them believed he was weird, because he never dated women, or men––or anyone, for that matter.

We were shown to the Editor's office. James Nixon sat tall in his leather chair. Behind him on the newly painted wall was that oversized portrait, an Impasto oil painting, within a heavily filigreed gold frame.

At first, when we began to question him, he was almost standoffish; but then he became oddly peaceful, and began telling us much more than we'd asked for.

We learned about the contest between Janet Sofel and Ben. The Sales Rep bringing in the highest grossing advertisement accounts would receive the highly sought after promotion to Assistant Editor.

"Can you tell us about your working relationship with the deceased?" I asked.

"The truth is, we never really saw eye to eye on much. We both belonged to the same gun club. Ben was always the best shot––a true marksman. Sure, he gained a lot of respect, from most people. Well, it looks like now *I'll* be taking home all the trophies." He chuckled lightly at his own candor.

"When was the last time you saw Ben alive?" I asked.

"Yesterday," said Nixon. "When he delivered the hospital contract. He won the contest fair and square. I had offered the winner a free steak dinner. He was going to turn me down, but I insisted. He left the office around quitting time, and that was it. He never showed up at the Grill last night. I guess I know why, now."

"Is it true, Janet Sofel was Ben's fiercest competitor? That she might have done anything to win? Maybe even murder?"

"Unfortunately, that's the truth." James nodded. "She can be vicious. But she's smart, maybe a little conniving. After all, she's a bit like me––she hates to lose."

I began to wonder––was that motive enough for murder? Funny thing was, I knew Janet. I'd gone to high school with her... graduating class of 2002.

* * * * *

She wasn't at work today; she'd called in sick. Janet lived roughly five miles away from the newspaper. When she answered the door, she was wearing a pink sweater, in spite of the 80-degree temperature outside. Her red eyes almost matched her sweater. She gave me a look, the kind of stare that told me she was trying to place my face and name.

Nathan held up his badge. "Good afternoon, Ms. Sofel. I'm–"

"You must be here about Ben's death. Come on in," she interrupted. Her apartment had a foul odor that reminded me of the trash cans at the park on a hot summer's day. She brushed magazines and newspapers from the couch, but I was afraid to sit down. From the moment I had walked in, it felt like something was crawling on me. I noticed Nathan nervously cracking his neck––a lot. He does that when something's happening beyond his control. Reluctantly, I sat down on the edge of the cushion.

"Nixon promised Ben and me the Assistant Editor position. Like everything else, he turned it into a competition. The Sales Rep who could bring in the most revenue would win the job."

"That would have been a very big pay raise for you," I said. "Get you out of this apartment and into something really nice. So, when Ben got landed the hospital account worth twelve grand, he shot way ahead of you. You got angry and killed him, didn't you?"

"No." She wrapped her sweater closer around herself. Holding her head high, she said, "I worked hard to get that account. That asshole Silverstein snatched it right out from under me. Sure, I was mad. But that doesn't mean I killed him."

"But it does give you motive," I said.

She squinted, staring hard at me. Her eyes suddenly narrowed. "I remember you, now. Michael Hasson." She sneered. "We were in Mrs. Lockhart's class together, eleventh grade English. As I recall, you didn't do very well in her class. Not much has changed since school––I mean with your marriage failing, and all. Oops, did I just say that out loud?"

Bitch! No––Super bitch! No. Don't say anything. Try to keep your mouth shut. After all, you are a professional. Then I couldn't stop myself...

"Didn't you get expelled a few times for cheating?" I retorted with a snarky edge to my voice.

Janet looked miffed. "Oh, that," she said, smoothing her hands against the fabric on her jeans. "They were only rumors, nothing more." She stood up awkwardly. "I'm really not feeling well." She dramatically rested the back of her hand on her forehead. "I'd like you to leave now."

I was sizing her up, trying to figure out what her deal was. I was hoping she was the killer because now I wanted to slap cuffs on her wrists and haul her ass off to jail. I wondered what she was hiding. Unfortunately, Janet didn't look strong enough to lift a man the size of Ben, but she could have had help––maybe from Scott Rickers?

"Where were you last night around three?" I asked, ignoring her request.

"I was sleeping like the rest of the normal world. But where were you, Mike?"

I could feel the skin on my face heating up. Nathan must have sensed my anger because he stood up right then. "Thank you for your time, Ms. Sofel––we'll be in touch."

When I rose to my feet, I grimaced feeling something sticking to my pant leg. I ran my hand over the material and I was right; an envelope was attached to my ass. I peeled it off, turned it over to read the name, and frowned.

Janet snatched the envelope from my hands. "That's personal property. You don't have a warrant. Get out." All semblance of her headache seemed to have vanished.

"Well, that was a dead end," said Nathan, once we reached the cruiser.

"I don't think so," I said, slipping inside. "I think she's guilty. That envelope that stuck to my leg was addressed to that ice cream clown, Scott Rickers."

Nathan scowled. "What's she doing involved with him? Rickers has been tangled up in some nasty shit, but there's never been enough evidence to put him away."

* * * * *

Staring at the ceiling, I was terrified to close my eyes; afraid of where I might end up in the middle of the night. I tried doing the meditation exercises the doctor recommended, but there was no settling my brain down––not tonight.

I picked up the bottle of melatonin that our tech guy, Tommy Shannon, had given to me, swearing that it worked. I read the label––every last word—nothing. Well, maybe it wouldn't hurt to take just one.

Yup. That didn't help. I woke up naked again, standing on the edge of my neighbors' diving board. I nearly lost my balance—caught myself, thought I had it together––but I didn't. I fell right into the cold water. Thank goodness tonight I didn't have my revolver. It was safe with the Captain.

If I'd taken one more step in my sleep and fallen in, would I have taken a stroll across the pool, forgetting I couldn't breathe underwater? I might have drowned before I woke up. Cameron was right to leave me. I was a danger to myself.

I was relieved that my neighbors' house remained dark and quiet. I didn't wait around; I hauled my dripping wet, naked self out of the pool, and rushed home before I could be discovered.

* * * * *

Scott Rickers lived in Cedarwood Mobile Home Park, in a 1960 Ghost Moon trailer, with typical thin metal siding. Peeling paint hung in long curling strips from the siding, and most of the rotted wooden skirting was gone. Weeds grew up nearly five foot high. The rusty old ice cream panel truck sat next to the shed.

Nathan rapped ten times on the metal door, bellowing Scott's name until the narrow door creaked open. A cigarette hung from the corner of his sneering lips. He was still wearing faded clown make-up around his eyes and mouth.

You know those scary killer clown movies? Yup, Rickers would have had a starring role. A permanent red smile was plastered on a chalky white face, eyes so dark they made you gulp hard. He gave you pause; made you wonder if he'd just escaped from some far away mental hospital.

His dark eyes fell on me. There was something in that gaze, half hidden under all that make-up. It was a weird expression, almost as if he knew me––intimately.

"I paid all my parking fines." He scoffed behind his disturbed smile.

"We're not here because of that," said Nathan. "We want to talk to you about Ben Silverstein's murder."

He flicked the cigarette butt out the door, over our shoulders. "I had nothing to do with that."

"We saw your truck on Haverhill Road. What were you doing out in the early morning hours, around 3:00 am?"

"I was picking up my ice cream order. Is that a crime?"

"No." I held up an official warrant. "We're here to search your place."

He chuckled. It grew into maniacal, unhinged laughter that went on too long, longer than normal. "Go ahead." He finally squeaked out. "Don't let the rats bite you."

Nathan headed down into the bedroom, but the moment I stepped into his kitchen and dining area, that familiar smell filled my nostrils; the same sweet sugary fragrance that had lingered around Ben Silverstein's body. Now I was more than convinced that Rickers had something to do with the murder.

I searched around under the kitchen cabinets, always keeping my eye on Scott. I watched the beads of sweat break out on his forehead, as his eyes darted from me out into the hallway and back. Suddenly he moved behind the collapsible kitchen table. I got the feeling that he was hiding something there.

"Move," I ordered. "Stand next to the sink. Right there. Keep your hands where I can see them." I slapped one cuff on his wrist and the other end of the galvanized metal vent pipe. I hollered for Nathan when Scott tried to shake free of my grip, but I caught his other hand and zip-tied it to his cuffed wrist.

"This is police brutality!" he snapped, as Nathan came out from the bedroom.

I turned the table over and sure enough, there was a gun. Another Colt .45, duct taped to the underside. Nathan slipped on a pair of gloves, tore off the tape, and dropped the gun into an evidence bag.

* * * * *

I had never touched that gun––so how could it have my fingerprints all over it? More damning evidence linking me to the murder. And without all the fired rounds, we had no way to pin the murder rap on Rickers' weapon.

Time was running out and I was desperate to clear my good name. Nathan let it slip that in the morning I would be detained, probably even booked for murder one, because Hurley had no choice. I would have to be arraigned for the murder of Ben Silverstein.

I kept fixating on those Colt .45 revolvers. Maybe it was a little too ironic that we had come across so many of the same weapon? We'd found three––one in Ben's apartment, one in James Nixon's office, and another one at Rickers' mobile home––surely, one of them had to be the murder weapon. Without those fired bullets, it was going to be nearly impossible to find the murderer.

The *Amesbury News* office was closed. I rapped on the window and flashed my badge, and the cleaning crew let me inside. I went to Ben's desk first. I stood quietly surveying the wall plaques. At this time of day, the late afternoon sunlight coming in reflected all of his awards onto the glass wall in front of his desk.

I stood up and took a few steps across the hall into James Nixon's desk, and sat down in his chair, staring at his desktop. There was something about that margarita glass... The Colt was gone now, sitting in the evidence room––but it kept bothering me. It was something James Nixon had said that was eating at me, "*...we never really saw eye to eye on much... It looks like now I'll be taking home all the trophies.*"

Ballistics hadn't found any residue on the inside of the gun barrel––in fact, the gun was clean––like never-been-fired, brand new clean. If the gun wasn't anything special, then why would James have it on display?

And suddenly the pieces started falling into place. I knew who the murderer was. I still had no weapon, no bullets, no proof–– but I had motive, and I was quickly putting together all the details––and I was certain I knew where the murder had taken place.

I swiveled the desk chair and was staring at the painting on Nixon's office wall. I got out of the chair and felt around the picture frame until my fingers grazed a button. When I pushed it, the heavy portrait slid to the side.

I smiled. I believed I had solved the murder, but I was racing against the clock. The first thing I did was send a text to Nathan, telling him about everything I believed was true.

The moment I stepped outside the newspaper office, I realized, too late, that someone was waiting for me. Something me hard in the back of the head. Everything went black.

* * * * *

When I opened my eyes, I had a pounding headache. Blood was crusted on my temples and in my ears. All sound was muffled. All I could think about was my ex-wife, Cameron. I had to find a way to get back with her.

I stood up slowly, feeling nauseous. My head dizzy, and stomach lurching, I tried to get my bearings, waiting for my eyes to adjust to the small low light coming in from a high, narrow window. I saw hanging pots and pans, shelves stacked with dishes, and industrial-sized rolls of foil and plastic wrap.

I was inside the back room of a restaurant kitchen; *The Margarita Grill* to be exact if the labeled boxes were correct.

Nixon.

He must have been at the newspaper office, watching me and waiting for me to step outside. I reached into my pocket for my cell phone, but it was gone.

I could make out three doors. One was clearly marked *Basement*. The others could have been a pantry or broom closet for all I knew. In the near darkness, I shuffled along holding the walls to steady myself, until I reached the first door––it was locked.

From the glow of my watch, a tiny glint of light caught my eye... so small I might have dismissed it. I leaned in close and ran my fingernail over the indents. Two bullets were lodged into the drywall.

I was wishing I had my cell phone––I needed to get a message to Nathan to pry the bullets out of the wall and bag them as evidence––when the door behind me opened and the lights came on. I squinted to adjust my eyes until they finally focused––on James Nixon's hand, brandishing a new Colt .45 revolver––aimed straight at my heart.

"You bastard! You tried to frame me for Silverstein's murder! Why me?"

He hesitated at first, then he started to chuckle. "I have a perfect alibi. You're going to take the fall for me. You see, your wife and mine use the same beauty parlor. Once I discovered the reason for your divorce, that little sleepwalking problem you have; well, I knew I had someone to pin the murder on. You know those magic pills you've been taking? It's not your prescription. The dosage you're on makes you susceptible to suggestions, almost like hypnosis. A couple of weeks on that dosage and you were the perfect fall guy. Everything would have come together flawlessly, if it wasn't for that imbecile, Rickers. He was not supposed to show up in the video. I didn't have time to fix his screw-up."

"They're going to arrest me, tomorrow," I said. "Sitting in your office helped me to figure it out. But tell me––why did you kill Silverstein?"

He shrugged, chuckling. "Okay, fine. What have I got to lose? You'll be dead in a minute anyway. Nobody will ever convict me, so I'll tell you. That pompous ass Silverstein loved to wave his trophies in my face every time he won a shooting match. Did you know I earned Expert Marksman in the military? Yeah, that good-for-nothing Silverstein never served our fine country. You know where he learned to shoot? College! And you know how he got there? The Whittier Scholarship! It wasn't right! Quakers are Pacifists, and I know, because my mother's people were Whittier's great-grandparents. I didn't get a free ride to college––I had to earn it! Every time he beat me, I wanted to kill him. So, I finally did." He paused to take a breath.

"Tell me, Mike," he asked like we were best buddies. "How did you figure it out?"

I was looking around trying to find a weapon. There were pots and pans, wine and margarita glasses––but no knives. I slowly started to side step toward the pans, hoping he wouldn't catch my movement.

"You wanted a trophy," I said, pointing at the glasses. "The margarita glass on your desk with the Colt. It came from your restaurant, here––that was your trophy––you earned it. You made a successful business of this place."

"You're smarter than you look, Hasson. But other than my confession, you don't have any proof. My Colt was never fired."

"You know I kept asking myself this same question, what would Nixon do with the murder weapon? It's funny because most scumbag murderers would buy an unmarked gun from some lowlife dealer on the street; they'd do the job and then dispose of it––toss it in the river or something, but not you. No. You were not only proud of what you'd done, you wanted to show off. It took me a while to put it all together, but it wasn't until I focused on your personality that I finally understood.

He nervously drew closer. "And you'll never find that gun. I destroyed it."

"You're a lousy liar, Nixon," I retorted. "That gun was your trophy! You finally won. You wanted that Colt to be on display for the world to see. No way would you *ever* destroy it."

That's what I'd been doing in his office earlier, searching for the missing Colt .45. I knew I had figured it out, and yet, I wasn't ready to tell him what I knew––no, not yet, because I still had more questions.

"What about Janet Sofel? How did she help you?"

"She was just as incompetent as Rickers. I asked her to do one thing; Call your cell phone at the right time. She called too early."

So that was the voice I recognized!

"How did you move the body?" I asked.

"Contractor garbage bag and plastic food wrap." He pointed to the industrial-sized clear plastic rolls.

"So," I said, keeping him talking because I was closer now to the racks of pots and pans. "I bet if we ran a light over this kitchen we'd find plenty of Ben's blood."

Now, I could just reach up and grab the pan. I'd have to be fast, and do some serious damage before he could get a round off.

"I'm done talking," James announced. "I've been looking forward to using my new gun all day." As he took a step forward, a noise from the basement drew our attention.

That's when I lunged at him, a large cast iron pan in hand. I slammed it against the arm holding his gun. The Colt discharged at the same moment it went flying in the air. The round whistled over my head, as the revolver went spinning and sliding across the floor.

Nixon staggered backward and quickly drew out another gun, a Highpoint he had hidden inside a back waistband holster. His hands were trembling as he drew back the hammer.

"Drop the gun!" shouted Nathan, as he stepped through the basement doorway, holding his .40 caliber Sig Sauer leveled at Nixon's head. "One move," he growled. "Just give me an excuse to shoot."

Nixon slowly lowered his gun to the floor and raised his hands. "You can't convict me of Ben's murder. My lawyer will have me out fast."

"Actually, I can," said Nathan. He drew from his pocket an evidence bag with the Colt .45.

James Nixon's face suddenly fell. "How-how did you find it?"

"Mike sent me a text before he left your office. You know, before you assaulted a police officer and kidnapped him? He remembered you bragging to us about how you'd had some work done on your trophy wall recently. I just had to make a quick call to my brother, who said he installed your pistol locker behind that god awful portrait.

"Yeah, I'll bet once Ballistics runs tests on these bullets in the wall," I said, pointing beyond Nathan. "They'll find them to be a perfect match. Put your hands on your head, Nixon. You have the right to remain silent..."

* * * * *

Word of James Nixon's arrest and how he'd tried to frame me was big news and it got around town quickly. Since then, I learned that Nixon's cousin, a pharmacist who would be sweeping floors in jail as his new career, was the one who swapped out my prescription. Captain Hurley sent me to the doctor for fresh blood work, and a pharmacy across town filled my new prescription.

I didn't return to the station that night; instead, I went home and got ready for bed. I couldn't fall asleep. I lay staring at the ceiling, my thoughts on James Nixon and how he tried to ruin my life—and how he had almost succeeded. It kind of put everything into perspective. Made me realize just how fragile life could be.

It was around 10:30 when I picked up the phone and dialed Cameron's number. When I heard her voice on the other end, I couldn't be sure, but I thought maybe, it sounded like maybe—just maybe—she was happy to hear my voice.

The Skeleton on the Ski Lift

D. G. Critchley

Mt. Whittier Ski Lift
To escape the summer heat, poets John Greenleaf Whittier and Lucy Larcom visited the Bearcamp River House in West Ossipee. The building burned in 1880 and the poets found a new summer destination, but Mounts Whittier and Larcom were named in their honor. None of which has to do with the defunct ski area. Because of confusion at the US Geologic Survey, official maps identified Mount Whittier as Nickerson Mountain and labeled another mountain to the west as Mount Whittier. The ski area was on Nickerson Mountain, which after a successful start in the mid-1940s, struggled as taller mountains with better slopes drew business north. A series of dry winters marked the beginning of the end – the ski area had never invested in snowmaking equipment and ceased operation in 1985.

One of the few advantages to living in Florida is the winter in Florida. That particular thought was never more evident to me as it was at the moment when I was standing ankle deep in slush at the base of an abandoned ski area in New Hampshire struggling with my video drone. The drone, allegedly "easy to disassemble for storage," had apparently bonded to its frame at a molecular level. My attempts had taken 20 minutes with no results except skinned knuckles. Just as I was thinking it was a bad as it could get, my phone rang. The ringtone meant it was my brother Robert – Things had just gotten worse.

"This is Jake Grymm, can I help you?" My teeth were already gritted to keep them from chattering, so I answered the phone. When I'm out filming, I'm Jake Grymm, the low budget film impresario. Granted there was no one around for miles, but it was the principle of the matter. It was Robert's idea so that no one would figure out Dr. Robert van der Grimmen was also "Bobby Grey," the silent partner in Grymm Films, LLC. It's not that he was embarrassed to be the executive producer of the profitable but low budget films I made, in fact, I don't think Robert was familiar enough with human emotion to even know when he should be embarrassed. It was that Robert has more degrees than a protractor and even more ongoing research projects. He just didn't want to be distracted from his work by unsolicited scripts and agents. Confused? Good, and welcome to my world.

"I take it you're still at Mount Whittier? Mr. Pomeroy called to remind us that we needed to finish filming today."

Louis Pomeroy was the property owner's smarmy attorney/representative and a pain in my ass. He knew I was filming by myself, shooting aerial footage with the drone. He could have just as easily called me directly. I disliked him from the first phone call, and this was his way of reminding me that the feeling was mutual.

Unfortunately, we had to tolerate each other. The owner gave permission to film but Pomeroy fought it with anything he could come up with – liability insurance, security deposits, anything he could think of. Fortunately, he wasn't an entertainment law specialist, and Robert, out of necessity, had become one. Of course, the fact that state film commission didn't like Pomeroy either helped too. Robert's budget for this film required me to use frequent flyer points, and Colorado was out of the question with what few points had accumulated – the flight into Manchester was pushing it.

And I did like the location. The ski area had shut down back in the mid-80s and was overgrown and decrepit. In other words, perfect for filming scenes of an abandoned ski resort for my latest movie, *Attack of the Abominable Snow Bunnies*.

I willed my teeth to stop grinding. "Well, I used the drone to film aerials along the old ski trails yesterday. I shot a few extra scenes this morning. All I need to do today head up to the gondola station at the summit to shoot looking down the trail. I still wish you'd managed to convince Pomeroy to let me shoot in some of the old buildings"

"Our contract specifies outdoors scenes. He's worried about liability with how badly the buildings have deteriorated. Don't do anything foolish, like sneak into a building and take pictures." Robert knows me too well.

"Robert, it's getting very overcast, and I still need to hike up to the top to get the scenic vista and the exterior of a couple of the buildings. And this early in April in New Hampshire, I don't know if I'll get rained on or snowed on."

"Very good. Just be careful, Thomas. Your production budget doesn't include a search and rescue bill."

I tucked the phone back in my pocket and attempted to think of a new epithet to call him. It was getting harder as the years went by. I resumed struggling with the drone. With a snap that probably meant I broke either another camera or another propeller, the infernal device came apart. I packed it back in its case and packed the case in the trunk. I stuffed the video camera in its waterproof bag and headed up one of the old trails.

I stopped to film one of the gondola towers that had a particularly unhealthy collection of dead vines climbing up it. It would make a decent drop-in shot. I noticed the memory was filling up. With the weather turning bad, I decided I'd risk maxing out the card instead of losing time by stopping to pull the memory card to pop into the phone and send the memory to the cloud for Robert to retrieve.

I reached the summit as the wind started kicking up. I started filming. The wind whipping through the scrub pines growing around the weathered brick building was giving it a real horror vibe. That's when the skies opened up with a combination of freezing rain and sleet. The nearest shelter was the gondola building. Pomeroy said I couldn't film in the building, but no one said anything about using it for shelter. It had no doors, so it's not like I was breaking and entering.

I stepped into the building. The center of the room was the old bullwheel that carried the cable that carried the gondolas to the summit which then continued around the wheel and back down the hill. Pomeroy be damned, I pulled out the camera. Using the viewfinder to frame the shot on the fly, I quickly scanned the room, half expecting Pomeroy to jump out and start screaming. The lighting was bad, but digital videography is very forgiving in postproduction. I panned across the walls, focusing on details like settlement cracks and an old work schedule still scrawled on a chalkboard. In the corner was an old gondola car, covered in dust, but looking sturdy enough to be hooked back to the cable and start ascending the hill at any time. Of course, the dust covered motors and rusty cables were a different story, but still…

I switched on the light and zoomed in on the car, moving closer to film in detail. It sounded like the rain was letting off, but I couldn't resist opening the car door and shooting the interior. I panned the inside until the interior stared back. I pulled the camera down – the light was hitting a grinning skull of a corpse sitting in the gondola.

I scrambled backward, tripped, but kept crawling away. When my heart started again, I stood up and cautiously approached the gondola again. Using the light on the camera I poked my head in again. The dead passenger had been there long enough to become a skeleton but not long enough that the clothing had rotted away. It was wearing some sort of ugly ski jacket in a mustard color with neon green piping on the sleeves. I shot a little more footage and then half-ran out of the building. I pulled my phone out and called the county sheriff office to report finding the body. A dispatcher told me to stay put and they'd send someone out to investigate. Looking at the sky, I hoped it was soon because it still looked threatening and I really didn't relish the thought of sharing a shelter with the dead guy. As I waited, it occurred to me that my camera could be considered evidence. I decided to transmit the footage to the cloud while I waited for the deputies. That way, if the camera was confiscated, I still had a copy.

In about 15 minutes, two ATVs with sheriff markings came roaring up the trail. The first vehicle stopped and a deputy stood up. He was slightly smaller than King Kong. The second ATV pulled up and an older man stepped off. He pulled off the helmet and walked over. His jacket said County Sheriff. He looked over at King Kong, who still hadn't moved.

"Joe, go take a look." Kong nodded and went into the building. The sheriff turned to me and we eyed each other warily. His hair was an ex-military cut and a color I knew came from a bottle – when you dye your gray hair, always remember the eyebrows never lie.

He glanced at the camera. "I'm Sheriff Chuck Griffith. You're Jake Grymm. Lou Pomeroy spent a week trying to convince to require you to have a security detail."

I smiled weakly. "Mr. Pomeroy is not a fan of my shooting here. That was probably his last ditch effort to make filming here too expensive."

He suddenly smiled and slapped my shoulder. "Anyone who can piss off that waddling pain in my ass is a friend of mine." He gestured toward the wheel house. "Shall we see what you found?"

Deputy Kong walked out of the building, ducking to clear the entry. "It's a body alright. Been here a while. No identification." He sounded threatening even when there was no one to threaten.

"Thanks, Joe." He strolled past the deputy, and I followed. To my credit, I did not flinch when he glanced at me.

I caught up with the Sheriff who was looking around the room. "Look at this place – no graffiti, no fire pits, and not an empty beer bottle. Damn kids today – too lazy to walk up a hill to party."

I really wasn't sure what I suppose to stay, so I just stood there. The sheriff sighed and looked around, stopping at the gondola. He hooked his thumb over toward it and looked at me. I nodded. We walked over as he pulled out a flashlight. I stood a few steps behind him as he stuck his head into the gondola.

He pulled his head out. "Yep. That's a dead guy. Looks like I'll need to call the State Police to see if they want to send up a CSI team. They won't find much – there are too many mouse droppings contaminating the remains."

We stepped back outside. "I didn't notice the mouse thing. Messes up the DNA?"

The sheriff looked at me. "Sort of - the mice steal the hair from the skull and makes nests, which means there's no way prove which evidence came from the body and which was brought in from somewhere else."

I looked at him. He shrugged. "We've had a couple of cross-country skiers vanish over the years. By the time we find them, Mother Nature has had her way with them."

I stood by as the sheriff said something to the deputy, who nodded and headed down the trail. "I send Deputy Young down to town to see who got stuck being the coroner this month."

He glanced at the camera clutched in my hand. "I assume you shot film inside the building?"

I nodded. "I assume this is now evidence?"

He took it from my hand. "Yep. Footage before you, Joe and I disturbed the crime scene." We walked over to the ATV where he went rummaging in duffle bag hooked to the back, finally pulling out an evidence bag.

As he sealed the bag, he glanced at me. "You can have it back in the morning. I'll have the IT guy download the footage and you can be merrily on your way tomorrow."

I didn't mention he could keep the chip and give me the camera. He didn't strike me as all that tech savvy, and I had watched enough TV to know something called chain of evidence or something drove cops crazy and made lawyers happy enough to get a two-part episode. The Sheriff offered to give me a lift down to the base, but I decided to take my chances on foot – I had seen him drive up the hill.

As soon as he headed down the hill, I called Robert. If I was going to have to be miserable walking down the hill, I might as well be miserable walking down the hill talking to my brother.

He answered on the third ring. "Robert," I began, "a couple of minor updates. First, I've finished filming. Second, I found a body up here. The sheriff took my camera and I can't get it back until the morning."

There was dead silence on the phone. Finally, he said "That answers my first question, which was when you added a skeleton to the script. Do they know who it is you found?"

I glanced at the sky and increased my gait. "No, there was no ID. Just a skeleton in an ugly parka sitting in a gondola."

Robert was silent again. "Very well, as your attorney, I will make a call to the sheriff and see where we stand."

"Robert," I pleaded, "please don't get me tossed in jail again. The hotel is a dump, but at least it has basic cable."

I could feel the look he was giving me, 1200 miles away, his patented "cold glare over the spectacles" look. "This time, Thomas, you're not a suspect. I'll advise him of your real name, make him aware we have a copy of the footage but will not use the section with the human remains. I'll make sure you can get the camera and still catch an evening flight out of Manchester tomorrow night."

The sleet started coming down again as I reached the parking lot. I jumped in the rental and headed into town. After a hot shower, dry socks, and a late lunch at the hotel's bar, I almost felt human again. I decided to see the sheriff. Officially, I was checking in to make sure Robert called. Unofficially, I had just had an idea for a film about a skeleton haunting a ski lift and wanted to get a feel for how the police process worked in case I needed it for the script.

I rounded the corner to the police station and stopped dead in my tracks. The sheriff was out front, arguing with a giant egg in a wool coat that probably cost more than my last two films combined. It was hovering around the freezing mark and yet the fat guy was sweating like it was August. I instinctively knew it was Lou Pomeroy, the bane of my existence. The sheriff shrugged and handed him an envelope. Pomeroy stuffed it in a pocket and waddled off in a huff, which I suspected was his normal state. The sheriff gestured at me and I followed him into a bar next to the station.

I sat down on a stool next to him. "Lou Pomeroy?"

He looked at me. You've never met him? How the hell did you get so lucky?"

I shrugged. "I'm not allowed to interact with people I'll probably end up punching in the throat."

"Wise move. It's worse for me. I carry a gun. People like Lou Pomeroy allow me to impress myself with my remarkable self-restraint."

The sheriff motioned to the bartender and brought over a couple of mugs of coffee. He looked at it and sighed. "Still on duty. Lou Pomeroy, as you saw, is bent out of shape because I made him come to my office. He's the last person around here who worked for the ski resort. I asked him to look at a DVD of your footage to see if he sees anything out of place in the machinery room – other than the skeleton."

I poured some milk into the coffee. It didn't look like it helped. "So is there any chance of identifying the poor guy?"

The sheriff shrugged. "Aside from the godawful color of the parka, there's nothing distinctive – what's left of the rest of the clothes are brands from a department store that shut down 20 years ago. There's no ID, and even f the wildlife didn't get to him, there's no DNA on file to compare against. I'm thinking it's going to be a John Doe case buried at the county's expense."

I cautiously sipped the coffee. I'd had worse but the shimmer of what I hoped was just grease on the surface was not encouraging.

The sheriff drank half his mug in one swallow. "Your brother called. I'm still not sure how all the pieces fit together. He's your brother, your partner, and your producer?"

"Robert is one of those super geniuses that are only supposed to exist on television. Doctorates in whatever fields strike his interest at the time. He bailed out my film company after a couple of problems, and then came up with some sort of algorithm on making profitable indie films. I give him the script, he makes minor changes to the plot and gives me a budget. I don't understand a thing about it, but I haven't lost money on a film since."

The sheriff sipped the coffee. "He offered me some thoughts on the case. It was an odd conversation – he knew more about the Haskell embezzling case than I did, and I was one of the investigators."

I just looked at him as I poured more sugar into the coffee. "What embezzlement case?"

The sheriff motioned to the bartender. "Back in the mid 80's, Mount Whittier was being passed over for larger mountains nearby. Money was getting tight, so they started running the gondola all year so tourists could see the scenery. They were struggling, but between leaf peepers and the restaurant, they were breaking even. Then someone redirected the cash reserves into a dummy account down in Massachusetts and cleaned out the company. It was a death sentence for the whole operation and they were in receivership within months."

I took another sip and reached for the sugar again. The coffee got nastier as it cooled down. "Never caught the guy?"

The sheriff shook his head. "The bookkeeper disappeared about the same time, Jerry Haskell. We assumed he was the embezzler, but we never found him. The money was transferred between banks until we lost the trail. I think Jerry Haskell is sitting on a beach in Caymans enjoying his retirement."

The bartender refilled the sheriff's coffee and topped off mine, which was now the unhealthiest shade of brown I could imagine. "So," I said, carefully sliding the cup a little further way, "So our friend on the mountain was fully dressed but had no ID. To a layman like me, that sounds a little off."

The sheriff took a healthy swig from his mug. "I can't say. It's an ongoing investigation." He looked around and lowered his voice. "Coroner says the cause of death was blunt force trauma to the back of the head. Poor guy never knew what hit him. It also means it was someone he trusted enough to get behind him."

The sheriff's cell phone rang. He answered it and began a series of monosyllabic answers. He put the phone away. "Well, that settles that. Lou Pomeroy called and confirmed that the parka was Jerry Haskell's"

I glanced at the mug of river sludge congealing on the counter. "So I can have my camera and get out of town?"

The sheriff drained his mug and put it down. I suppressed a shudder. "Well, I need to finish up the paperwork, but I can do that this evening. I promised lard-ass Pomeroy an update at 10

AM. Why don't you show up as well? I can release your camera and introduce you my dear friend Lou."

The fact he was carrying a weapon was the only reason I didn't tell him what I thought of the plan, Instead, I nodded. I got up, we shook hands, and I headed back to the hotel. I called Robert again to bring up to speed. I explained that Pomeroy had confirmed the identity of Jerry Haskell based on the color of the parka and that I would be gleefully heading to the airport as soon as Sheriff Griffith gave me my camera back in the morning.

Robert was uncharacteristically silent. "So," he finally said, "The case is closed because Mr. Pomeroy identified Mr. Haskell?"

I don't know, Robert. I get the impression the sheriff is the type who won't close the case until he finds the money or at least the partner."

"I believe you're correct about the sheriff. Very well, Thomas. I'll call tomorrow to confirm you have the camera back."

"Can't I just call you when I'm heading to the airport?"

"Thomas, with all due respect, you have a remarkable gift for complicating simple plans. As such, I haven't made new airline reservations. When you're actually leaving for the airport, I'll book airfare."

"All right Robert, you win. I'm queasy from bad coffee, so I just want to find some solid food and call it an early night." I hung up before he could reply. I would normally argue, but considering I just discovered a murder while shooting simple background footage, he did have a point.

I stalled as long as I could in the morning. The only upside of being trapped in an office with Pomeroy I could imagine is that if he mouthed off to the sheriff, deputy King Kong would club him upside the head. It was a cheering thought, even if unlikely. I was ushered into the sheriff's office where the festivities were already underway. The sheriff was simply sitting there, looking faintly amused, as Pomeroy ranted and raved about something or other. I just stood quietly in the back of the room. The sheriff glanced at me but went to staring at Pomeroy, who just got louder and madder. I was picking up enough of Pomeroy's diatribe to realize that he wanted me arrested, hanged, and thrown in jail for entering the building. He was launching into another scream fest about criminal trespass when my phone went off. The room fell silent as Pomeroy hoisted himself around to glower at me as I answered the phone.

"Not really a good time to call, Mr. Gray. I'm in the middle of a 'meeting' with the sheriff." I said it with enough sincerity that even Robert should have been able to take the hint. I should have known better.

"Good." He said, instead of taking the hint. Robert was not strong on verbal cues. "Let me talk to the sheriff while you're all there." I sighed and handed my phone to the sheriff. He stood up and took the phone.

The sheriff listened carefully to Robert but didn't get the pained look normally associated with such a conversation. In fact, he looked downright interested. "That's a very good question, Mr. Gray. Hold on a minute and I'll put you on the speaker."

Sheriff Griffith sat back down. "Well, I think we're pretty much done here. Mr. Grymm, you can have your camera back. There'll be some more paperwork for Mr. Pomeroy, but the murder is unsolved and neither of you is a suspect."

Pomeroy hoisted his ample girth from the chair and waddled toward the door. Griffith sat forward. "By the way, Lou, just to be positive. There are no fingerprints, and I can't test for DNA even if we had a sample to compare it against. You're absolutely sure that's Jerry Haskell's jacket you saw in the video?"

Pomeroy paused at the door and turned around. "Yes, Chuck. Jerry was very proud of that ugly jacket. I doubt there's another one of that ugly shade of yellow color in the state. I think he custom-ordered it."

The sheriff made a note on the pad in front of him. He looked up at Pomeroy over his glasses. "Good, that will help. One last thing, Mr. Pomeroy. How did you know the jacket was yellow?"

Pomeroy went white. "I-I told you. You gave me that DVD of the film to look at. That color is hard to miss."

The sheriff looked at my phone. "Mr. Gray, what's your opinion of the color of that jacket, since you also saw that footage."

My brother's voice came into the suddenly silent room. "The jacket is gray in that footage. Mr. Grymm broke yet another camera. I assume when disconnecting it from the drone - again. It was filming in black and white the entire time it was in the building. There's no way to determine the color of that jacket."

Pomeroy looked like a deer in the headlights – a big, fat, balding, guilty deer. He didn't say anything. I noticed that deputy Kong has quietly moved in front of the door.

My brother continued. "I've run every video program I can find, and there is no way to convert the footage to color."

Sheriff Griffith disconnected the call and handed me my phone. Pomeroy went for a gun in his jacket. He'd watched too many crime dramas. Even I know an amateur can't get a pistol out of a winter jacket pocket quickly. King Kong clubbed him upside the head before Pomeroy even had the gun out of his pocket. He slumped to the floor. My new best friend Deputy Joe handed the gun to the sheriff. For the first time, King Kong smiled. It was a chilling effect and gave me an idea for a movie.

It took 3 deputies and the burly-looking lady from the reception desk to half-drag/half-carry Pomeroy out to a cell. The Sheriff smiled. He motioned for me to come over to his desk. As I slowly walked toward him, he looked at the computer screen. "Your brother is a very clever man. I assume you never played poker with him."

I wasn't sure where we were going with the conversation. He turned the monitor toward me and I saw an error message about an "unrecognized file format." Griffith smiled. "He called me early this morning and had me ask the computer guy about how he transferred the file to the DVD I gave Lou yesterday. Apparently, your camera records in –" He looked down at looked at his notes, "AVCHD format, which won't play on regular DVD players. The tech guy burned the file to the DVD for Pomeroy, but didn't bother testing to see if was playable."

I was lost. The way Robert's brain worked, it happened a lot. The sheriff apparently recognized the look.

"Your brother reviewed all the old newspapers from the original crime on one of those fancy online databases. Apparently, Haskell had no friends and apparently didn't ski. A bookkeeper who doesn't ski and has no friends doesn't hop a gondola up the mountain, never mind wander into the machinery room unless he was meeting a partner in the scam – or getting set up to take the fall."

"I was a deputy back when it happened. We knew Haskell at least had to have had a partner. The sheriff never liked Haskell for the crime, but without an arrest, we couldn't prove whether Haskell was the mastermind or a patsy. He assumed the partner was someone at the bank with Haskell at the ski lodge. The one person we never thought of was the company's lawyer. Your brother asked me to look at the old case files. Turns out Pomeroy not only first reported the discrepancies, he handled the forensic accounting to see how extensive the theft was."

Suddenly I saw where he was going. "Pomeroy covered his own tracks by assisting the investigation."

The sheriff shrugged. "Thirty years ago, Carroll County's budget barely covered gas for the squad cars, never mind funds for anything as fancy as a forensic accountant. Pomeroy wasn't a suspect, so the help was gladly accepted."

"Your brother thought that if Pomeroy was the killer, he wouldn't bother watching the video. Call it a guilty conscience or whatever, but he wouldn't need to – he already knew who it was and what color his jacket was. If he was innocent, he'd have tried to watch it and wouldn't be able to and would have come in here this morning screaming about that instead. So the black and white thing was to make him admit he hadn't watched it."

I turned to go. I was not aware my brother had any background in criminal psychology. Didn't surprise me either. "Thank you, sheriff. I am relieved."

"Relieved? You were never a suspect."

"I'm glad you caught your killer, but I'm relieved I didn't break the camera. Robert would remind me about that for years to come– that would be murder!"

Contributors

Whittier's First Desk

Guests entering the Whittier Homestead sign a guest register that rests on the desk of Joseph Whittier, the poet's great-grandfather. Although the desk in his home in Amesbury is where his most famous works were composed, this is where his first pamphlet on slavery "justice and Expediency" was written. When his Elizabeth niece married Samuel Pickard and moved to Maine, the desk was given to her. She had the desk restored and in 1891, it was returned to Whittier, making the desk where Whittier wrote his last poems the same one where he wrote his first. Courtesy of Nathan Schoonover.

David Bernard ("The Death Clock") is a native New Englander who now lives (albeit under protest) in South Florida, a paradoxical place where, when temperatures drop below 60°, locals break out parkas to wear over their shorts and sandals. His previous works include short stories in anthologies such as *Twice upon an Apocalypse*, *Strangely Funny*, and *Legacy of the Reanimator*.

William Cullen Bryant ("The Murdered Traveller") was an American romantic poet, journalist, and long-time editor of the *New York Evening Post*. Along with Whittier, he was part of that most exclusive group of American literary superstars known as The Fireside Poets.

Judi Calhoun ("Exposed for Murder") lives with ferocious black bears and wild wolves that howl at the moon every night in the Great North Woods of New Hampshire. A member of the New England Horror Writers, her stories regularly appear in e-zines, most recently in *Portable NOUNS, Crimson Street, Theme of Absence,* and *Great Jones Street*, just to name a few. Her stories have also appeared such anthologies as the N.H. Pulp Fiction Series, *Pernicious Invaders, Canopic Jars,* and *The Passion of Cat*. She was also in last year's Whittier anthology *Snowbound with Zombies*.

Tim Coco (Introduction) is the president of the Trustees of the John Greenleaf Whittier Homestead. He is the founding president of non-profit Public Media of New England Inc., operator of radio station WHAV 97.9 FM. He is a commissioner of the Essex National Heritage Commission, and a member of the City of Haverhill's License Commission. In his spare time, he is CEO of COCO+CO. Inc., an advertising and marketing agency.

D.G. Critchley ("Skeleton on the Ski Lift") lives in northern New Jersey but will deny it if pressed on the issue. A novice mystery writer, he feels actually writing mysteries is the logical culmination of a life-long fascination with pulp detective magazines.

Ken Faig, Jr. ("The Goodwife and the Bookseller") is one of the leading scholars on the Amateur Journalism movement as well as the genealogy of H. P. Lovecraft. *Lovecraft's Pillow and Other Strange Stories*, a collection of his stories, was released by Hippocampus Press. The collected casebooks of this tale's protagonist, Wilmott Watkyns, are currently being collected for publication.

David Goudsward (editor) lives in Lake Worth, Florida but was raised on the summit of Haverhill's Scotland Hill. The author of 10 books on various nonfiction topics, his latest book is *Horror Guide to*

Northern New England. He can be seen on reruns of the Travel Channel shows *Mysteries at the Museum* and *Mysteries at the Monument.*

Lucy Larcom ("The Murderer's Request") was an educator, editor, and publisher. Whittier became her mentor after "discovering" her work in *Lowell Offering*, a publication Larcom produced of literature by her fellow mill workers. A highly regarded poet in her lifetime, she is best remembered today for writing *A New England Girlhood* (1889), an autobiographical look at the advent of the industrial age and her role in it as an 11-year old laborer in a textile mill.

Edith Maxwell ("Murder in the Summer Kitchen") is an Agatha-nominated mystery writer and a national best-selling author. *Called to Justice*, her second novel about 1888 Quaker midwife Rose Carroll, released in April 2017. A resident of Whittier's hometown of Amesbury and a docent-trainee at the John Greenleaf Whittier Home Museum, Edith also writes the Local Foods Mysteries, set on an organic farm, and award-winning short crime fiction. As Maddie Day she writes the Country Store Mysteries and the Cozy Capers Book Group Mysteries.

Rock Neely ("Cane Fishing") is a Professor of Communications and English in the Cincinnati area. He is the author the Purple Heart Mystery series about combat-wounded veterans turned private detectives.

Gregory L. Norris ("Antiques") is a prolific fiction writer. He was screenwriter on two episodes *of Star Trek: Voyager*, and recently penned the screenplay for the feature film *Brutal Colors* (Royal Blue Pictures). His most recent collection, *Tales from the Robot Graveyard*, is a collection of cyber-centric novellas.

Susan Oleksiw ("Miss Larcom Meets the Neighbors") writes two mystery series, one featuring Chief of Police Joe Silva in the New England coastal village of Mellingham, and the second featuring Anita Ray, an Indian-American photographer living in South India. She was the founder and editor of *The Larcom Review: A Journal of the Arts and Literature of New England,* and is the co-founder of Level Best Books.

Peter Rawlik ("Black Ice") is the author of more than twenty-five short stories, a smattering of poetry, and the Cthulhu Mythos novel series *Reanimators, The Weird Company*, and *Reanimatrix*. His short story "Revenge of the Reanimator" was nominated for a 2014 New Pulp Award. He lives in southern Florida where he works on Everglades issues.

Kristi Petersen Schoonover ("A Cricket in the Wall") has appeared in countless magazines and anthologies. *Skeletons in the Swimmin' Hole*, her collection of Disney World-themed horror, appeared in 2011, and her first novel, *Bad Apple*, was published in 2012. She was also in last year's Whittier anthology *Snowbound with Zombies*.

Celia Thaxter ("A Memorable Murder") was born in Portsmouth, New Hampshire and raised on the Isles of Shoals. After 10 years of marriage on the mainland, she returned to Appledore, writing poetry about the Isles that captured the public's imagination. Her success brought literary giants to call, and the hotel parlor served as a salon with visits from Emerson, Hawthorne, Longfellow, and of course, Whittier.

Vicki Weisfeld ("The Flock") is a writer, reader, active blogger, and reviewer of books, movies, theater, and socio-cultural phenomena. Find her online at vweisfeld.com. Her stories have appeared in *Ellery Queen Mystery Magazine, Betty Fedora, King's River Life*, and *Big Muddy Literary Magazine* of Southeast Missouri State University, among others.

John Greenleaf Whittier ("A Mother's Revenge" and "The Murdered Lady") was a poet, journalist, editor and abolitionist. His first book, *Legends of New England in Prose and Verse*, was published in 1831. In 1866, with slavery abolished, he turned toward religious and nostalgic themes, one of which would be his most popular work. "Snow-Bound," brought him widespread popular acclaim and the financial security to focus exclusively on his poetry.

About Post Mortem Press

Since its inception in 2010, Post Mortem Press has published over 100 titles in the genres of dark fiction, suspense/mystery, horror, and dark fantasy. The goal is to provide a showcase for talented authors, affording exposure and opportunity to "get noticed" by the mainstream publishing community. Post Mortem Press has quickly become a powerful voice in the small genre press community. The result has been five years of steady growth and successful endeavors that have garnered attention from all across the publishing world.